CROSS ROADS

Also by Wm Paul Young

The Shack

CROSS ROADS

WM PAUL YOUNG

HODDER &
STOUGHTON

First published in Great Britain in 2012 by Hodder & Stoughton
An Hachette UK company

Published in association with FaithWords, a division of Hachette Book
Group USA, 237 Park Avenue, New York, NY 10017.

1

A CIP catalogue record for this title is available from the British Library

ISBN 978 1 444 74597 9
eBook 978 1 444 74598 6

Printed and bound in Great Britain by Clays Ltd, St Ives plc

Hodder & Stoughton policy is to use papers that are natural, renewable and recyclable prod-
ucts and made from wood grown in sustainable forests. The logging and manufacturing
processes are expected to conform to the environmental regulations of the country of origin.

Hodder & Stoughton Ltd
338 Euston Road
London NW1 3BH

www.hodder.co.uk

This story is dedicated to our grandchildren,
each a unique reflection of their parents,
each their own universe unexplored,
carriers of delight and wonder,
infecting our hearts and lives profoundly and eternally.
One day when you read this story,
may it be a small window through which
you better understand your Grandpa,
your God,
and your world!

CONTENTS

CROSS ROADS

1

A CONGREGATION OF STORM

*The most pitiable among men is he who turns his
dreams into silver and gold.*
—Khalil Gibran

Some years in Portland, Oregon, winter is a bully, spitting sleet and spewing snow in fits and starts as it violently wrestles days from spring, claiming some archaic right to remain king of the seasons—ultimately the vain attempt of another pretender. This year was not like that. Winter simply bowed out like a beaten woman, leaving head down in tattered garments of dirty whites and browns with barely a whimper or promise of return. The difference between her presence and absence was scarcely discernible.

Anthony Spencer didn't care either way. Winter was a nuisance and spring not much better. Given the power, he would remove both from the calendar along with the wet and rainy part of autumn. A five-month year would be just about right, certainly preferable to lingering periods of uncertainty. Every cusp of spring he wondered why he stayed in the Northwest, but each year found him again asking the same question. Maybe disappointing familiarity had its own comforts. The idea of actual change was daunting. The more entrenched in his habits and securities, the less inclined he was to believe that anything else was worth the effort if even possible. Known routines, even though painful at times, at least had their own predictability.

He leaned back in his chair and looked up from the desk cluttered with papers and into his computer screen. With each tap of a key he could watch the monitoring feed from his personal properties; the condo in the building adjacent to where he sat, his central workplace situated strategically in downtown Portland midway up a midsized office scraper, his getaway house at the coast and larger home in the West Hills. He watched and restlessly tapped his right index finger on his knee. All was quiet as if the world was holding her breath. There are many ways to be alone.

Although people who interacted with Tony in business or social situations would have thought otherwise, he was not a cheerful man. He was determined and ever in search of the next advantage. That often required an outgoing and gregarious presence, broad smiles, eye contact, and firm handshakes, not because of any true consideration, but because everyone potentially held information that would be valuable in positioning for success. His many questions created the aura of genuine interest, leaving others with both a sense of significance but also a lingering emptiness. Known for gestures of philanthropy, he understood the value of compassion as a means to more important objectives. Caring made people that much easier to manipulate. After a few halting attempts he has concluded that friends of any depth were a bad investment. So little return. Actual caring was inconvenient and a luxury for which he had no time or energy.

Instead he defined success in real estate property management and development, diverse business ventures, and a growing investment portfolio, where he was respected and feared as a severe negotiator and master deal maker. For Tony, happiness was a silly and transient sentiment, a vapor compared to the smell of a potential deal and the addicting aftertaste of the win. Like Scrooge of old, he took delight in wresting the last vestiges of dignity from those around him, especially employees who toiled from fear if not respect. Surely such a man is worthy of neither love nor compassion.

When he smiled, Tony could almost be mistaken for handsome. Genetics had gifted him with a six-foot-plus frame and good hair, which even now in his mid-forties showed no evidence of leaving even though the lawyer's gray had started to salt his temples. Obviously Anglo-Saxon, a hint of something darker and finer softened his features, especially noticeable during rare moments when he was transported out of his customary business demeanor by some fancy or unhinged laughter.

By most standards he was wealthy, successful, and an eligible bachelor. A bit of a womanizer, he exercised enough to stay competitive, sporting only a barely sagging belly that could be sucked in appropriately. And the women came and went, the wiser the sooner, and each feeling less valuable for the experience.

He had married twice, to the same woman. The first union, while both were in their early twenties, had produced a son and a daughter, the latter now an angry young adult living across the country near her mother. Their son was another story. That marriage had ended in divorce for irreconcilable differences, a poster story of calculated disaffection and a callous lack of consideration. In only a few short years Tony had battered Loree's sense of worth and value into barely recognizable bits and pieces.

The problem was she bowed out gracefully, and this could not be counted as a proper win. So Tony spent the next two years wooing her back, throwing a magnificent remarriage celebration, and then two weeks later serving her divorce papers for a second time. Rumor was these had been prepared even before the signatures were inked on the second set of marriage certificates. But this time she came at him with all the fury of a woman scorned, and he had financially, legally, and psychologically crushed her. This certainly could be chalked up as a win. It had been a ruthless game, but only to him.

The price he paid was losing his daughter in the process, something that rose like a specter in the shadows of a little too much Scotch, a little haunting that could soon be buried in the busyness of work and winning. Their son was a significant reason for the Scotch in the first place; over-the-counter medicine that softened the ragged edges of memory and regret and tempered the painful migraines that had become an occasional companion.

If freedom is an incremental process, so, too, is the encroachment of evil. Small adjustments to truth and minor justifications over time build an edifice that would never have been predicted. True for any Hitler or Stalin or common person. The inside house of the soul is magnificent but fragile; any betrayals and lies embedded in its walls and foundation shift its construction in directions unimagined.

The mystery of every human soul, even Anthony Spencer, is profound. He had been birthed in an explosion of life, an inner expanding universe coalescing its own internal solar systems and galaxies with unimagined symmetry and elegance. Here even chaos played her part and order emerged as a by-product. Places of substance entered the dance of competing gravitational forces, each adding their own rotation to the mix, shifting the members of the cosmic waltz and spreading them out in a constant give-and-take of space and time and music. Along this road, pain and loss came crushing, causing this depth to lose its profoundly delicate structure and begin to collapse in on itself. The deterioration rippled on the surface in self-protective fear, selfish ambition, and the hardening of anything tender. What had been a living entity, a heart of flesh, became stone; a small hardened rock lived in the husk, the shell of the body. Once the form was an expression of inward wonder and magnificence. Now it must find its way with no support, a facade in search of a heart, a dying star ravenous in its own emptiness.

Pain, loss, and finally abandonment are each a hard taskmaster, but combined they become a desolation almost unendurable. These had weaponized Tony's existence, equipping him with the ability to hide knives inside words, erect walls protecting the within from any approach, and keeping him locked in an imagination of safety while isolated and solitary. Little true music now existed in Tony's life; scraps of creativity barely audible. The sound track of his subsistence didn't even qualify as Muzak—unsurprising elevator melodies accompanying his predictable elevator pitches.

Those who recognized him on the streets nodded their greetings, the more perceptive spitting their disdain onto the sidewalk once he passed. But plenty of others were taken in; fawning sycophants awaited his next directive, desperate to win a scrap of approval or perceived affection. In the wake of alleged success, others are carried along by a need to secure their own significance, identity, and agenda. Perception is reality, even if the perception is a lie.

Tony owned an expansive house on acreage in the upper

West Hills, and unless he was hosting a party for some advantage, kept only one small portion heated. Though he rarely bothered to stay there, he retained the place as a monument to vanquishing his wife. Loree won it as part of their first divorce settlement but had sold it to pay her mounting legal bills relating to their second. Through a third party he bought it from her for pennies on the dollar and then threw a surprise eviction party, complete with police to escort a stunned ex-wife off the premises on the day the sale closed.

He leaned forward again and switched off his computer, reaching for his Scotch, and rotated his chair so he could stare at a list of names he had written on a whiteboard. He got up, erased four names and added one, and then slumped back into his chair, the horses in his fingers again tapping their cadence onto his desk. Today he was in a fouler mood than usual. Business obligations had required attending a conference in Boston that held little interest for him, and then a minor crisis in personnel management meant he was returning a day earlier than planned. While it was annoying that he had to deal with a situation easily handled by subordinates in the company, he was grateful for the excuse to withdraw from the barely tolerable seminars and return to the barely tolerable routines over which he had more control.

But something had changed. What began as a hint of a shadow of uneasiness had grown to a conscious voice. For a few weeks Tony had felt a nagging sense he was being followed. At first he dismissed it as stress overreaching itself, the fabrications of an overworked mind. But once implanted, the thought had found fertile soil; and what began as a seed easily washed away by serious consideration spread roots that soon expressed itself in nervous hypervigilance, sapping even more energy from a mind constantly alert.

He began noticing details in minor events, which individually would draw barely a wonder. But together they became in his consciousness a chorus of warning. The black SUV he sometimes spotted shadowing him on his way to the main office, the gas attendant who forgot to return his credit card for minutes, the alarm company that notified him about three power failures at his home that seemed to affect only his property while his neighbors' remained undimmed, each outage lasting exactly twenty-two minutes at the same time three days in a row. Tony began to pay more attention to trivial discrepancies and even how others looked at him—the barista at Stumptown Coffee, the security guard on the first-floor entry, and even the personnel manning the desks at work. He noted how they glanced away when he would turn in their direction, averting their eyes and quickly changing their body language to indicate they were busy and involved elsewhere.

There was an unnerving similarity in the responses of these disparate people, as if by collusion. Theirs was a secret to which he was not privy. The more he looked, the more he noticed, so the more he looked. He had always been a little paranoid, but it now escalated to constant considerations of conspiracy, and he lived agitated and unnerved.

Tony kept this small private office complete with a bedroom, kitchen, and bathroom, its whereabouts not even known to his personal lawyer. This was his retreat down by the river just off Macadam Avenue for the times when he simply wanted to disappear for a few hours or spend the night off the grid.

The larger property that housed this hidden hidey-hole he also owned, but had years before transferred the title to a nondescript shell company. He had then renovated a portion of its basement, equipping it with state-of-the-art surveillance and security technology. Other than the original contractors, who had all been hired at arm's length, no one had seen these rooms. Even the building blueprints did not disclose their existence, thanks to construction payoffs and well-placed donations to local governmental chains of command. When the proper code was entered in what appeared to be a rusty telephone junction box keypad at the back of an unused janitorial closet, a wall slid sideways to reveal a steel fire door and modern camera and keypad entry system.

The place was almost completely self-contained, tied to power and Internet sources independent from the rest of the complex. Additionally, if his monitoring security software discovered any attempt to backtrace the location, it would shut and lock the system down until reset by entering a new and automatically generated code. This could be done from only one of two places: his downtown office desk or inside the secret lair itself. As a habit, before he entered he would turn off his mobile phone and remove its SIM card and battery. He had an unlisted landline that could be activated should there ever be the need.

There was no show here. The furnishings and art were simple, almost spartan. No one else would ever see this place, so everything in these rooms meant something to him. Books lined the walls, many he had never opened but had belonged to his father. Others, especially classics, his mother had read to him and his brother. The works of C. S. Lewis and George MacDonald were among the most prominent of these, childhood favorites. An early edition of Oscar Wilde's *The Picture of Dorian Gray* was prominently displayed, for his eyes alone. Crammed into one end of the bookshelf were a plethora of business books, well read and marked, an arsenal of mentors. A few works by Escher and

Doolittle haphazardly hung on the walls and an old phono-graph player sat in one corner. He kept a collection of vinyl records whose scratches were like comforting reminders of times long gone.

It was in this hidden office that he also kept his criti-cally important items and documents: deeds, titles, and especially his official Last Will and Testament. This he fre-quently reviewed and changed, adding or subtracting peo-ple as they intersected his life and their actions angered or pleased him. He imagined the impact of a gift or the lack thereof on those who would care about his wealth once he had joined the ranks of the "dearly departed."

His own personal lawyer, different from his general counsel, had a key to a safety-deposit box secured in the downtown main branch of Wells Fargo. This could be accessed only with his death certificate. Inside were instruc-tions revealing the location of the private apartment and office, how to gain entry, and where to find the codes for opening the concealed safe buried in the foundation floor. Should anyone ever attempt to gain access to the box with-out a certified death certificate, the bank was required to notify Tony immediately; and as he had warned the attor-ney, if such ever occurred, their relationship would termi-nate without consideration, along with the healthy retainer that arrived promptly the first business day of every month.

Tony kept an older Last Will and Testament, for show, in the safe at the main office. A few of his partners and col-leagues had access for business purposes, and he secretly hoped that curiosity would overtake one or the other, imag-ining their initial pleasure at knowing its contents followed by the sobering event of the reading of his actual will.

It was public information that Tony owned and man-aged the property adjacent to the building that housed his secret place. It was a similar structure with storefronts on the first floor and condos above. The two buildings shared underground parking, with strategically placed cameras that seemed to blanket the area completely but actually left a corridor that one could invisibly pass through. Tony could quickly access his hidden refuge unnoticed.

In order to justify his regular presence on this side of town, he publicly purchased a two-bedroom condominium on the second floor of the building next to his hidden office. The apartment was complete and lavishly apportioned, a perfect front, and he spent more nights here than at either his West Hills house or his getaway at the coast near Depoe Bay.

Tony had timed the walking distance between the condo and his secret sanctuary through the parking garage, and knew he could be sequestered away in his special sanctuary in less than three minutes. From the security of this enclosed and protected asylum he was connected to the outside world through recordable video feeds that monitored his personal properties and downtown office. The extensive electronic hardware was more for self-protection than it was for advantage. But nowhere had he hidden cameras in bedrooms or bathrooms, knowing that others would occasionally use them with his permission. He might have been many things distasteful, but a voyeur was not one of them.

Anyone recognizing his car driving into the garage would simply assume, and usually correctly, that he was coming to spend the night in his condo unit. He had become a routine fixture, part of the background noise of everyday activity, and his presence or absence sent no signal, drew no attention, which was just the way he wanted it. Even so, in his heightened state of anxiety, Tony was more cautious than usual. He altered his routines just enough that it would allow him to catch a glimpse of someone who might be tailing him, but not enough to create suspicion.

What he couldn't understand was why anyone would be following him in the first place, or what might be their motivations and intentions. He had burned bridges, most bridges actually, and he supposed that therein he would find the answers. *It has to be about money,* he surmised. Wasn't everything about money? Maybe it was his ex-wife? Perhaps his partners were preparing a coup to wrest his portion from him, or maybe a competitor? Tony spent hours, days, poring over the financial data of every transaction past and current, every merger and acquisition, looking for a pattern that was out of place, but found nothing. He then buried himself in the operations processes of the multiple holdings, again looking for...what? Something unusual, some hint or clue that would explain what was happening? He found some anomalies, but when he subtly raised them as issues with his partners, they were either swiftly corrected or explained in a manner that was consistent with the standard operating procedures he himself had created.

Even in a struggling economy, business was steady. It was Tony who had convinced his partners to maintain a strong liquid-asset base, and now they were carefully purchasing property and diversifying into enterprises at better than liquidation values, independent of the banks that had withdrawn themselves into self-protective credit hoarding. He was currently the office hero, but this did not give him much peace. Any respite would be short-lived, and every success simply raised the bar of performance expectations. It was an exhausting way to live, but he resisted other options as irresponsible and lazy.

He spent less and less time at the main office. Not that anyone looked for opportunities to be around him anyway.

His heightened paranoia made him more testy than normal and the slightest irregularity set him off. Even his partners preferred that he work off-site, and when his office remained dark, everyone sighed in collective relief and actually worked harder and in more creatively focused ways. Such is the debilitative power of micromanagement, a strategy that Tony often took great pride in wielding.

But it was into this space, this momentary reprieve, that his fears had surfaced, his sense of being a target, the object of someone's or something's attention, unwanted and unwelcome. To make matters worse, his headaches had come back with a vengeance. These migraines were usually precipitated by vision loss, followed closely by slurred speech as he struggled to complete sentences. It all warned of an impending slam of an invisible spike through his skull into the space behind his right eye. Light and sound sensitive, he would notify his personal assistant before crawling into the darkened recesses of his condo. Armed with painkillers and white noise, he slept until it hurt only when he laughed or shook his head. Tony convinced himself that Scotch helped the recovery process, but he looked for any excuse to pour himself another.

So why now? After months without a single migraine, they were happening almost weekly. He began watching what he consumed, concerned that someone might be trying to slip poison into his food or drink. Increasingly he was desperately tired, and even with prescription-enhanced sleep felt exhausted. Finally, he set an appointment for a physical with his doctor, which he failed to keep because an unexpected meeting required his presence to resolve issues pertinent to an important acquisition that had gone sideways. He rescheduled the appointment for two weeks later.

When uncertainty impinges upon routine, one begins to think about one's life as a whole, about who matters and why. Overall, Tony was not displeased with his. He was prosperous, better than most, which was not bad for a foster child whom the system had failed, and who had quit crying about it. He had made mistakes and hurt people, but who hadn't? He was alone, but most of the time preferred it that way. He had a house in the West Hills, a beach retreat at Depoe Bay, his condo by the Willamette River, strong investments, and the freedom to do almost anything he wanted. He was alone, but most of the time preferred it...He had reached every objective he had set, at least every realistic goal, and now in his forties he survived with a brooding sense of emptiness and percolating regrets. These he quickly stuffed down inside, into that invisible vault that human beings create to protect themselves from themselves. Sure he was alone, but most of the time...

Upon landing in Portland from Boston, Tony had driven directly to the main office and initiated a particularly volatile argument with two of his partners. It was then that the idea occurred to create a list of those he trusted. Not of people he would *say* he trusted, but those he actually did trust. Those he would tell secrets to, share dreams with, and with whom he would expose his weaknesses. For this reason he had cloistered himself away in his hidden office, pulled out a whiteboard and Scotch, and began writing down and erasing names. The list was never long, and originally included business partners, a few others who worked for him, one or two he had encountered outside of the job, and a couple of people he had met through private clubs and travel. But after an hour's contemplation he whittled even that down to six people. He sat back and shook his head. It had turned into an exercise in futility. The only people he truly trusted were all dead, although there was some question about the last name.

His father and particularly his mother topped the six. He knew rationally that much of his memory of them was idealized by time and trauma, their negative attributes swallowed up by his ache for them. He treasured the faded photograph, the last one taken before a teenage partyer lost control and turned glory into rubble. He opened the safe and pulled it out, now protected inside a laminated sheet, but he tried to smooth out its wrinkles anyway, as if caressing it could somehow let them know. His father had talked some stranger into taking their picture outside the now-extinct Farrell's Ice Cream shop, he a gangly eleven-year-old with his seven-year-old kid brother, Jacob, standing in front of him. They had been laughing about something, his mother's face upturned with the joy of the moment written large upon her beautiful features, his father grinning wryly, the best he could do. It was enough, his father's grin. He remembered it clearly. An engineer not given to much emotional expression, it would unexpectedly slip out anyway and almost meant more because it was not easily accessible. Tony had tried to recall what they had all been laughing about, staring his question into the photograph for hours as if it might yield the secret, but try as he might, it lay just outside his grasp, tantalizing and maddening.

Next on his list came Mother Teresa, followed closely by Mahatma Gandhi and Martin Luther King Jr. All great, all idealized, each very human, vulnerable, wonderful, and now dead. Pulling out a small notepad he wrote down the names, tore off the single sheet, and then toyed with it between his right forefinger and thumb. Why had he written down the names of these people? It had been almost without thought, this final list, perhaps a true reflection of a source very deep and maybe even real, perhaps even a *longing*. He detested that word, but loved it somewhere. It sounded weak on the surface, but it had sure staying power, outlasting most other things that had come and gone in his life. These three iconic personages represented, along with the last name on the list, something larger than himself, a hint of a song never sung but still calling, the possibility of someone he might have been, an invitation, a belonging, a tender *yearning*.

The last name was the most difficult and yet the easiest: Jesus. Jesus, Bethlehem's gift to the world, the woodworker who supposedly was God joining our humanity, who might not be dead, according to the religious rumors. Tony knew why Jesus was on the list. The name bridged to the strongest memories he had of his mother. She loved this carpenter and anything and everything to do with him. Sure, his dad loved Jesus, too, but not like his mom. The last gift she had ever given him lay inside his safe, in the foundation of the building that housed his secret place, and it was the single most precious thing he possessed.

Not two days before his parents were so forcefully stolen from his life, she had inexplicably come to his bedroom. The memory was etched into his soul. He was eleven years old, working on homework, and there she stood, leaning against the door, a slip of a woman in a floral apron, flour highlighting one cheek where she had brushed away hair that escaped the tie holding her tresses up and away from activity. It was because of the flour that he knew she had been crying, the trail of tears running a jagged course down her face.

"Mom, are you okay? What's wrong?" he had asked, getting up from his books.

"Oh," she exclaimed, wiping her face with the backs of her closed hands, "nothing at all. You know me, I sometimes start thinking about things, things that I am so grateful for, like you and your brother, and I just get all emotional." She paused. "I don't know why, my dearest, but I was thinking about how big you're getting, a teenager in a couple years; then you will be driving and off to college and then you'll get married, and as I thought about all this, do you know what I felt?" She paused. "I felt joy. I felt like my heart was about to burst out of my chest. Tony, I am so thankful to God for you. So I decided to make you your favorite dessert, Marion-berry Cobbler, and some caramel rolls. But as I was standing there, looking out the window at everything we have been given, all the gifts, and especially about you and Jake, I suddenly wanted to give you something, something that's especially precious to me."

It was then that Tony noticed her clenched fist; she was holding something. Whatever it was fit in the small grasp of this woman already shorter than he. She held out her hand and slowly opened it. Curled up on her palm was a flour-anointed necklace with a gold cross at the end, fragile and feminine.

"Here." She held it out. "I want you to have this. Your grandmother gave it to me, and her mother to her. I thought I would one day give it to a daughter, but I don't think that's going to happen and I don't know why, but as I was think-ing and praying for you, today seemed to be the right day to give it to you."

Tony had not known what else to do so he opened his hand, allowing his mother to drop the finely woven thread onto his palm, adorned with the small delicate gold cross.

"Someday, I want you to give this to the woman you

love, and I want you to tell her where it came from." The tears were now rolling down her face.

"But Mom, you can give it to her."

"No, Anthony, I feel this strongly. I don't exactly understand why, but it is for you to give, not me. Now don't get me wrong, I plan to be there, but just like my mother gave it to me to give, I now give it to you, for you to give."

"But how will I know—"

"You will," she interrupted. "Trust me, you will!" She wrapped her arms around him and hugged him long, unconcerned for the flour that might be transferred. He had not cared either. None of it had made any sense to him, but he knew it was important.

"Hold on to Jesus, Anthony. You can never go wrong by holding on to Jesus. And know this," she said as she pulled back and looked up into his eyes. "He will never stop holding on to you."

Two days later she was gone, swallowed up in the selfish choice of another barely older than he. The necklace still lay in his safe. He had never given it away. Had she known? He had often wondered if this had been a premonition, some warning or gesture by God to give him a remembrance. Her loss had destroyed his life, sending it careering down a path that had made him who he was, strong, tough, and able to withstand things that others struggled with. But there were moments, fleeting and intangible, when the tender longing would slip in between the rocks of his presentation and sing to him, or begin to sing as he would quickly shut such music away.

Was Jesus still holding him? Tony didn't know, but probably not. He wasn't much like his mother anymore, but because of her, he had read the Bible along with some of her favorite books, trying to find in the pages of Lewis, MacDonald, Williams, and Tolkien a hint of her presence. He even joined, for a short time, the Young Life group in his high school where he tried to learn more about Jesus, but the foster system in which he and his brother landed shuttled them from home to home and school to school, and when every hello is just a good-bye waiting to happen, social clubs and affiliations become painful. He felt that Jesus had said good-bye like everyone else.

So the fact that he had kept Jesus on the list was a bit of a surprise. He hadn't given him much thought in years. In college he had briefly renewed the quest, but after a season of conversation and study had quickly relegated Jesus to the list of great dead teachers.

Even so, he could understand why his mother had been so enamored. What wasn't there to like about him? A man's man, yet good with children, kind to those unacceptable to religion and culture, a person full of infectious compassion, someone who challenged the status quo and yet loved those he challenged. He was everything that Tony sometimes wished he was, but knew he wasn't. Perhaps Jesus was an example of that bigger-than-yourself life, but it was too late to change. The older he got, the thought of transformation seemed increasingly remote.

And it was the God-thing that he couldn't understand, especially as it related to Jesus. Tony had long decided that if there was a God, he or she or it was something or someone terrible and malevolent, capricious and untrustworthy, at best some form of cold dark matter, impersonal and uncaring, and at worst a monster taking pleasure in devastating the hearts of children.

"It's all wishful thinking," he mumbled as he crumpled up the paper and indignantly tossed it at the garbage can across the room. Living people couldn't be trusted. Reaching for a fresh bottle of Balvenie Portwood, he poured himself a triple and turned back toward his computer, switching it back on.

He brought up his official Last Will and Testament and spent the next hour expressing his suspicion and antipathy by making major revisions and printing off a new copy, which he signed, dated, and tossed with the old back onto a pile of others already in the safe, locking and resetting the alarms and turning off his desk lights. As he sat in the darkness thinking about his existence and who might be pursuing him, little did he know he was drinking his last Scotch.

2

Dust to Dust

God moves in a mysterious way, his wonders to
  perform.
He plants his footsteps in the sea, and rides upon the
  storm.

—William Cowper

Morning burst through his uncovered window with a
vengeance. Bright sunlight mixed with remnants of Scotch
sent his head into spasms, a morning migraine to murder the day. But this was different. Tony not only couldn't
remember how he had gotten back to his condo, but he was
in the grip of pain unlike any he had ever known. Sprawled
and passed out on his couch in an awkward position might
account for the stiffness in his neck and shoulders, but nothing in his memory compared with this piercing pounding,
as if someone had unleashed an unstoppable series of thun-
derclaps inside his head. Something was extremely wrong!

Sudden nausea propelled him toward the toilet, but
he didn't make it before forcefully ejecting everything
that remained in his stomach from the night before. The

exertion only accentuated the excruciating pain. Tony felt raw fear, long imprisoned by sheer willful determination, now bursting its bonds like a beast, feeding off expanding uncertainty. Fighting the debilitating terror, he staggered out the door of his condo, pressing both hands hard over his ears as if it would keep his head from exploding. He leaned into the hallway wall, frantically searching for his ever-present smart phone. A frenzy of pocket rifling produced nothing but a set of keys, and he was suddenly hopelessly awash in a terrible vacancy, an absence of connectedness. His would-be savior, the electronic purveyor of all things immediate but temporary, was missing.

The thought occurred to him that his cell phone might be in his coat, which he usually hung on the back of the kitchen chair, but the condo door had automatically locked when he exited. One eye wasn't functioning properly, so he squinted with the other at a blurry keypad, trying to remember the code that would allow him back inside, but the numbers spilled over one another and none of them made any sense. Closing his eyes he tried to concentrate, his heart pounding, his head on fire while growing desperation continued to build inside. Tony began weeping uncontrollably, which infuriated him, and in a flurry of profanity-empowered panic he began punching numbers randomly, frantic for a miracle. A wave of blackness dropped him to his knees and he slammed his head against the door. It only exacerbated the pain. Blood now streamed down his face from a gash where he had engaged the edge of the doorjamb.

Tony's confusion and agony increased until he was entirely disoriented, staring at an unfamiliar electronic keypad and in one hand holding a set of unfamiliar keys. Maybe he had a car nearby? Reeling along a short hall, he tripped down a flight of carpeted stairs and out into a parking garage. Now what? Pushing all the buttons on the key fobs, he was rewarded by the flashing lights of a gray sedan not thirty feet away. Another upwelling of darkness yanked him off his feet and down he went a second time. On his hands and knees, he crawled frantically toward the car as if life depended on it. Finally he made it as far as the trunk, hoisted himself to a stand, steadied for a moment while the world spun, and once again dropped, this time swallowed into a comforting nothingness. Everything that hurt and tugged so desperately for his attention stopped.

If anyone had witnessed him fall, which no one had, they might have described a sack of potatoes tossed from the back of a moving truck, collapsing in a heap as though no bones inhabited his body, dead weight pulled down by gravity. The back of his head struck the top of the trunk hard; his momentum spun him toward the concrete floor where his head bounced a second time with a sickening thud. Blood now oozed from his left ear and pooled from the gashes in his forehead and face. For almost ten minutes he lay in the dimly lit underground garage before a passerby busy looking for car keys in her purse stumbled over his leg. Her shriek echoed off the concrete. No one heard. Visibly shaking, she dialed 911.

The dispatcher, sitting in front of an array of screens, took the call at 8:41 a.m. "Nine-one-one. What is the location of the emergency?"

"Oh my God! He's bleeding everywhere! I think he's dead…" The woman was hysterical and on the verge of shock.

Trained for this, the dispatcher slowed the cadence of her voice. "Ma'am, I need you to calm down. I need you to tell me where you are, so I can send help." While listening she muted the call and on a separate line prenotified Portland Fire of the potential medical emergency. She quickly typed information and codes into the call log, maintaining communication to an expanding set of first responders. "Ma'am, can you tell me what you see?" She muted and switched, quickly stating, "Engine 10. M333 respond Code 3 on a UN3 at 5040 SW Macadam Avenue, cross street is Richardson Court, just north of the US Bank and beneath Weston Manor, in the first level of an underground parking garage on the river side."

"Medic 333 copy, switching to ops 1," came the response through her headphones.

"All right, ma'am, slow down and take a deep breath. You found a man who appears unconscious and there is blood...Okay, help is on the way and should be there in a couple minutes. I want you to stand to the side and wait for them to arrive...Uh-huh, that's right...I will stay on the line with you until help gets there. You did great! They are on their way and almost there."

Portland Fire arrived on-scene first and, locating Tony, did a quick initial assessment before beginning medical procedures to stabilize him while one of their crew calmed and interviewed the distraught witness. The ambulance operated by American Medical Response (AMR) was there only minutes later.

"Hey, guys, what do you have? What can I do to help?" asked the AMR paramedic.

"We have a fortyish male who the lady over there found laying on the ground next to his car. He's vomited and reeks of alcohol. He's got a large gash to his head and facial cuts and has been unresponsive. We did a manual c-spine, and he's on a non-rebreather."

"Did you get vitals yet?"

"Blood pressure is 260 over 140. Heart rate, 56.

Respiration's 12 but irregular. Right pupil is blown and he's bleeding from the right ear."

"Looks like a pretty significant head injury?"

"Yeah, that's what I'm thinking."

"Okay, then, let's get him on the board."

They carefully logrolled Tony and placed him on a full backboard. The fire crew securely strapped him down while the AMR paramedic started an IV.

"He's still pretty unresponsive and his breathing is erratic," offered the fire EMT. "What do you think about tubing him?"

"Good idea, but let's do it in the back of the ambulance."

"University COREL status is green," called out the driver.

They put Tony on a gurney and quickly loaded him into the ambulance while the driver called in.

Tony's vitals plummeted and he went into asystole, a type of cardiac arrest. A flurry of activity, including an injection of epinephrine, got his heart restarted.

"University, Medic 333. We are coming to your facility Code 3 with a fortyish-year-old male found down in a parking garage. The patient has an obvious head injury and was unresponsive upon arrival. Patient is 5 on the Glasgow Scale and is in full spinal precautions. He had a brief period of asystole, but return of pulse after 1 milligram epi. Last BP was 80/60. HR 72, and we are currently bagging him at a rate of 12 breaths per minute and preparing to intubate. We have an ETA to your facility of about five minutes, do you have any questions?"

"No questions. Administer 500 cc's of mannitol."

"Copy."

"Dispatch, Medic 333 is transporting with two firefighters aboard."

Siren howling, they exited the garage. It took less than five minutes to climb the winding hill to Oregon Health and Science University (OHSU), the hospital sitting like a gargoyle above the city. Wheeling Tony into the resuscitation rooms where incoming trauma patients are triaged, a crowd of doctors, nurses, techs, and residents converged and what ensued was orderly chaos, an intricate dance where each knew their role and expected participation. Rapid-fire questions punctuated the conversation with the first responders until the doctor in charge was satisfied, and the crew released to ease down from the adrenaline charge that usually accompanied such a call.

An initial CT scan and later CT angiography (CTA) revealed subarachnoid bleeding, as well as a brain tumor located in the frontal lobe. Hours later Tony was finally admitted to 7C, Neuro ICU, room 17. Attached to tubes and medical paraphernalia that both fed and kept him breathing, he was oblivious to being the center of so much attention.

⚜ ∞ 🎋 ✦ ∞ ❋ ⑤ ﷽

Tony could feel himself drifting, upward, as if drawn insistently toward something with a gentle but firm gravitational field. It was more like a mother's love than a solid object, and he didn't resist. He had a fuzzy remembrance of being in a fight that had exhausted him, but now the conflict was fading.

As he rose, an inner suggestion emerged that he was dying, and the thought easily anchored itself. Internally, he braced as if he might have the power to resist being absorbed into...what? Nothingness? Was he merging with the impersonal all-spirit?

No. He had long decided that death was the simple end,

the cessation of all conscious awareness, dust relentlessly returning to dust.

Such a philosophy had granted him solace in his selfishness. When all was said and done, wasn't he justified in looking out for himself, controlling not only his life but also others' lives for his benefit and advantage? There was no single right thing, no absolute truth, just legislated social mores and guilt-based conformity. Death as he viewed it meant that nothing truly mattered. Life was a violent evolutionary gasp of meaninglessness, the temporary survival of the smartest or most cunning. A thousand years from now, providing the human race survived, no one would know he had even existed or care how he lived his life.

As he floated upward with the invisible current, his philosophy began to sound rather ugly and something in him resisted, didn't want to accept that when the curtain was finally drawn, nothing and no one had meaning, that everything was part of the chaos of random self-interest pushing and pulling for position and power, the best techniques manipulative and egotistical. But what were the alternatives?

On one specific day, hope for anything more had died. That stormy November morning, for almost a minute, he held the first shovelful of dirt. Standing in wind-driven rain, he stared down at the small ornate box that held his Gabriel. Barely five years old and hardly a breath, his little boy had fought courageously to hold on to everything beautiful and good, only to be torn from the tenderness of the ones who loved him most.

Tony finally let the soil fall into that abyss. Shattered bits of his broken heart tumbled in also, along with any remaining scraps of hope. But no tears. Rage against God, against the machine, against even the decay in his own soul, had not saved or kept his son. Begging, promises, prayers, all bounced off the sky and returned empty, mocking his impotence. Nothing...nothing had made any difference as Gabriel's voice went silent.

With these remembrances his drift upward slowed and he hung in the inky blackness, suspended in a moment of question. If Gabe had lived, could that precious little boy have saved Tony's pathetic existence? Three other faces flashed to mind, three people he had failed intensely and miserably: Loree, teenage sweetheart and twice his wife; Angela, his daughter who probably hated him almost as much as he hated himself; and Jake...oh, Jake, I'm so sorry, little man.

But what did any of it matter anyway? Wishful thinking, that was the real foe. The what-if, or what could have been or should have been or might have been, was all a sucking waste of energy and an impediment to success and in-the-moment self-gratification. The very idea that anything mattered was a lie, a delusion, a false comfort as one drifted toward the ax. Once annihilated, what remained of him would be the illusions of those still living, retaining temporary but fleeting recollections, bad or good, all momentary bits of a mirage that his life had significance. Of course, if nothing had meaning, then even the idea that wishful thinking was the enemy became absurd.

Since hope was a myth, it could not be an enemy.

No, death was death and that was the final word. But, he then mused, this could not be rationally believable either. It meant that death itself would have meaning. Nonsense. He shut out his thoughts as just ridiculous and incongruous wonderings to avoid embracing the irrelevance of an empty and futile life.

He was rising again and could see in the far distance

a pinpoint of light. As it approached, or as he drew nearer, he wasn't sure which, it grew in substance and intensity. This would be the locus of his death; of this he was now certain. He had read about people who died and saw a light but always considered it no more than the final firings of neuro-circuitry. The brain was greedy for one last, pointless grasp of any vestige of thought and memory, a desperate clutch at something as elusive as quicksilver in a calloused hand.

Tony let himself go. He felt caught in an invisible river, engulfed in an antigravitational wave that propelled his consciousness toward the point of brightness. Its brilliance increased until he had to turn his head, squinting to protect himself from the luminescence that both pierced and warmed. He now realized he had been cold in the grip of whatever was suspending him. But even while he turned his face away, something within him was reaching out, as if responding to an invitation inherent in this dazzling.

Abruptly, his feet scraped against what felt like rocky ground and his hands brushed against walls on either side. Smells of dirt and leaves filled his senses. Was he buried and looking up from the bottom of a grave? The terrible thought occurred to him, and corresponding fear instantly squeezed breath from his lungs. Was he not completely dead and mourners had gathered to pay their last respects, not knowing that he was in fact still alive?

The rush of alarm was brief. It was finished and he was being undone. He gave himself reluctantly to his end, folding his arms across his chest. The intensity of the light was so overpowering he was forced to turn completely away. The rush was terrifying and exhilarating. He was propelled into the dismantling fire and blinded by...

3

ONCE UPON A TIME

Some day you will be old enough to start reading
fairy tales again.
—C. S. Lewis

Sunlight?

It was sunlight! How could it be sunlight? Any clarity of thought Tony had established disappeared in a rush of sensory overload. He again closed his eyes, letting the distant radiance warm his face and wrap his chill in her golden blanket. For a moment he cared about nothing. Then, like an impending dawn, the impossibility of his situation crashed his reverie.

Where was he? How had he gotten here?

Tony opened his eyes carefully and looked down, squinting to allow them to adjust. He was clothed in familiar old jeans and the pair of hiking boots he wore to navigate low-tide beach rocks at Depoe Bay. Tony had always been more comfortable in these clothes than the suits he wore to his daily grind. *These boots should be in my beach house closet*, was his first thought. They bore the recognizable scores from scraping against the ancient coastal lava along the Oregon seashore.

Looking around deepened his bewilderment. No clues indicated where he was or even when he was. Behind him lay the opening of a small black hole, supposedly the place from which he had been so unceremoniously ejected. The shaft looked barely large enough to fit through, and he couldn't see a foot past its entrance. Turning back, he shielded his eyes against the sunshine and scanned the landscape spread before him, mentally cataloging his growing number of questions.

However he had come to this place, whether expelled, delivered, or propelled through the dark tunnel, he was now centered in a narrow mountain meadow strewn with wildflowers: orange agoseris, a scattering of purple anemone and the delicate whites of alumroot interspersed with the daisy-like yellow arnica. It was an invitation to take a deep breath, and when he did he could almost taste the scents, strong and savory with barely a touch of salt in the wind as if an ocean lay just beyond the range of sight. The air itself was crisp and clean, no hint of anything not native to the place. Below him lay the expanse of a huge valley surrounded by a range of mountains similar to the Canadian Rockies, postcard picturesque and panoramic. Central to the valley was a lake radiant with the early afternoon's reflections. An irregular shoreline cast shadows into attending valleys and river feeders that were invisible from where he looked. Thirty feet in front of him the meadow vanished sharply and dangerously into a ravine, the floor at least a thousand feet below. Everything was stunning and vivid, as if his senses had been unleashed from their usual tethers. He breathed deeply.

The lea in which he stood was not more than a hundred feet in length, sleeping between borders marked by the precipice along one side and the steep mountain slope on the other. To his left its floral-colored patterns abruptly ended at sheer rock walls, but in the opposite direction there was a single path barely discernible and disappearing into the tree line and encroaching thickness of bushy green foliage. A slight breeze kissed his cheek and teased his hair, a waft of perfumed fragrances lingering in the air as if a woman had passed by.

Tony stood absolutely still, as if that would help quiet the storm inside his head. His thoughts were a cascade of confusion. Was he dreaming or insane? Was he dead? Obviously not, unless…unless he was completely wrong about death, a thought too disconcerting to take seriously. He reached up and touched his face as if that might confirm something.

The last thing he remembered was what? The images were a jumble of meetings and migraines, and then a quick jolt of alarm. He remembered careering out of control from his condo, clutching his head because it felt about to explode, and stumbling his way to the parking structure in search of his car. Being drawn toward a light was his last memory. Now he was here, with no idea where "here" was.

Assuming he wasn't dead, maybe he was in a hospital, loaded with drugs that were trying to calm an electrical storm firing inside his brain. Perhaps he was caught in the backwash, creating unrealities in his own head, neural net connections of incongruent hallucinations collected over a lifetime's expanse. What if he were sitting in a padded cell, locked in a straitjacket and drooling on himself? Death would be preferable. But then again, it was more than tolerable if comas or insanity delivered one to shores like this.

Another cooler wind bussed his face and he again

inhaled deeply, feeling a wave of...what, exactly? He wasn't sure. Euphoria? No. This had more substance than that. Tony didn't have a word for this, but it clearly resonated inside like the dim remembrance of a first kiss, now ethereal yet eternally haunting.

So what now? It seemed that he had two choices, besides just staying in this place and waiting to see what came to him. He had never been one for waiting...not for anything. Actually, there were three choices if he included stepping off the cliff to see what would happen. He couldn't help but grin as he shrugged that idea away. That would make for a short adventure; to find out he was not dreaming and not dead.

He turned back to the cave, startled to see that it had vanished, absorbed back into the wall of granite without a trace. That option removed, he was down to only one obvious choice, the path.

Tony hesitated at the trail's beginning, letting his eyes adjust to the darker interior of the forest. He glanced back at the vista behind him, reluctant to leave its embracing warmth in exchange for this cooler uncertainty. Again, he had to wait while his vision corrected and he could see the trail dissolve into the underbrush not thirty feet ahead. The woods were chillier but not uncomfortable, the sun filtering through the canopy above casting shards of light that captured dust motes and occasional insects in its beams. Lush dense undergrowth hemmed in the rocky and defined path, which almost appeared as if it had been freshly laid and awaiting him.

He could smell this world, a mixture of life and decay, the piney dampness of old growth, moldy and yet sweet. Tony took another deep breath, trying to hold the scent. It was almost an intoxication, a remembrance of Scotch, similar to his beloved Balvenie Portwood, but richer, purer, and with a stronger aftertaste. He grinned, at no one, and plunged into the woods.

Not a hundred yards from where he began there was a branching of the trail, one to the right that inclined away, another that dropped downward to the left, and a third that went directly ahead. He stood for a moment considering the options.

It is an odd feeling, trying to make a decision about matters where not only the outcomes are unforeseeable, but the present situation is unknown. He didn't know where he had come from, didn't know where he was going, and was now faced with choices with no knowledge of what each might mean, or cost.

Standing suspended between options, Tony was struck by the thought that he had been here before. Not actually, but in some sense truly. Life had been a long series of encountered choices, intersections, and he had bluffed his way to decisions, convincing himself and others that he completely understood where each would take them, that each was a simple extension of his own correct evaluations and brilliant judgments.

Tony had labored diligently to extract certainty out of option, to somehow control the future and its outcomes by exuding an aura of intelligent prophetic prescience. The truth, he now understood, was that eventualities and consequences were never inevitable, and marketing and image-making were the tools of choice to cover the disparity. There were always interfering variables outside the range of probability that muddied the waters of control. Creating the illusion that he knew and then bluffing became his method of operation. It was a grueling challenge to remain a prophet when things were so unpredictable.

He stood facing three choices with not one clue as to where each would lead. Surprisingly, there was an unexpected freedom in not knowing, the absence of any expectation that would eventually find him guilty of a wrong decision. He was free in this moment to pick any direction, and that autonomy was both exhilarating and frightening, a tightrope walk potentially between fire and ice.

A closer examination of each of the particular paths did not help. One might initially appear easier than another, but that was no guarantee of what lay around the next bend. He stood, frozen by the freedom inherent in the moment.

"You can't steer a docked ship," he mumbled, and took the middle path, making a mental note in case he had to find his way back. Back to where? He didn't know.

Less than two hundred yards down the trail of choice he encountered another three-way branch, and again had to evaluate and choose. He simply shook his head, hardly pausing, and took the one that climbed upward to the right, adding the turn to his imaginary notebook. Within the first mile or so, Tony faced more than twenty such decisions and quit the mental gymnastics required to track where he had come from. To be safe he probably should have always picked the middle path. Instead, his journey had become a jumble of right, left, up, down, and straight. He felt hopelessly lost, not that he had been found to begin with or had any sense of a destination, which only added to his feeling of bewilderment.

What if it's not about getting anywhere? he wondered. What if there was no goal or objective here? As the pressure to "arrive" eased, Tony unintentionally slowed down and began paying attention to the world around him. This felt like a living place, almost as if it were breathing along with him. The wing-tunes of insects, the calls and color flashes of birds announcing his presence, and the occasional movement of invisible animals through the underbrush only added to the sensation of unsettled wonder. Not having an objective had inherent gifts—no timetable demands and no agendas—and Tony hesitantly allowed the surroundings to begin assuaging the nagging frustration of being so utterly disoriented.

At times the footpaths took him through old-growth timber, a wonder of massive trees standing almost shoulder to shoulder in their grandeur, twisted arms locked in seeming solidarity that darkened the floor beneath their conjoined canopy. *Not a lot of old growth left in my life*, he thought and shrugged. *What I didn't sell, I burned.*

One trail took him under a cleft in the rocky face of the mountain, almost but not quite a cave, and he couldn't help but quicken his pace in case this little gap closed and crushed him in a stony grip. Another choice took him through a scarred area where fire had some time past ripped the heart out of the woods, leaving stubs and relics of the aged along with scatterings of a new generation of tender growth, feeding off the death of the past and emerging to salvage what had been lost, and more. One path merged and followed an ancient and dried sandy riverbed, while another was a barely discernible climb on velvet moss that swallowed his footprints as he passed. But always another crossing, and more alternatives.

After several hours of hiking, wandering, and wondering, it occurred to Tony that the number of direction decisions was diminishing; options were significantly decreasing. The singular footpath slowly widened into something that could easily be a narrow lane, the trees and brush on either side closing ranks to form an almost impenetrable barrier. Perhaps he was finally getting somewhere. His steps quickened. The thoroughfare, now a road, began an easy descent, the woods thickening until he had the sense of striding down a green-and-brown carpeted hallway with a blue cloud–dotted ceiling.

Turning another corner, he stopped. A quarter mile in front and sloping away from him, the walls of emerald turned to stone. The road ended at a massive door built into what appeared to be the ramparts of a colossal rock structure. The construction was not unlike fortified cities Tony had seen pictured in books and modeled in museums, except this was gargantuan in comparison.

He continued toward what he now believed was the imaginary door of an imaginary fortification. He had never questioned the profoundly inventive power of the human mind, one of evolution's most impressive accidents, but this creation was staggering and beyond any expectations. He surmised it was the combined result of neurologically stimulating drugs and an imagination unleashed, the collected residue of children's fables with castles and ramparts. But it felt so real and tangible, like those few dreams he vividly remembered in which the details never escaped, the kind that felt so actual you had to trace your steps to conclude they were impossible. This was like that; real but impossible. The only explanation was that he was caught in the chaos of a most vivid dream!

Such a conclusion was an instant relief, as if he had been holding his breath waiting, and finally his mind had found an organizing principle. It had been stated. This was his dream. This was a projection of an unleashed psyche empowered by medicine's best psychotropic drugs. He raised his hands into the air and shouted, "A dream! My dream! Incredible! I'm awesome!" It echoed back off the distant walls and he laughed.

His mind's creativity was inspiring and impressive. As

if hearing the accompanying sound track to this movie of his hallucination, Tony did a little dance, arms still raised, head upturned, slow spin to the left, then the right. He had never been much of a dancer, but here no one could see him and so there was no chance of embarrassment. If he wanted to dance, he would dance. This was "his" dream, and he possessed the power and authority to do whatsoever he wanted.

This did not quite turn out to be the truth.

As if to prove a point, Tony pointed his palms toward the distant rock monstrosity, and as if he were a magician's apprentice, commanded, "Open sesame!" Nothing happened. Well, it was worth an attempt. It only meant that even in vivid dreams, his control was limited. There was no turning back and so Tony continued his walk, enthralled by the grandeur and scope of his imagination. Since this was his mind at work, then all this must mean something, maybe even something significant.

By the time he reached the door, Tony had come to no conclusions about the meaning and import of his vision. Although it almost seemed trivial in comparison to the structure into which it was carved, the portal was massive and made him feel tiny and insignificant. He took time to examine it without touching it. While obviously a point of entry, there were no visible means of access, no knob or keyhole, nothing that would allow him admission. It seemed it could be opened only from the inside, which meant that something, or someone, had to be in there to open it.

"Well, this should be interesting," he muttered to himself, and raised his fist to knock. Tony froze! He heard a knock, but it wasn't him; his hand was still raised. He looked at his fist, confused. He heard another knock, strong and loud. Three raps on the door, from the other side. He even waved his fist around in front of his face, to see if somehow he was inadvertently creating the knocking sound, but nothing happened.

And then it came a third time, three raps, strong but not insistent. He looked back at the door. A clasp had appeared where he hadn't seen one before. How could he have missed it? Hesitantly, he reached out and felt it, a piece of metal cold to the touch that operated a very simple lever that lifted a bar keeping the door in place. He didn't remember seeing the bar earlier either. Without another thought, as if on command, Tony raised the latch and stepped aside as the immense portal easily and without a sound swung inward.

On the other side stood a man Tony didn't recognize leaning against the massive doorjamb. His face lit up in a wide and welcoming smile. But the biggest shock was that when Tony looked past him, he was looking up the road he himself had so recently traveled. He was inside the edifice, and without realizing it had somehow opened the door from within. Slowly he turned around to be certain, and it was true. He was already standing inside, looking farther into a sweeping open land, likely more than half a dozen square miles in area. The property was confined inside gigantic stone walls, a boundaried fortress in contrast to the wild and free world outside.

Reaching for the wall to steady himself, he turned back. The man was still there, leaning against the doorjamb, smiling at him. As if caught in vertigo, Tony felt the world tilting and his footing slip, his knees buckled, and a familiar darkness began clouding his vision. Perhaps the dream was ending and he was returning to the place he had come from, where things made more sense, and where at least he knew what he didn't know.

Strong arms caught and gently helped him to the ground, leaning him against the wall on the other side of the entrance he had just opened.

"Here, drink this." Through a muddy haze he felt cool liquid being poured into his mouth. Water! It had been hours since he'd had any water. Maybe that was what had happened, dehydration. He had been walking in the woods; wait…that couldn't be right? No, he was lying in a parking structure and now he was in a castle? A castle, with…with who? The prince?

That's stupid, he mused, his thoughts a jumble. *I'm not a princess.* And that made him chuckle. As he slowly sipped the refreshing fluid, the mist gradually lifted and his senses began to clear.

"Dare say," came the voice, strongly accented, British or Australian if Tony was to hazard a guess, "if you were a princess, you would scarcely fit the fables, being as homely as you are."

Tony leaned back against the rock and looked up at the gentleman hovering over him with a flask outstretched. Hazelnut-brown eyes sparkled back. He had a mildly stocky build, probably only an inch or two shorter than Tony, and appeared to be in his late fifties, maybe even older. A high forehead and receding hairline gave him an air of intelligence, as if he needed the extra room for deep thought. His dress was old-fashioned, wrinkled gray flannel trousers and a worn brown tweed jacket that had seen better days and fit a little too snug. He looked bookish, his skin the pasty white of long periods indoors, but his hands were those of a butcher, thick and rough. Childlikeness danced on the edges of a playful grin as he patiently waited for Tony to collect his thoughts and finally find his voice.

"So"—Tony cleared his throat—"do all those trails end

up here?" The question seemed rather shallow, but in the myriad of so many it was the first to surface.

"No," the man answered, his voice strong and resonant. "Quite the opposite, actually. All those paths originate from here. Not often traveled these days."

That didn't make sense to Tony, and in the moment it felt complicated so he asked another simpler question: "Are you British?"

"Ha!" The man threw back his head and laughed. "Oh, heavens no! Irish! The true English," he said as he leaned forward again, "although, in the spirit of accuracy, though I was born in Ireland, I am probably thoroughly British by culture. There wasn't much of a difference when I was young so your mistake is entirely forgivable." He laughed again and lowered himself to sit on a flat rock next to Tony, his knees up so his elbows could rest comfortably.

Both of them looked back up the road quarantined by woods.

"I will admit," the Irishman continued, "just between you and me, I have continued to grow in my appreciation for the contribution the British made to my life. However, they almost accidently killed a few of us during the Great War by shelling short. Too few mathematicians, I suppose. Thank God we were on their side."

As if to celebrate his sarcasm, the man removed a small pipe from the tweed pocket that covered his heart, inhaled, and slowly blew out the smoke like a sigh of relief. The scent was pleasant and lingered until absorbed by the stronger forest fragrances. Without looking, he offered the pipe to Tony.

"Would you like to try? Three Nuns sitting cozy in a Tetley Lightweight, another 'thank you' to the British." He bowed slightly as he finished his sentence.

"Uh, no thank you, I don't smoke," Tony answered.

"Just as well, Mr. Spencer," the man responded wryly. "I've been told it can kill you."

With that he slipped it back into his jacket pocket, bowl down, still lit. A piece of unrelated cloth, trouser maybe, had been sewn into the pocket. Most assuredly smoldering embers had eaten away the original.

"You know me?" asked Tony, trying to place this stranger in his memory, but nothing connected.

"We all know you, Mr. Spencer. But please, forgive my poor manners. Truly bad form. My name is Jack, and I am honored to finally meet you, face-to-face, that is." He held out his hand and Tony took it, out of habit if nothing more.

"Uh, Tony... but you already knew that? How do you know me exactly? Have we met before?"

"Not directly. It was your mother that first introduced me to you. It is small wonder that you have little recollection. I never considered myself that memorable anyway. Nonetheless, childhood influences have staggering formative consequences, for good and evil, or for life."

"But how...," Tony stammered, confused.

"As I stated before, we all know you. Knowing is quite layered. Even our own souls we hardly apprehend until the veils are lifted, until we come out of the hiding and into the place of being known."

"I'm sorry?" interrupted Tony, feeling rising aggravation. "What you just said makes no sense to me at all and frankly seems utterly irrelevant. I have no idea where I am or even when I am, and you are not being very helpful!"

"Indeed." Jack nodded soberly, as if that might comfort.

Tony buried his head in his hands trying to think, resisting as best he could the irritation he felt growing. They both sat silently looking back up the road.

"Anthony, you do know me, not well and not truly, but substantially, hence your invitation." Jack's voice was sure and measured, and Tony concentrated on what he was saying. "I was an influence on you when you were a young man. That *guidance and perspective*, shall we call it, has undoubtedly faded, but its roots remain."

"My invitation? I don't remember inviting anyone to anything! And you don't look familiar to me at all," Tony asserted. "I don't know who you are! I don't know Jack from Ireland!"

Jack's voice remained calm. "Your invitation was many years ago and probably remains at best but a vague feeling or longing for you. If I had thought to bring a book and you could smell its pages, that most assuredly would help, but I didn't. We never actually met, at least not in person, until now. Would it surprise you to know that I died a few years before you were born?"

"Oh, this just gets better," Tony exploded, standing up a little too quickly. His legs were rubbery, but his anger propelled him a few steps back up the road in the direction from which he had come. He stopped and turned around. "Did you just say that you died a few years before I was born?"

"I did. On the same day Kennedy was assassinated and Huxley died. Quite the trio turning up, as they say, at the 'pearly gates'…" He said this using his fingers to form quotation marks. "You should have seen the look on Aldous's face. Brave new world, indeed!"

"So then, Jack from Ireland, who says he knows me"— Tony again moved closer, his tone controlled even while he could feel his ire and fear pushing the perimeters of internal boundaries—"where the hell am I?"

Jack hoisted himself to a stand and took a position not even a foot away from Tony's face. He paused, his head slightly cocked as if listening to another conversation before he spoke, carefully emphasizing his next words.

"There is indeed a sense that the word *hell* might be an appropriate word for here, but then, so would the word *home*."

Tony took a step back, trying to process what Jack had said.

"Are you telling me that this is hell, that I'm in hell?"

"Not exactly, at least not in the sense that you imagine it. I am certain Dante is not lurking anywhere nearby."

"Dante?"

"Dante, with his inferno and pitchforks and all. Poor boy is still apologizing."

"You said, not exactly? What do you mean, not exactly?"

"Tony, what exactly do you think hell is?" Jack's question was calm and measured.

It was now Tony's turn to pause. This conversation was not going in any direction he'd anticipated, but he quickly made a mental decision to humor this curious man. After all, he might have information that would prove useful or at least helpful.

"Uh, I don't know…exactly." No one had ever asked him so directly. The question of hell had always been an assumption. As a result, Tony's response came out more a question than a statement. "A place of eternal torment with fire and gnashing of teeth and stuff?"

Jack stood listening as if waiting for more.

"Uh, a place where God punishes people he is angry with because they are sinners," continued Tony. "Uh, where bad people are separated from God and good people go to heaven?"

"And you believe that?" asked Jack, again cocking his head to one side.

"No," responded Tony adamantly. "I think that when you die you die. You become worm-meal, dust to dust, no rhyme, no reason, just dead."

Jack grinned. "Ah, spoken with the certainty of a man who has never died. If I may, might I ask you another question?"

Tony barely nodded, but it was enough and Jack continued, "Does your believing this, that dead is simply dead and that is 'all she wrote'; does your believing it make it true?"

"Sure! It's real to me," retorted Tony.

"I didn't ask if it was real to you. Obviously it is real to you, but what I asked was if it was true."

Tony looked down, thinking. "I don't get it. What's the difference? If it's real, isn't it true?"

"Oh, not at all Tony! And to make matters even more convoluted, something might be real but not actually exist at all, while truth remains independent from what is real or perceived to be real."

Tony raised his palms and shrugged, shaking his head. "Sorry, this is way beyond me. I don't understand—"

"Oh, but you do," interrupted Jack, "much more than you realize, no pun intended; so let me give you examples that will clarify."

"Do I have a choice?" Tony acquiesced, still at a loss but more interested than aggravated. Somewhere in this man's words was hidden a compliment, and while he couldn't grasp it, he could sense it.

Jack smiled. "Choice? Hmm, good question, but for another time. To my point, there are those who 'really' believe there was no Holocaust, that no one has actually walked on the moon, that the earth is flat, that there are monsters living under the bed. Real to them, but not true. Closer to home, your Loree believed..."

"What does my wife have to do with any of this?" reacted Tony, more than a little defensively. "I suppose you know her, too, and just so you understand, in case she's lurking around here, too, somewhere, I have no interest in talking to her."

Jack held up his hands in surrender. "Tony, calm down, this is just an illustration, not a reprimand. May I continue?"

Tony folded his arms and nodded. "Yeah, sorry; as you can see, not a favorite topic of conversation."

"Yes, I do understand," resumed Jack. "That is also for another time. Again, my question: Did Loree at any time believe that your love for her was real?"

It was bold and almost absurdly personal in the current circumstances, and Tony took a moment before answering candidly. "Yes," he admitted. "There was probably a time when she believed my love for her was real."

"So, you think it was real to her?"

"If she believed it was real, then yes, it was real to her."

"Then it begs the question, was your love for her real to you, Tony? Did you truly love her?"

Instantly Tony felt an internal guard go up, the discomfort associated with a perceived accusation. Normally, now would be the time to change the subject, to make a witty or sarcastic remark to deflect the emotions being exposed and turn the river of words toward more lighthearted and irrelevant banter. But Tony had nothing to lose in this exchange. He would never see this man again, and he was intrigued by the moment. It had been a long time, he thought, since a conversation had gone so deep so quickly, and he had allowed it. Such was the safety of dreaming.

"Honestly?" He paused. "Honestly, I don't think I knew how to love her, or how to love anyone for that matter."

"Thank you, Anthony, for that admission. I am certain

you are correct. But the point is that she believed in your love, and even though it didn't exist, it became so real to her that she built a world and life around it...twice."

"You didn't have to bring that up," muttered Tony, again looking away.

"Just an observation, son, not a judgment. On to a second illustration, shall we?" He waited for Tony to catch up and then began. "Let's just suppose, for the sake of this example, that there is truly a God, a being of—"

"I don't believe any of that stuff," interjected Tony.

"I am not trying to convince you of anything, Tony," maintained Jack. "Not my job. Keep in mind that I am dead, and you are...confused. I am simply positing something to amplify the difference between real and true. That is our subject if you recall." He smiled, and Tony couldn't help but respond with one of his own. There was a kindness in this man that was disarming, almost deeper than genuine.

"So let's suppose this God is good all the time, never a liar, never a deceiver, always a truth-teller. One day this God comes to you, Anthony Spencer, and says this: 'Tony, nothing will ever separate you from my love, neither death nor life, not a messenger from heaven nor a monarch of earth, neither what happens today nor what may happen tomorrow, neither a power from on high nor a power from below, nor anything else in God's entire created cosmos; nothing has the power to separate you from my love.'

"So, you listen to God tell you this, but you don't believe it. Not believing it becomes what is real to you, and you then create a world that holds not believing the word of this God, or the love of this God, or even in this God at all, as a fundamental cornerstone of your life's construction. Here is one question nestled among many others: Does your inability to believe the word of this God make what this God has said not true?"

"Yes," Tony responded too quickly, and then, thinking, changed his mind. "I mean no. Wait, let me think about this a second."

Jack paused, allowing Tony to sift through his thoughts before speaking.

"Okay," Tony replied, "if what you assume about this God is true...and real, then I guess my belief wouldn't change anything. I think I'm beginning to understand what you're saying."

"Do you?" challenged Jack. "Then let me ask this: If you choose not to believe the word of this God, what would you 'experience' in relationship to this God?"

"Uh, I would experience..." Tony was struggling, looking for the right words.

"Separation?" Jack filled in the blank. "Tony, you would experience a sense of separation, because separation is what you thought was 'real.' Real is what you believe, even if what you believe does not exist. God tells you that separation is not true, that nothing can 'really' separate you from the love of God—not things, behaviors, experiences, or even death and hell, however you choose to imagine it; but you believe separation is real, and so you create your own reality based on a lie."

It was too much for Tony and he turned away, rubbing his hands through his hair. "Then how does one ever know what is true? What is truth?"

"Aha!" exclaimed Jack, slapping Tony on the shoulder. "Pontius Pilate speaks from the dead. And there, lad, is an ultimate irony! Standing at the fulcrum of history in the very presence and face-to-face with truth, he, as so many of us are wont to do, declared it nonexistent, or, to be more accurate, declared 'him' to be nonexistent. Thankfully, for all our sakes, Pilate did not have the power to turn something real into something that wasn't true." He paused before saying, "And Tony, neither do you."

The moment was frozen for a brief second and then the ground shook slightly, as if a small tremor had occurred deep beneath their feet. Jack smiled his enigmatic best and declared, "Well, I think that means my time with you, for now, is finished."

"Wait!" objected Tony. "I have questions. Where are you going? Can't you stay? I still don't understand where I am. Why am I here? If this isn't hell exactly, what is this? And you said something about it not being exactly home either? What does that mean?"

Jack turned back to face Tony one last time. "Tony, hell is believing and living in the real when it is not the truth. Potentially you could do that forever, but let me say something that is true, whether or not you choose to believe it, and whether or not it is real to you." He again waited. "Whatever you believe about death and hell, it is truly not separation."

The ground shook again, this time a larger statement than previously, and Tony steadied himself against the rock wall. When he turned back Jack was gone, and night had fallen.

Suddenly, Tony felt exhausted, tired to the center of his bones. He sat down once again, rested against the colossal structure, and looked out at the road and scenery that were quickly exchanging their colors for shades of gray. His mouth dry and clammy, he felt around him, hoping Jack had left his flask, but his searching hands found nothing. Drawing his knees up into his body, he secured a little place of protection, a huddle against the cold that had begun a relentless creep inside, like a thief stealing away fragmented pieces of warmth.

It was too much! An icy wind had risen, blowing his questions away like bits of paper scattered by a gale. Was this now the end? Finally? Could he hear the groaning approach of emptiness, a swallowing nothingness determined to extract from him the last vestige of heat?

He was shivering uncontrollably when a light appeared, a bluish luminescence that surrounded the most beautiful dark brown eyes he had ever seen. It reminded him of someone, but he couldn't remember who. Someone important.

Fighting to stay conscious, Tony managed to form the question, "Who am I? No, wait, where am I?" A man sat and cradled Tony in his arms, and carefully poured another warmer liquid into Tony's mouth; he could feel it expanding and soaking into his frozen center, spreading outward. His shaking slowed, then stopped, and he relaxed into the man's embrace.

"Safe," the man whispered, and stroked his head. "You are safe, Tony."

"Safe?" Again Tony could feel darkness descending. His eyes were heavy, his thoughts thick and slowing. "Safe? Never been safe."

"Shhhh." Again that voice. "It's time to rest a little. I am not leaving. I will always hold you, Tony."

"Who are you?"

If the man answered, Tony didn't hear him as the night, like a blanket, wrapped him in a tender caress and he slept safely without dream or even wishful thought.

4

HOME IS WHERE THE HEART IS

I long, as every human being does, to be at home
wherever I find myself.
—Maya Angelou

Sunlight?

It was sunlight, again. But this time different, muted and softer. Tony sat up with a start. Now where was he? With the question everything instantly returned: the tunnel, the trails with the myriad of choices, the door, Irishman Jack, the other man.

The other man? That was the last he remembered. Was he still dreaming? Was he in a dream inside a dream? He had been asleep, or dreaming that he slept. The sun streamed through curtains, lighting the room well enough to reveal he had awoken in a makeshift bedroom. A thin mattress covered a sagging spring frame. The blanket he had slept under was tattered and ragged, but clean.

Pulling back the curtain, he spied the same sprawling countryside he had briefly seen from the portal in the wall.

When had that happened? Last night or yesterday or never? Stone walls rose in the faraway, and inside of them were terraced open spaces, trees growing haphazardly, some in clumps, others solitary. A few buildings dotted the landscape, barely noticeable and unremarkable.

Tony heard a knock at the door. Three taps, like before, and Tony steadied himself against the wall, prepared for another inside-outside switch.

"Come in?" It came out more a question than an invitation, but it didn't seem to matter.

"Can you grab the door?" came a vaguely familiar voice from the other side. "My hands are full and I can't open it."

"Uh, sure, sorry," apologized Tony as he pulled the door inward.

There stood the stranger from before, with the penetrating dark brown eyes, and suddenly Tony remembered "safe." This man said he was "safe." "Safe" had been a relief, but was now deeply perplexing.

"Okay if I come in?" the man said with a grin, holding a tray of coffee and pastries. He appeared about the same age as Tony. Dressed in jeans and a woodsy shirt, the man had dark bronze skin that looked hued by sun and wind.

Tony suddenly became aware that he was wearing a blue-and-white hospital gown, a draft notifying him that it was open at the back. It seemed oddly appropriate and disturbing. Feeling exposed, he used one hand to clutch and close the opening as best he could. "Of course, sorry," he apologized again, not knowing what else to do, and stepping aside, he held the door open so the man could enter.

"I've got some of your favorites: coffee from Barista, a McMinnville Cream and Mango Tango from Voodoo Donuts, and a jelly from Heavenly Donuts. The almost perfect way to start a day."

"Uh, thank you!" Tony picked up a large mug of steaming coffee, a vanilla latte with perfect foam, a feather design etched into its surface. He took a sip, piping hot, letting the flavors settle before he swallowed, and then sat down carefully on the edge of the spring-loaded bed. "You're not having any?"

"Nah, tea man myself, and already had enough this morning." The man pulled a chair closer to Tony and sat down. "I suppose you have more than a few questions, son, so you ask and I will answer as best you can understand."

"Am I dreaming?"

The man sat back in the chair and smiled. "Well, for a first question you ask an involved one, and I am afraid the answer will not be very satisfying. Are you dreaming? Yes and no. Let me see if I can answer the question you meant and not just the one you asked. Anthony, you are in a coma, up the hill at OHSU, and you are here, too."

"Wait, I'm in a coma?"

"Yup, I'm right here, and I heard me say that, too."

"I am in a coma?" Tony was incredulous. He sat back, and without thinking, took another sip of his scalding drink.

"And this?" He nodded at the coffee.

"That is coffee."

"I know it's coffee, but is it, you know, real? How can I be in a coma and drinking a latte?"

"That's part of what you wouldn't understand if I tried to explain it."

"I can't believe it, I'm in a coma," he repeated, stunned.

The man stood up and put his hand on Tony's shoulder. "Tell you what, I have a couple things that I want to do, so I'll be right outside. Why don't you gather up your questions and meet me out there. Your clothes are hanging in the closet over there, and you'll find your boots there, too. When you're ready, just find your way out."

"Okay" was all Tony could manage, hardly glancing up as the man slipped out of the room. It strangely made sense. If he was in a coma, then these occurrences were only expressions of deep subconscious wanderings. He would remember none of it. None of this was real, or true. The thought reminded him of Irishman Jack, and he grinned to himself. The realization was attended by a sense of relief. At least he wasn't dead.

He slurped his latte. It certainly tasted real, but there must be triggers in the brain that could stimulate other parts like memory and together could manufacture a pseudoreality, like drinking coffee, or, he thought as he reached for a Mango Tango and took a bite, like one of these. Wow, if you could package this somehow, you could make a killing—no calories, no coffee or sugar side effects, and no supply-chain issues.

He shook his head at the sheer lunacy of this experience, if it could even be categorized as one. Does an event that isn't real and will never be remembered qualify as an experience?

With the last bite of donut, Tony felt it was time to face what awaited him on the other side of the door. Though he assuredly would remember none of this, here he was, with nothing to lose by going along with whatever this was. So he quickly dressed, grateful his imagination supplied warm water to wash his face. Taking a deep breath, he stepped outside the bedroom.

He found himself emerging from the wing of a rambling ranch-style house that had seen better days. Paint was flaking off the woodwork and everything felt tired. Sad and tidy, it was much below the standard to which Tony had grown accustomed and definitely was not ostentatious or pretentious. His room opened onto a wide wraparound deck, it, too, worse for wear. The stranger stood leaning against the railing, picking at his teeth with a piece of grass, waiting.

Tony joined him and looked out over the expanse of property. It was an odd mix, this place. Parts of it looked somewhat managed but much of it was unkempt and disorganized. Behind nearby broken fencing he noticed the barely recognizable suggestion of an abandoned garden overrun by thistle and thorn and dense weeds, an ancient oak at its center from which hung a dilapidated children's swing barely moving in the breeze. Beyond that lay an old orchard, unpruned and fruitless. In general, the land looked worn and abused, spent. Thankfully, patches of mountain wildflowers and the occasional rose had populated some of the worst scars, as if softening a loss or grieving a death.

Probably something wrong with the soil, Tony surmised. It seemed water and sun were in supply but so much depends on what lies beneath the surface. The breeze shifted and Tony picked up the unmistakable scent of daphne, sweet and gentle, a reminder of his mother. It was her favorite plant.

If, as he suspected, all this was a manifestation of his brain trying to find its way by connecting stored thoughts and images, it made sense that he felt a surprising, unexpected ease here. Something here called to him, or at least resonated. "Safe" had been the word this man had spoken over him. Not exactly a word he would have chosen.

"What is this place?" he asked.

"It's a habitation," the man responded, looking into the distance.

"A habitation? What exactly is a habitation?"

"A place to dwell, to abide, to be at home in, a habitation." The man said these words as if he loved this place.

"Home? Huh, that's something Jack said about this place, although he said it wasn't 'exactly' home. He also said it wasn't 'exactly' hell either, whatever that meant."

The man grinned. "You don't know Jack. Extraordinarily clever with words, that one."

"I didn't understand everything he said, but I started to get the gist of one thing—the difference between real and true."

"Hmmm," the man grunted and remained silent, as if not to interrupt Tony's processing. They stood for a time, side by side, each seeing the place through different eyes— one compassionate, the other uneasy and a little dismayed.

"So, when you say this is a habitation, are you talking about this old run-down house or does that include the property, too?"

"It includes everything, everything you saw yesterday and more; all that is inside this enclosure and all that is outside of it, everything. But here," he said, his hand spanning the entire enclosure, "is the center, the heart of the habitation. What happens here changes everything."

"Who owns it?"

"No one. This place was never intended to be 'owned.'" He enunciated the last word as if it were slightly repulsive and didn't belong in his mouth. "It was intended to be free, open, unrestricted...never owned."

There were a few seconds of quiet as Tony considered the right words for his next question. "So then, who 'belongs' here?"

A smile toyed at the corner of the man's mouth before he answered, "I do!"

"You live here?" he asked before thinking. Of course he did. This stranger was a complex projection of Tony's own subconscious, and somehow he was interacting with it. Besides, no one would actually live here, in the middle of nowhere, alone like this.

"I certainly do."

"You like living alone?"

"Don't know. I've never lived alone."

That piqued Tony's curiosity. "What do you mean? I haven't seen anyone else here. Ohhh, you mean Jack? Are there others like him? Can I meet them sometime?"

"There's no one like Jack, and as for the others, in due time." He paused. "There's no hurry." Another silence followed, almost awkward in duration. During these spaces between conversation, Tony had been trying to conjure up some image or memory that would begin to make sense of what he was seeing, but nothing came. No picture, no idea, and as far as he could remember not even an imagining that resonated with any of this. How was it possible that all this was simply a projection of his drugged brain scrambled inside a coma? He was drawing a blank.

"So, how long have you lived here?"

"Forty-some years, give 'r take. A lifetime, some would say. Barely a drop, really."

"No kidding," retorted Tony, shaking his head, the tone of his voice disingenuous and tinged with superiority. What crazy person would choose to live in this wilderness for forty years? He'd go stir-crazy in forty hours, let alone forty years.

Trying not to be obvious, Tony glanced sideways at the stranger, who either didn't notice or simply didn't care. Tony already liked him. He seemed to be one of those rare people who felt completely comfortable inside their own skin, and at peace with everything around him. There was no detectable agenda, no sense of someone looking for an advantage or angle like most everyone else he knew. Maybe *content* was the word, not that anyone in his or her right mind could ever be content out here in this loneliness. To Tony, *contentment* and *boredom* were synonyms. Maybe the guy was just ignorant, didn't know better, untraveled and uneducated. But here he was, an unexpected element inside some projection of Tony's subconscious. He must mean something.

"So tell me, if you would, who are you?" It was the obvious question.

The man deliberately turned to face him, and Tony found himself looking into those incredibly penetrating eyes. "Tony, I am the one your mother told you would never stop holding on to you."

It took a moment for the answer to register, and Tony took a step back. "Jesus? You? Are you *the* Jesus?"

The man said nothing, only returning his gaze until Tony looked down at the dirt in order to focus, and then suddenly it made sense. Of course it was Jesus! He had written his name on the list. Who better to conjure up in a drug-induced comatose state than Jesus, the archetype of all archetypes, an imagination buried in the deepest recesses of his neural network? And here he stood, a neurological projection that had no actual existence and no real substance.

He looked up just as the stranger cracked him across the face with an open hand, hard enough to sting but not hard enough to leave a mark. Tony was stunned and instantly felt anger surface.

"Just helping you perceive how active your imagination really is." The man laughed, his eyes still kind and gentle.

"It is amazing how a projection with no actual existence or real substance can pack a wallop, eh?"

If anyone else had been present, Tony would have been embarrassed and furious. But he was more startled and surprised than anything. "Perfect!" he announced after collecting his thoughts. "See, that's proof right there! The real Jesus would never slap anyone," he claimed.

"And you know this how, exactly? From personal experience?" The Jesus person was grinning, enjoying himself. "Keep in mind, Tony, you have convinced yourself that I am a Jesus generated by a drug-addled subconscious. You yourself introduced this dilemma. Either I am who I say I am, or you believe deep down inside in a Jesus who would slap a person across the face. Which is it?"

He stood there, this Jesus guy, arms folded, watching Tony struggle with the logic. Finally, Tony looked up again, and answered, "Then I guess I must actually believe that Jesus is a person who would slap me across the face."

"Ha! Good for you! Dead people *do* bleed!" Jesus laughed and put his arm around Tony's shoulder. "At least you try and remain consistent with your assumptions, even when they aren't true and regardless of the difficulty they add to your life. Hard way to live, but understandable."

Tony shrugged and laughed along, thoroughly mystified by the reference to bleeding dead people. As if they both knew their destination, they together descended the steps and began walking up a hill toward a distant grove of trees. From below, these appeared to be congregated at the highest point of the property, nestled into the gray stone wall somewhere near but above where he had first encountered Jack. From that vantage point it was likely that one could see the entire enclosure and perhaps even over the far walls and into the valley beyond. As they walked Tony continued to ask questions, the businessman in him puzzled.

"Forty-some years and this place looks pretty tired and broken. No offense, but is this all you've managed in all that time?" If he had intended to mask his insinuation, he was unsuccessful. Instead of reacting, the Jesus-man absorbed the implication.

"You might be right. Guess I'm not too good at this. This place is only a shadow now of what it once was in its beginning. At one time it was all a wild and magnificent garden, open, lovely, and free."

"I didn't mean to sound...," Tony began apologetically, but Jesus waved it off with a grin. "It just doesn't look much like a garden," Tony offered.

"Yeah, work in progress," Jesus sighed, a sound both resigned and determined.

"Looks to me like an uphill battle," Tony added, trying not to be too negative. He couldn't help himself; it was an old habit, finding a way to gain the superior position in conversations.

"It might take some time, but I don't lose," came the unruffled reply.

"I certainly don't mean to be rude, but don't you think this project is taking way too long? There's a lot you could do to clear the land, plant it, fertilize it, see it grow. I think it has potential. A few professionals with the right tools could come in here and make rather short work of it. Couple bulldozers? I noticed a few places where the walls are starting to crumble and deteriorate. You could get an engineer and an architect in here and stonemasons could get this place shipshape in about six months, and that would include a crew to tear down and rebuild your house, too."

"This, Tony, is a living land, not a construction site. This is real and breathing, not a fabrication that can be bullied into being. When you choose technique over relationship and process, when you try and shortcut the speed of growing awareness and force understanding and maturity before its time, this"—he pointed down and over the length and width of the property—"this is what you become."

Tony couldn't tell if Jesus was using the editorial inclusive "you" or the "you" that meant him. In case he was talking about him, he didn't ask.

"We are only able," Jesus continued, "to move at the speed and in the direction the land itself allows. One must relate to it with honor and reverence and let the land speak its own heart. Then, out of respect we must choose to submit to its idea of 'real' and still remain ones who love it toward the true, without faltering, regardless of the cost. To not live for the land in this way is to join its aggressors, ravagers, users, and benefactors, and then all hope for its healing would be lost."

"Sir." Tony was growing a little perturbed as he tried again to grasp what he was hearing. "You're talking in metaphor, and I'm losing you somewhere in the translation. You are referring to this land as if it were personal, like someone that you know and love. How can that be, when it's just dirt and rocks and hills, wildflowers, weeds, and water and stuff."

"And that," Jesus said as he touched Tony on the shoulder and squeezed gently, "is exactly why you cannot understand what I am saying. I have not used a metaphor once, while you have done so many times. Because you continue to inhabit and believe your metaphors, you cannot see what is true."

Tony stopped on the trail, raised his hands up as if taking in the expanse of the place, and dramatically announced to make his point, "But it's just dirt! It's not a living person. It's dirt!"

"Ah, Tony, you already said it yourself...from dust to dust. Dirt!"

This was the connection he had been missing! The very idea was a shock, staggering in its implications. He looked up into those eyes again and found the words, afraid of what he was about to suggest. "Are you telling me that all of this, and not just what I saw inside the walls but everything outside as well, all of this is a living being?"

The Jesus-man did not waver in his gaze. "I am telling you much more than that, Tony. I am telling you that this living being...is you!"

"Me? No, that can't be true. That's impossible. It can't be!" He felt crushed beneath an invisible fist that hammered him in the stomach. He turned, staggering a few steps away, looking back and out. In an instant, his vision had changed, his eyes had opened, but now he desperately did not want to see through them. He had already judged this place from a superior position of aloof noninvolvement, and declared it a no-man's-land of loss, a scrap heap not worth saving. That was his assessment. He was being polite and trying to be encouraging, but it hadn't reflected at all what he really felt about this place. He would level everything that lived, bury it under asphalt, and then replace it with concrete and steel. It was ugly and without value, worthy only of destruction.

Tony dropped to his knees and covered his eyes with his hands as if to conjure new lies to conceal the gaping emptiness left by the absence of the old ones, or secure a new delusion that might offer refuge, protection, and comfort. But once you "see," you can't "un-see." Honesty compelled him to rip his hands from his face; clarity demanded a hearing. He looked again and this time looked deep. He found nothing he admired or felt affection toward. This place was a shattered waste, a complete and utter loss, a sad blemish in an otherwise potentially appealing world. Were this truly him, his own heart, he was a staggering disappointment, at best. At worst, he hated everything about himself.

Crying was a weakness that Tony detested, an activity he had vowed as a boy never again to indulge in. But now he couldn't help himself. The weeping became a sob. A dam, years in the making, broke, and he felt utterly helpless in the onslaught. He couldn't tell if his emotions were causing him to shake and tremble or whether the earth was literally quaking beneath him.

"It can't be true, it just can't be," he bawled, trying not to look at this Jesus-man. Then came the unexpected cry from somewhere deep within him, "I don't want this to be true!" He begged, "Please, tell me it isn't true. Is this all I am, a sick and pitiful waste of a human being? Is this all my life is? Am I ugly and disgusting? Please, tell me it isn't true."

Waves of self-pity and self-loathing pounded him until he felt the fabric of his soul was going to tear apart at its seams. A shock wave knocked him off his knees and slammed him to the ground. The Jesus-man knelt down and held him, letting him wail in his arms, strong enough to keep unbearable pain and loss inside a grasp of tender kindness. It felt as if the only thing holding him in one piece was the presence of this man.

Caught in an emotional hurricane, Tony felt his mind tearing from its moorings; everything he had considered real and right was now turning to dust and ashes. But then, like a bolt of light, the opposite presented itself: What if he were actually finding his mind, his heart, his soul? He shut his eyes tight and sobbed, wanting to never open them again, to never again see the shame of what he was, what he had become.

The Jesus-man understood and pressed Tony's weeping and snot-smeared face into his shoulder. As one wave of emotion would ease, a new upswelling would pummel him and he was washed away again, the pressure at times so intense he thought he was turning inside out. Surge after surge, years of buried emotions, waiting for jubilee, expressed, finally voiced.

Slowly the onslaught hesitated, then subsided and finally receded. A quiet descended, occasionally interspersed with short spasms that rocked him. All the while he was held by this Jesus person who wouldn't let go. Finally, when calm fully settled, the man spoke.

5

AND THEN THERE WAS ONE

Pain may well remind us that we are alive, but
love reminds us why we are alive.
—Trystan Owain Hughes

Listen to my voice, Tony." Jesus was again stroking his hair, as he would a child, a son. "Every human being is a universe within themselves. Your mother and father participated with God to create a soul who would never cease to exist. Your parents, as cocreators, supplied the stuff, genetics and more, uniquely combined to form a masterpiece, not flawless but still astounding; and we took from their hands what they brought to us, submitting to their timing and history and added what only we could bring to them—life. You were conceived, a living wonder who exploded into being, a universe within a multiverse, not isolated and disconnected, but entangled and designed for community, even as God is community."

"Ha! Living wonder?" Tony sniffled, limp from the exertion of fighting the flood. He thought the tears had drained, his reservoir empty, but a few more presented themselves at the thought, running down and trickling off his chin. "I'm not."

"For there to be an 'I am not,' there must first be an 'I am,'" Jesus encouraged. "Image and appearance tell you little. The inside is bigger than the outside when you have the eyes to see."

"I'm not sure I want to see, or know," mumbled Tony. "It hurts too much. Anyway, I don't believe any of this, including you, is real. And yet I still feel so ashamed. I would rather go back to my blindness, to not seeing."

"The hurt is real, and true. Trust me, Tony. Transformation without work and pain, without suffering, without a sense of loss is just an illusion of true change."

"I hate it," declared Tony, another but brief spasm racking his body. "I can't do this. And trust? That's not a word I've had in my vocabulary. Trust is not my thing."

"That's for sure," Jesus said and chuckled. "But it is *my* thing!"

Tony still had not moved or opened his eyes, his head down and resting on the chest of this man. He felt stupid and vulnerable, but he didn't want to move.

"I don't know what to do," confessed Tony. "Can I tell you who I miss most right now?" Tony opened his eyes and took a deep breath. "I really miss my mom." From somewhere Jesus produced a folded red handkerchief, which Tony gratefully accepted and blew his nose.

"Tony, your mother was the last person you trusted. You can't do any of this on your own or even on your own terms. You were created by a community to exist in community, made in the image of a God who has never known anything except community."

"God, a community?"

"Always. I told you I have never been alone. I've never

done anything by myself. Relationship is at the very heart of who I am."

"I never understood any of that."

"No worries. It was not meant to be understood. It was meant to be experienced."

Tony took another deep breath. "So, what happened to me? If this place is really me, how did I end up a lifeless and devastated wasteland?"

"From your point of view, you would say that 'life' happened to you: big and little losses inside the everyday; the accumulation and embracing of lies and betrayals; the absence of parents when you needed them; the failure of systems; the choices to protect yourself, which, while keeping you alive, also inhibited your ability to be open to the very things that would heal your heart."

"And from your perspective?"

"From my perspective, it was death not life, an unreality you were never designed for. It was un-love, un-light, un-truth, un-freedom...It was death."

"So, am I dying? Is that why all this is happening?"

"Son, you have been dying since the day you were conceived. And even though death is a monstrous evil, human beings have imagined it into something much more powerful than it deserves, than it actually is, as if light were casting death's shadows in horrific proportions onto the backdrop of your existence and now you are terrified by even the shadow of death."

"I don't understand."

"It's a conversation with many layers, much of it not for today. For now, understand that a significant reason why you fear death is because of your atrophied and minuscule perception of life. The immensity and grandeur of *life* continually absorb and eradicate death's power and presence. You believe death is the end, an event causing a cessation of things that truly matter, and therefore it becomes the great wall, the inevitable inhibitor of joy, love, and relationship. You see death as the last word, the final separation.

"The truth is," he continued, "death has only been a shadow of those things. What you call death is indeed a separation of sorts, but not anything like you imagine it. You have focused yourself and defined your existence with reference to the fear of that singular last-breath event rather than recognizing death's ubiquitous presence all around you—in your words, your touch, your choices, your sorrows, your unbelief, your lies, your judgment, your unforgiveness, your prejudices, your power-seeking, your betrayals, your hiding. The 'event' of death is only one small expression of that presence, but you have made that expression everything, not realizing that you swim in death's ocean every single day.

"Tony, you were not designed for death, but neither was death intended for this universe. Inherent in the event of death is a promise, a baptism in this ocean that rescues, not drowns. Human beings uncreated life and brought that un-life into your experience, so out of respect for you, we wove it from the beginning into the larger tapestry. You now experience this underlying tension between life and death every day until you are released through the event of death, but you were designed to deal with its encroachment in community, inside relationship, not in self-centered isolation like your little place here."

"And all those paths, the many trails leaving here?"

"Tony, they originated here, inside all this damage. No one is coming. They all left."

For a moment grief rose like a stalking predator but as

quickly vanished. He decided to acknowledge what he was thinking. "I sent them away, didn't I? They didn't just leave."

"When you don't deal with death, Tony, everyone in your world becomes either a catalyst for pain or dead to you. Sometimes it's easier to bury them somewhere on your property than to simply send them away."

"So death wins?" Tony knew what he was really asking, and if this Jesus-man was really...who he said he was, then he would know, too.

"Sometimes it feels like it, doesn't it? But no, life won! Life continues to win. I am living proof."

"So you're not just a myth, then, a children's story? You really expect me to believe that you rose from the dead?" He wanted to hear him say it.

"Ha, it takes a lot more faith to believe that I didn't. That I was beaten unrecognizable, hung on the torture cross, speared through the side into the heart, buried dead in a tomb, and yet somehow resuscitated, unwrapped myself, rolled away a ton of rock, subdued the elite temple guard, and started a movement that is supposedly all about the truth of life and resurrection, but actually based on a lie? Yeah, much easier to believe."

Tony glanced at this man, his words framed by edges of humor and triumph, but the canvas a portrait of grief.

"It's just a story!" Tony exclaimed. "A story to make us feel better or fool us into thinking that life has some kind of meaning or purpose. It is a morality fable told by weak people to sick people."

"Tony, I rose from the dead. We broke death's illusion of power and dominance. Papa God loved me to life in the power of the Spirit, and demonstrated that any ideology of separation would forever be insufficient."

"You know that I don't believe any of this, right?" Tony

snapped. "I still don't even believe that you exist. I don't know what overcame me. I mean, sure, there was a Jewish guy, a rabbi named Jesus who did a lot of good and so people made up all sorts of stuff about him doing miracles and even rising from the dead, and they started a religion, but he died. Like everyone else, he died, and death is death, so you can't exist. You are nothing more than my mother's voice echoing somewhere in my subconscious mind."

"You almost convinced me," Jesus stated with a touch of sarcasm and laughed. "What you are in the middle of at this moment, Tony, is called a crisis of faith. More often it happens in the moment of your physical death, the event, but since there have never been formulas governing relationships and you are not actually dead yet, something special and mysterious must be afoot."

Tony was surprised. "Are you telling me that you don't know why I'm here?"

"No! Papa hasn't shared that piece of purpose with me so far." He leaned in as if to share a secret. "He knows I like surprises."

"Wait. I thought you were supposed to be God?"

"I'm not supposed to be God, I am God!"

"Then how come you don't know why I am here?"

"Like I said, because my Dad hasn't told me."

"But if you are God, don't you know everything?"

"I do."

"But you just said you didn't—"

"Tony," Jesus interrupted, "you don't think in terms of relationship. You see everything through the grid of an isolated independence. There are answers to your questions that will absolutely bewilder you, make no sense whatsoever, because you don't even have a frame of reference that would allow them."

Tony was nodding, appearing as bewildered as Jesus had suggested.

"Part of the wonder of me, always God, joining the human race, is that I was not some actor added to the cast of characters, but literally became fully human as a forever reality. I never stopped being fully God, fully the creator. It is true now and has been since the beginning of time that the entire cosmos exists inside me and that I hold it all together, sustaining it, even now, right this moment, and that would include you along with every created thing. Death could never say that. Death holds nothing together."

Tony was shaking his head, trying to understand yet at the same time resisting internally.

Jesus continued, "So, yes, I could draw upon my knowledge as God to know why you are here, but I am in relationship with my Father, and he hasn't told me, and I trust him to let me know if it becomes important for me to know. Until then, I will walk this out in real time and space with you, in faith and trust, and see what surprises Papa has in store for us."

"You are absolutely blowing my mind!" Tony raised his hands and shook his head. "I am so confused."

"That was the easiest answer I could give you," Jesus said, chuckling, "that might even begin to make some sense."

"Well, thank you for that!" Tony retorted. "So, bottom line, if I understand you correctly, you are God, but you don't know why I'm here."

"Exactly, but my Dad and the Holy Spirit know and if I need to, I will also."

Tony was still shaking his head as he stood up and brushed himself off. How could this be a projection of his internal subconscious? They were talking about things he had never even considered. It was all so baffling. Slowly they turned and began again working their way up the hill.

"So let me get this right," Tony began. "There is Father, that's your Dad, and you would be the Son?"

"And the Holy Spirit," offered Jesus.

"So, who is the Holy Spirit?"

"God."

"This is a Christian thing, right? So you are telling me that anyone who believes in you believes in three gods? Christians are polytheists?"

"There are lots of folks besides Christians who believe in me. 'Believer' is an activity, not a category. Christians have only been around a couple thousand years. As for the question about them being polytheists? Not at all."

Jesus stopped and turned once again to face Tony, indicating that what he was about to say was significant and important.

"Listen carefully, Tony. There is only... hear me carefully: there is only one God. The darkness of the choice for independence has blinded humanity to the simplicity of the truth. So first things first—one God. As much as they disagree about the details, and the details and disagreements are significant and important; but the Jews with their sects, the Christians of every stripe and color, the Muslims with their internal diversity, all are in agreement about this: there is only one God, not two, not three, not more, just one."

"Wait, but you just said...," Tony interjected, but Jesus held up a hand, stopping him from finishing.

"The Jews were the first to put it best in their Shema: 'Hear, O Israel: The Lord our God is one Lord!' But the Jewish Scriptures speak of this 'one' God as a plurality. 'Let 'us' make Man in 'our' image.' That was never intended as a contradiction about God being only one, but an expansion of what the nature of the 'one' was like. Rooted in the Jewish understanding was that *essentially*, and I use that word carefully, essentially the one was singular in essence and yet a plurality of persons, a community."

"But..." Again Jesus raised his hand and Tony quieted.

"This is a gross oversimplification, but the Greeks, whom I love dearly, beginning especially with Plato and Aristotle, got the world consumed in thinking about the one God, but they didn't get the plurality part, so they opted for an indivisible singularity beyond all being and relationship, an unmoved mover, impersonal and unapproachable but at least good, whatever that meant."

"And then I show up, in no way contradicting the Shema, but expanding on it. I declared in the simplest possible terms, 'The Father and I are one and we are good,' which is essentially a relational declaration. As you probably know, that solved everything, and finally the religious got their ideologies and doctrines straight and everyone agreed and lived happily..." Jesus glanced at Tony, who was looking at him, his eyebrows raised in question.

"I'm being sarcastic, Tony." He grinned as they again turned and continued to walk.

"To stay with my story, in the first few hundred years after my incarnation, there were many, like Irenaeus and Athanasius, who got it. They saw that God's very being is relational, three distinct persons who are so wonderfully close we are oneness. 'Oneness,' Tony, is different than an isolated and independent 'one,' and the difference is relationship, three persons distinctly together."

Jesus paused.

Tony shook his head, trying to grasp what Jesus had said. This was a conversation like none he could remember, and that bothered him. He was intrigued but not sure why. "Would you like to know what happened next? Where things went sideways?"

Tony nodded and Jesus continued.

"The Greeks, with their love for isolation, influence Augustine and later Aquinas, to name only a couple, and a nonrelational religious Christianity is born. Along come the Reformers, like Luther and Calvin, who do their best to send the Greeks back outside the Holy of Holies, but they are barely in the grave before the Greeks are resuscitated and invited back to teach in their schools of religion. The tenacity of bad ideas is rather remarkable, don't you think?"

"I'm starting to realize that," admitted Tony, "but I'm not sure I understand any better than when you started. It's all fascinating but irrelevant to me."

"Ah, all you need to know is this: at the heart of all existence is a great dance of self-giving, other-centered love—oneness. Nothing is deeper, simpler, and purer."

"That sounds beautiful; if only it were—"

"Look, we're here," interrupted Jesus. The pathway entered a grove of trees and narrowed until only wide enough for one person. Tony led the way, grateful that the trail did not deviate. As he broke from the trees and into a glade, he realized he was alone. The clearing butted up against a massive boundary of stone that stretched almost out of sight. An earthen stairway climbed up to an insignificant mud building, a hovel, maybe large enough for two rooms but from which the entire valley could be viewed. He made out the silhouette of a woman sitting on a wooden bench and resting against the wall of what he presumed was her dwelling. The Jesus-man already stood talking to her, his hand lovingly resting on her shoulder.

As Tony climbed the hundred or so steps he could see

she was an elderly round woman, jet-black hair falling in two braids wrapped in faceted cut beads of many colors. She wore a simple flowing calico dress, tightened by an ornate belt of more beads, and a sunburst starquilt blanket draped around her shoulders. Her eyes were closed, her face upturned. She was an Indian, a Native American or First Nations woman.

"Anthony," greeted Jesus as Tony approached the pair, "this is Wiyan Wanagi. You can call her Kusi (kuen-shee), or Grandmother, if you prefer. You have some things to discuss. She knows why you are here, so I will leave you for a time, although I am never absent." In less than a blink, he was maybe not gone but not visible.

"Thank you, Anpo Wicapi," she said tenderly.

"Sit!" She motioned to the bench and space next to her, not opening her eyes, her voice deep and resonant. He obeyed. They sat in silence, she with her eyes shut, he looking down the expanse of land that lay like a mantle beneath them. From here he could almost see to the far wall, at least a few miles away, and to the left, clearly discernible, the ramshackle homestead where he had woken. So this desolate place was supposed to be his heart, if what he had been told could be believed. It was not exactly home, but not exactly hell either. The latter felt truer at the moment than the former.

They were silent for what seemed hours, but was probably only a dozen minutes or so. Tony was not used to either stillness or quiet. He waited, an internal pressure building.

He cleared his throat. "Do you want..."

"Shhhh! Busy!"

He waited again until he couldn't help himself. "Uh, busy doing what?"

"Gardening. So many weeds."

"Oh," not wanting to admit that it made no sense. "And what exactly am I doing here?"

"Agitating," she replied. "Sit. Breathe in, breathe out, be still."

And so he sat, trying to be still on the outside, the rush of images, emotions, and questions rising like a slowly flooding river. He lifted his right heel off the ground, a habit, until his foot began to bounce up and down. He did not even notice this nervous attempt to control inner energy and tension.

The woman, without opening her eyes and barely moving, reached over and put her hand on the bouncing knee and it slowed to a stop.

"Why you running so fast?" Her voice was soft and young for the body that produced it.

"I'm not," he responded. "I'm just sitting here like you told me to."

She didn't move her strong and calloused hand and he could feel warmth spreading from her touch. "Anthony, why do you always think invitations are expectations?"

He grinned. He knew he didn't have to answer, that she already knew his thoughts. Invitations *were* expectations. There was always an agenda, sometimes obvious, often hidden, but always. Was there any other way to live in the world? But her question left him wondering.

"So, we are just sitting here, then," he mused, not expecting any response.

"No, Anthony, not *just* sitting... praying."

"Praying? Who are you praying to?"

"I'm not praying to anyone," she replied, her eyes still closed. "I am praying with."

He tried to wait awhile, but it was not his habit. "So, who are you praying with?" he asked.

"With you!" The woman's face folded into a smile, the reflecting afternoon light hiding in and then softening the crevices of her face. "I am praying with you."

"But," he said, shaking his head as if she could see him, "I'm not praying."

She smiled again but didn't speak.

They sat for almost an hour, he mentally tossing his concerns and fears into little imaginary boats that in his fancy he set afloat down the tiny creek that ran not far from where they sat. He had learned this in an anger management class the courts had mandated. One by one they sailed out of view, each taking a little of the load, until there were none left and he sat in the comfort of this woman, breathing in deep a clarity of air. He couldn't explain it, but he again felt...safe.

He was the first to finally speak. "I'm sorry, I don't remember how to pronounce your name."

She grinned, a beaming that lit up her face, softening her features even more and seeming to radiate into the falling dusk. "Yeah, I'm sorta known for that. Grand-Mother... you pronounce it Grand-Mother."

He laughed. "Okay, then, Grandma," he stated, and patted her hand.

Her eyes opened for the first time and he found himself looking again into those same incredible brown origins of light. He was looking at Jesus, but different. "Not Grandma," she observed, "Grandmother. Understand?" She stated it with a nod, and he found himself nodding back.

"Uh, yes, Grandmother," he stammered apologetically. "I'm not sure I understand the difference."

"Obviously! But I forgive you for that."

"Excuse me?" He was surprised. "You're going to forgive me something that I don't even understand?"

"Listen to me, dearest..." She paused, and Tony felt a wave of something painful and sweet in her use of that particular term of endearment. He let it wash over him, and as if she knew when it subsided, she waited before continuing, "Much of what you must forgive others for, and especially yourself, is the ignorance that damages. People don't only hurt willfully. More often because they simply don't know anything else; they don't know how to be anything else, anything better."

Tony wanted to change the subject. She pushed at emotions better left dormant. It had already been a long day.

"So, where do you live?" He couldn't imagine anyone actually living in the adjacent outbuilding. It looked more like a poorly built gardening shed for tools.

"I live everywhere I am," came the curt reply.

"No, that's not what I meant—" he began, and she cut him off.

"I know what you meant, Anthony, but you don't know what you ask."

Tony didn't know how to respond to that. Finding himself at a loss for words was not usual.

Fortunately, she rescued him. "So," Grandmother said as she stood up and stretched, "do you have anything to eat?"

Even though he knew they were empty, he quickly checked his pockets to make sure. "No, sorry. I don't."

"That's okay." She smiled. "I have plenty." And with that she chuckled to herself and ambled in the direction of the mud shack, light warmly emanating through its cracks and crevices. He stood up and took one more look down the length of this place as the evening's descent muted and then began erasing its colors. From here he could see a few lights scattered unevenly, little dots of white mostly in or near the ramshackle homestead. He was also surprised to see in the farthest distance, near the bottom end of the property, a congregation of brighter lights. He hadn't remembered seeing any other buildings, but he hadn't been looking for any either.

He stretched one last time, getting the sitting kinks out, walked the few feet to the entrance, and stooped to peek. It was larger inside than it had appeared from the outside, but that could be just an illusion of how she used the space. A fire burned against one wall, the smoke rising and disappearing through a rather complex sequence of coverings, probably to keep rain from dousing the flames while allowing the smoke to escape.

"May I come in?" he asked.

"Of course, you are always welcome here!" She warmly waved him inside. He found blankets on the floor and, though taking the risk that he might be violating some protocol, sat down anyway, surprised by how soft and plush they were. She seemed to take no offense and he settled, watching as she swayed back and forth over what looked and smelled like a stew and some flatbread baking on a stone by the fire. Simple and inviting, and, he smiled to himself, without expectation.

He paused, watching her rhythmic movements between stew and bread, almost a dance. "May I ask you a question?"

"You want to know why I live here, in this 'hovel'; I think that is the word you used, based on your civilized and educated perception?"

There was no use denying it. "Yes, I was wondering. So why?"

"It was the best you could give me." She didn't turn from her work.

"Excuse me? The best 'I' could give you? I had nothing

to do with this. I could build you something much better, but not this. How could you think...?"

"It's all right, Anthony! I have no expectations. I am grateful to have found even this small place in your heart. I travel light"—she smiled as if at some secret thought—"and I make my home inside the simplest gifts. There is nothing to feel bad or ashamed about. I am thoroughly grateful, and being here is a joy!"

"So...because this is me, my world somehow, I have only made this small place for you? And for Jesus, I made a larger place, but it's still only a run-down ranch house...?" He was suddenly saddened, and he wasn't sure why.

"It is his joy, too, to be here. He gladly accepted the invitation."

"Invitation? I don't ever remember inviting him, or you for that matter. I'm not even sure who you are. I don't know if I ever knew enough to invite anyone."

Now she turned toward him, licking the spoon that she was using to stir the stew. "It wasn't your invitation, Anthony. If it had only been left up to you, we probably would never have had the opportunity to dwell here."

Again confused, Tony asked hesitantly, "But if not my invitation, then whose?"

"The Father's invitation. Papa God."

"Jesus's Father...you mean, like God the Father?" Tony was surprised and upset. "Why would he invite you here?"

"Well, despite everything you believe about him or don't, and by the way, almost nothing you believe about him is true...regardless, Papa God cares for you with relentless affection. That is why we are here. We share in his affection." With that she ladled out a bowl of stew and handed it to him, along with a clean rag to use as a napkin.

Now he was angry! Here was the catch, the hidden

agenda, the reason all of this was dangerous and a lie. Whoever this woman was, and despite being drawn to her much as he was to Jesus, she had uncovered his fundamental assumption, the true heartache that he knew lived in the belly of his pain. If there was a God, he was a monster, an evil trickster who played with people's hearts, who ran experiments to see how much suffering human beings could endure, who toyed with their longings so they opened the beginnings of trust only to have everything precious destroyed. Surprised at his own inner fury and trying to calm himself, he took a bite of her cooking. It worked. The flavors seemed to attack his ire and settle him down.

"Wow!" he exclaimed.

"Good word, *wow*, one of my favorites." She chuckled. "You are welcome, Anthony."

He looked at her. She was scooping out food for herself, her back to him. The fire highlighted her dignified presence and seemed to ignite an invisible perfume that wrapped the room in a sense of liturgy. It made no sense that Jesus and this woman were in any way related to the God they spoke about with such consideration. If she noticed he had tensed up, it didn't show.

"So does this Father God live here...in my world?" he asked, a brittle edge on the words, thinking about the collection of lights at the bottom of the property.

"He doesn't, not as a habitation anyway. Anthony, you have never made a place for him, at least not inside these walls. While he is never absent, he also waits for you in the forest, outside the walls of your heart. He is not one who forces relationship. He is too respectful." Her demeanor was as gentle as a feather. He would have preferred hearing disappointment in her voice. That was manageable. Kindness was too slippery and intangible. As quickly as the anger had risen he reburied it and took another bite of stew, changing the subject.

"This is spectacular! There are spices in here I don't recognize."

She smiled her appreciation. "Made it from scratch, secret family recipe; don't ask." She handed him flatbread, which he dipped and took a bite of. It, too, was unlike anything he had ever tasted.

"Well, if you opened a restaurant, you could make a killing."

"Always the businessman, Anthony. Joy and pleasure have value only if you can turn them into commodities? Nothing like damming a river and turning it into a swamp."

He realized how crass it had sounded and began to apologize. She raised a hand. "Anthony, don't. I was making an observation, not a value statement. I don't expect you to be any different than you are. I know you, but I also know how you were forged and designed, and I intend to keep calling that from the deep, from the lost."

He again felt uncomfortable, as if she had somehow unclothed him.

"Uh, thank you, Grandmother," he offered and again segued to another subject, hoping to find a safer one. "Speaking of food, in my state of being, you know, in a coma and all, is it necessary for me to eat?"

Her answer was quick and direct. "No! You are being sustained in the hospital through feeding tubes. That's just not my idea of a good meal."

Grandmother put down her bowl and leaned forward on her stool, drawing Tony's attention. "Listen, Anthony, you are dying."

"Well, I know that, Jesus said that we are all..."

"No, Anthony, that is not what I am talking about. You

are lying in a room at OHSU and you are approaching the event of physical death. You are dying."

He sat back and tried to take this in. "So, is that why I'm here, because I am dying? Does everyone go through this, whatever this is...this intervention? Is it to try and do what? Save my soul?" He could feel the hairs on his neck bristle as the blood began to rise with the flow of irritation now mounting. "If you guys are God, then why don't you do something? Why don't you just heal me? Why don't you send some church person up there and pray for me so that I don't die?"

"Anthony...," she began, but he was already standing.

"I am dying, and you are sitting here doing nothing. I may not be much, and I have obviously made a complete mess out of my life, but am I not worth anything to you? Am I not worth something? If for no other reason than that my mother loved me, and she was a good religious person, isn't that enough? Why am I here?" His voice was rising and his temper spilling through the cracks of his fears. He was desperate for some measure of control. "Why did you bring me here? So you could flaunt in my face what a worthless piece of crap I am?"

He stooped and walked out into the early evening. Fist clenched, he began pacing along the edge of the stairway, barely visible in the flickering light cast from the fire inside. In an instant, he turned back, stooped, and reentered, this time with a purpose.

Grandmother had not moved; she just watched him with those eyes. For the second time in less than hours he could feel another dam starting to collapse inside and with every ounce of strength he possessed, he tried to hold it back. It wasn't enough. He knew he should run, but his feet were planted and his words emerged in spits of emotion. He was losing control. Suddenly he was shouting and waving his arms, caught between fury and desolation.

"What exactly do you want from me? Do you want me to confess my sins? Do you want me to invite Jesus into my life? Seems a little late for that, don't you think? He seems to have found a way to be right in the middle of my mess. Don't you realize how ashamed of myself I am? Don't you see? I hate myself. What am I supposed to think? Now what am I supposed to do? Don't you understand? I was hoping…" He broke down as a realization burst to the surface, sweeping over him. The audacity of it drove him once more to his knees. He covered his face with his hands as new tears coursed their way down his face. "Don't you understand? I was hoping…" And then he said it, voiced the belief that had dominated his entire life, so deep that he was unaware of it even as he spoke it: "I was hoping…that death was the end." He was sobbing and words could barely find their way through. "How else can I get away from what I've done? How can I escape myself? If what you're saying is true, I have no hope. Don't you see? If death is not the end, I have no hope!"

6

HEATED CONVERSATIONS

What is to give light must endure the burning.
—Viktor Frankl

He awoke, still in Grandmother's small hovel. He sat up. It was fully dark outside and the coolness of the evening slid past the hanging blankets at the entrance, sending a slight shiver down his spine. By the open fire two figures huddled in conversation. It was Jesus and Grandmother talking in hushed tones, something about a perimeter wall that had been significantly damaged during the night's quakes. Aware he was awake, they now raised their voices to include him.

"Welcome back, Tony," acknowledged Jesus.

"Thanks, I think. Where have I been?"

"Combination of comatose and fury," indicated Grandmother.

"Yeah, about that, sorry."

"Oh, please, don't be," reassured Jesus. "What you admitted to yourself was astounding! Don't minimize it because you are embarrassed. We think it was profound."

"Great!" moaned Tony and flopped back onto the blankets. "I am in love with death. How comforting." He sat up again, a thought occurring to him. "But if that's true, why am I fighting so hard to stay alive?"

"Because life is the normal and death the anomaly," stated Jesus. He continued, "You were never designed or created for death, so by nature you fight it. It's not that you are in love with death, but you are driven to give yourself to something bigger than yourself, something out of your control that might save you from your sense of guilt and shame. You ashamed yourself to death."

"Reminds me of some others I know," piped up Grandmother.

"Oh, now I feel so much better about myself." Tony pulled a blanket over his head. "Just shoot me!"

"We have a better idea if you are open to listening."

Tony slowly pulled the blanket from his head and stood up, grabbed a stool, and pulled it toward the warmth of the flames.

"I'm all ears, not that I can't think of anything else to do and a million places I would rather be at this moment, but go ahead...not that I am going to agree or anything, and I'm still not sure any of this is believable anyway so...I'm rambling aren't I?"

Grandmother grinned. "You just let us know when you are finished. Time is something that we have plenty of."

"Okay, I'm done. You said you have a better idea than shooting me?" *This should be good*, he thought. God having an idea. Was that even possible? If you knew everything, how could you have an "idea"? He looked up at them looking at him. "Sorry, I'm done."

Jesus began, "Tony, this is an invitation, not an expectation."

"So tell me," Tony interrupted with a sigh, "am I going to agree to this? Thought I might save us some time."

Jesus looked at Grandmother, who nodded.

"Okay, then, let's get on with it. What do I have to do?"

"Don't you want to know what you are agreeing to?" asked Jesus.

"Did I freely choose to agree? I wasn't coerced in any way?"

"You freely chose."

"Okay, then, I believe you." He sat back, a little surprised at himself. "I almost hate to admit it, but this not knowing is kinda growing on me. You have to understand, I never do this; I mean, I never just take a risk or trust someone without some sort of guarantee or at least a nondisclosure agreement... You don't want an NDA, do you?"

"Never needed one before." Jesus laughed.

"So, what do I do?"

"We...wait. We watch the fire go out."

A strange ease had come over Tony, perhaps due to the recent confession and cathartic emotional release. Whatever the reason, he breathed deep and pulled his stool even closer to the logs that were dancing and popping, ablaze and excited by their own brilliance.

"Jesus, have I mentioned to you that you have..." He wanted to say "beautiful eyes," because it was what first came to mind, but concerned about being inappropriate he changed it to "remarkable eyes."

"Yeah, I get that a lot. Got them from my Dad."

"You mean Joseph?" queried Tony.

"No, not Joseph," answered Jesus. "Joseph was my step-dad, no direct genetic inheritance there. I was adopted."

"Oh, you mean"—Tony pointed up—"your God Dad?"

"Yes, my God Dad."

"I've never liked your God Dad," admitted Tony.

"You don't know him," asserted Jesus, his voice unwavering, warm and kind.

"I don't want to know him," responded Tony.

"Too late, my brother," returned Jesus. "Like Father, like Son."

"Hmm," grunted Tony, and again they were silent for a time, mesmerized by the dance of heat and gas as flames voraciously consumed their prey. Finally Tony asked, "Your Dad, isn't he the God of the Old Testament?"

It was Grandmother who responded, standing up and stretching. "Oh, the God of the Old Testament! He kinda freaks me out!" And with that she turned and headed through a net of blankets and back into the bedroom. Jesus looked at Tony and they both laughed, returning their gaze to the dying embers.

Tony lowered his voice. "Jesus, who exactly is that woman...Grandmother?"

"I heard that," came the voice from the other room. Tony grinned but otherwise ignored her.

Jesus leaned in. "She is like you. Lakota."

"Like me?" Tony was surprised. "What do you mean, like me?"

"Tony, all of us belong to a tribe, all members of the two-legged Nation. My tribe is Judah and you have Lakota blood in you."

"I do?" He was incredulous. "Is she my"—he paused— "is she my real grandmother?"

"Only according to blood, water, and Spirit, but not according to flesh. You are not related to her, but she is related to you."

"I don't understand."

Jesus smiled. "And that surprises you? Let me answer

your question another way. That strong, courageous, and beautiful woman in there is the Holy Spirit."

"That woman, that Indian woman is the Holy Spirit?"

Jesus nodded and Tony shook his head. "Not exactly what I expected. I thought the Holy Spirit would be, you know, more ghostly, oozier or something, like a force field, not," he whispered, "some old woman." He lowered his voice till it was almost inaudible and mouthed the words, "who lives in a shack."

"Ha!" Jesus laughed deeply and the voice from the other room spoke again: "I can do oozy. If you want oozy or ghostly, I can do that, too, and...if you don't think I like shacks, you don't know me very well."

The ease of their banter and relationship was entirely new to Tony. No underlying tension, no eggshells or mine-fields hidden in the conversations. He could not even detect agenda masked inside their words. It was real, authentic, compassionate, easy, enjoyable, and felt almost dangerous.

A few minutes passed before Jesus spoke, barely above a whisper, "Tony, you are about to go on a journey..."

He laughed. "That sounds more like something Grand-mother would say: 'You are about to go on a journey, grandson,'...as if this"—he opened up his arms to include everything around—"as if this couldn't qualify as a journey?"

Jesus chuckled softly. "Exactly like something she would say. Regardless, on your 'journey,' it is important that you remember you will never be alone, no matter what it looks or feels like."

"Do I really need to know this?" He reached over and touched Jesus's arm. "I've been sitting here trying not to remind myself that I already agreed to this, so if you're try-ing to make me nervous, it's working."

Again Jesus laughed, quietly and authentically, giving

Tony the comfort that he was indeed fully present to him, fully there for him. "I am not about making you feel nervous; just wanted you to know that I will never stop holding on to you."

Tony took a deep breath, searching for the right words before speaking. "I think I believe you, as much as I believe any of this. Not sure why, maybe because of my mom, but I think I do." He paused before adding, "Thank you, by the way, for all that, you know, when I came apart on the way up here."

Jesus patted him on the shoulder, a silent acknowledgment of what he had said, and continued, "Grandmother and I want to give you a gift that you can give to someone on your journey." As if on cue, Grandmother parted the blankets from the other room and returned to sit with them. She had taken her braids out; her inky hair falling loose and free created a contrast with her wizened but radiant face. She was comfortable and at ease in presence and movement.

She stretched and scratched herself below her chin where a button was missing from her smock.

"I'm getting old," she grumbled, "but what can you do?"

"Whatever!" Tony teased. This woman was supposedly older than the universe. "Exercise and diet," he offered with a smile, which she returned.

With that she plopped down on the stool next to Tony, squirmed a little until she appeared comfortable while at the same moment producing from the folds of her garment what looked like several strands of light. He watched transfixed as she deftly brought various ends together, matching and connecting without thought or intention, but as light touched light their colors merged and transformations began. A length of iridescent aquamarine became a thousand shades of dancing greens, reds undulating against purples while white continuously flashed throughout. With each new shade and hue, a barely audible tone would begin and together merged and grew into a harmony that Tony could physically feel inside his body. Between her fingers emerged shapes, dark spaces in between the light pieces that were three-dimensional or more.

These patterns and figures became increasingly complex, and suddenly within the rich blackness in the hanging spaces small explosions began, patterned fireworks like multicolored diamonds suspended on an inky backdrop. But they didn't disappear. First they hung in the emptiness, twinkly and shimmering, and as their tones united they stirred to a dance precisely choreographed yet free-form. It was utterly captivating, and Tony found he had been holding his breath as he watched. He sensed that the slightest breeze, even a whisper, might send her creations in directions unpredictable and maybe even ruinous. Grandmother's arms opened wider to contain this treasure, and Tony witnessed the evolving of design that seemed impossible, as if his eyes could observe in ways his mind could not process. He was now experiencing the harmonies within his chest, from the inside, and the music seemed to grow as did the complexity of configurations. Hairline waves of brilliant color entangled with purpose and intent, each penetration creating a quantum participation, filaments of random certainty, chains of chaotic order.

Suddenly Grandmother laughed like a little girl and gathered this grandeur inward until it was cupped in her hands. These she finally closed, until Tony could only see light pulsating through the spaces between her fingers. She brought it all slowly to her mouth as if to encourage embers, but instead blew like a cosmic magician, spreading her arms and opening her hands at the same moment to create a shape like a heart descending. The glory was gone.

She smiled at Tony, whose mouth was still open. "You like that?"

"There aren't words," he said, struggling to speak. "That was the single most thrilling thing I have ever seen, or heard, or even felt. What were those things?"

"Strings," she responded matter-of-factly. "You remember cat's cradle?" He nodded, thinking about the simple game of finger manipulations and shapes he played as a child. "That was my version. Helps me focus."

"So." He hesitated, not wanting his question to be ignorant, but still needing to ask. "So, what I just saw, that… whatever that was that you just did, did you just make that up as you went, or was that the design of something specific?"

"That is a brilliant question, Anthony. What you saw, heard, and felt is a very tiny presentation of something very specific."

"And what is that, specifically?" Tony was eager to know.

"Love! Self-giving, other-centered love!"

"That was love?" he asked, hardly believing what she was saying.

"A tiny presentation of love. Child's play, but real and true." She smiled again as Tony sat back, trying to grasp her words. "One more thing, Anthony. You couldn't have noticed, but there was something essential purposefully left out of my little composition. You heard and felt the harmonies of light, at least the surface of them, but you didn't notice, did you, that the melody was missing?"

It was true, Tony had not heard a melody, just a symphony of harmonies.

"I don't understand. What's the missing melody?" he asked.

"You, Anthony! You are the melody! You are the reason for the existence of what you witnessed and consider so immeasurably awe inspiring. Without you, what you perceived would have no meaning and no shape. Without you, it would have simply…fallen apart."

"I don't...," Tony began, looking down at the dirt floor, which he felt move slightly under his feet.

"It's okay, Anthony. I know you don't believe much of this yet. You are lost and looking up from a very deep hole just to see the superficial. This is not a test you can fail. Love will never condemn you for being lost, but love will not let you stay there alone, even though it will never force you to come out of your hiding places."

"Who are you?" He looked up and into those eyes, almost able to see in them what he had so recently witnessed in her hands. At this moment, "Holy Spirit" seemed a vague description and without much content.

Her gaze held his without waver or hesitation. "Anthony, I am she who is more than you can begin to imagine and yet anchors your deepest longings. I am she whose love for you, you are not powerful enough to change, and I am she whom you can trust. I am the voice in the wind, the smile in the moon, the refreshing of the life that is water. I am the common wind that catches you by surprise and your very breath. I am a fire and fury opposed to everything that you believe that is not the Truth, that is hurting you and keeping you from being free. I am the Weaver, you are a favorite color, and he"—she tilted her head toward Jesus—"he is the tapestry."

A holy hush descended, and for a time they only watched the cinders glowing, breathing bright, then fading, oscillating according to the whim of invisible breath.

"It is time," whispered Grandmother.

Jesus reached over and took Tony's hand. "The gift I spoke of earlier, Tony, is that on this journey you are taking, you can choose to physically heal one person, but only one, and when you choose the one, your journey will end."

"I can heal someone? Are you telling me that I am able

to heal anybody that I want to?" he asked, surprised by the very idea. His thoughts, without prompting, immediately returned to Gabriel's bedside as the five-year-old's hand slipped from his, and then skipped to his own body in an ICU room. He glanced down at what was left of the fire, hoping that no one else knew what he had been thinking, which he by now accepted as unlikely. He cleared his throat and asked, just to be certain he understood, "Anyone?"

"Providing they are not dead already," commented Grandmother. "Not impossible, but not usually a good idea."

Tony interrupted, his vision slowing, as if he were seeing frame by frame, and his words blurred, too. "So, lemme get it straight. Anyone! I can heal anyone I want to, I can heal?" Though he wasn't sure what he asked made any sense at all, he was confident that Grandmother and Jesus understood.

Jesus leaned closer. "You can't actually heal anyone, not alone, but I will be with you, and anyone you choose to pray for, I will heal through you. But this sort of physical healing is ultimately temporary. Even faith healers eventually die."

"Anybody?"

"Yes, Tony, anyone." Jesus was smiling, but his smile was beginning to come off his face, and Tony reached out into space to try to put it back.

"Okay, then," he mumbled, his words barely understandable. "Good! So lemme ask you, do I have to believe for this to work?" He again looked back at the fire, bare remnants remaining, yet heat emanating from it strong and certain. He wasn't certain he heard the answer, but thought later that Jesus had replied, "Healing isn't about you, Tony."

He lay back and began sliding.

7

Slip Sliding Away

You know the nearer your destination,
The more you're slip slidin' away.
—Paul Simon

Night had fallen in Portland. Somewhere above the seemingly ever-present clouds and precipitation flew a full moon, and the normal lunar patient increase had begun to clutter the waiting rooms of OHSU's emergency ward. Neurological Sciences ICU on the seventh floor was thankfully quiet except for routines, accompanied by the programmed repetitions of monitoring devices and other electronic gadgetry, medical staff and personnel dancing to the rhythms of well-established and predictable expectations.

Dr. Victoria Franklin, head of the Department of Neurosurgery, was making her evening rounds with a cadre of students who pursued and huddled like a flock of chicks trying to keep pace with their mother hen, each hopeful to impress while avoiding embarrassment. She was a smallish African American woman, a little frumpy but with eyes and a demeanor that demanded and maintained attention.

Her next stop, room 17. Walking to the end of the bed, the chief resident tapped the tablet and scanned the information. "Our patient is Mr. Anthony Spencer," she began, "who will be forty-six in a couple weeks, assuming he makes his birthday, a businessman who has graced our premises a couple times in the past, once for a torn Achilles tendon and another time a little sparring with pneumonia, but other than that has been mostly healthy. He came in yesterday and presented with head trauma in two places, a sizable gash on his forehead and a concussion probably occurring when he collapsed on-site where he was found, resulting in bleeding from the right ear.

"Bleeding like that is indicative of...?" queried Dr. Franklin.

"Battle sign for a basilar skull fracture," responded the resident. She continued, "The patient almost coded while first responders were attempting to stabilize, was transported immediately here, where imaging confirmed subarachnoid brain hemorrhaging and also revealed a subfascial meningioma tumor located in the frontal lobe, midline beneath the falx cerebri."

"So what do we have here?" the doctor asked.

"A highly unusual concurrence of three processes. Trauma, aneurysm, and tumor."

"What side of the brain is the tumor?"

"Uh, we don't know, but he was wearing his watch on his right."

"Significance?" She turned to another of the students.

"Uh, he's left-handed?"

"And that is important because?"

While the questions and responses in room 17 continued for a short time before the doctor and her entourage exited to the next room and next medical situation, another more heated interaction was taking place in the adjoining building on the tenth floor of Doernbecher Children's Hospital.

Molly Perkins was angry and tired. The life of a single mom was routinely difficult, but on days like today seemed impossible. God wasn't supposed to give you more than you could handle, but she felt at the last-straw point of the load. Did God include the baggage that she herself had added to the weight of what she was supposed to handle? Did God take into account what others brought and dumped on her? She hoped so.

Molly and the doctor on call were engaged in a conversation similar to others she had been having for almost four months. She knew that this particular man was not the cause of her pain, but in this moment it simply didn't matter. The unlucky recipient of her frustration, he kindly and patiently let her emotions spill in his direction. Her precious fourteen-year-old, Lindsay, lay dying only a stone's throw from where they stood, her physique ravaged not only by the spreading leukemia but also by the drugs that had been commissioned to take up combat inside this tiny, trembling, and weakening island of humanity. She was well aware that the hospital was filled with others like her Lindsay who were locked in war with their own bodies, but at the moment she was too exhausted to care for more than her one.

Compassionate people, like the doctor Molly was verbally castigating, were among the dedicated many in the trenches, and while these might later weep their losses into pillows in secure homes, on duty they held it together. They, too, knew the haunting guilt of continuing to live, laugh, play, and love while others, often young and innocent, slipped from their best attempts at rescue.

Parents like Molly Perkins needed answers and reassurances on which to hang the myriad of uncertainties, even when there simply weren't any. The doctors could provide only more facts and charts and attempts at explanations that might soften the potentials or the inevitabilities. Thankfully there were wins, but the losses seemed to carry much greater weight, especially when they ran in a series.

"We're going to run the set of tests again tomorrow, Ms. Perkins, and that will let us know how close we are to nadir, the point that the white blood count reaches zero. I know you've heard all this many times already, so I apologize if it feels condescending in any way. Are you going to be able to be here? It's easier for Lindsay when you are."

"Yeah, I'll be here." She tugged on the wisp of blond hair that always seemed to escape her best attempts at control. What was her boss going to say this time? At some point his patience would end. He couldn't keep asking the others to fill in for her. Although she was hourly, not paid unless she punched in, it still upset the schedules; and while most seemed to understand and bend with the wind that was so turbulent in her world, they had their own lives to live, their own families and children waiting.

She glanced over to a nearby chair to check on Cabby, sixteen years old and busy looking through the friends and extended family photo album that he often brought to occupy the wait, rocking back and forth gently to some invisible breeze or rhythm. He was engaged and that was good. Had to keep an eye on this one.

Cabby sensed her attention and looked up, beamed his gorgeous smile, and waved his affection. She blew him a kiss, this firstborn child, the offspring of what she thought had been true love. Ted was there faithfully, right up to the moment he first saw their newborn's rounded face, almond-shaped eyes, and small chin. Suddenly the romantic idealism that had fired her boyfriend's infatuation lost its orbit and crashed onto the realities of everyday commitments.

Both of them healthy, with the naive optimism of youth and the world their common enemy, they had ignored the advantages of prenatal visits or checkups offered freely through their state medical plan. Not that she would have made any other choice had she known. After the initial shock of her son's cognitive disability, she found within the rising of a ferocious love for her baby boy. It was the look of bitter disappointment on Ted's face that she would never forget, and just as she was falling in love with their challenged little man, he fell out of love with her. She refused to become weak or run, while he did both.

Some men, when confronted by their own mortality or the embarrassment, unwanted attention, and intrusion brought into their lives by a child beneath their expectations, justify their cowardice with noble language and slip out the back door. Ted didn't even bother to say good-bye. Three days after Cabby was born, she returned to the tiny three-room apartment above the bar she tended and found no trace that Ted had ever been present, and in all the years since, she had neither seen nor even heard from him.

The arrival of the unforeseen reveals the depths of one's heart. A small ambiguity, the exposure of a tiny lie, an extra bit of the twenty-first chromosome, the replacement of the imagination or ideal by the real, almost anything unexpected can cause life's wheels to lock up and the facade of control to reveal its inherent arrogance.

Thankfully, most women do not see escape as the option that some men do, and Molly responded to her losses by pouring her heart and soul into her son. She named him Carsten, after her great-grandfather, for no reason except she had always liked the name and had heard good stories about the man. Cabby was the name he had given himself, a name he found easier to say. *Better*, she thought, *than Taxi!*

About a year after bringing Cabby home, she had let herself be sweet-talked by a pub rat in heat and on the prowl, with a face of kind consideration and a touch that lingered. She knew better, but the daily weights of existence dulled the warnings and her heart's longings drowned out the flashing sirens. For him, she was another soulless conquest, a way to love himself through another's body for a night. For her, their liaison became a catalyst for change. With the help of social services, some friends, and a church whose rock walls held living hearts, she had relocated, found new work, and nine months later brought Lindsay Anne-Marie Perkins, seven pounds, eight ounces of dark-haired health, into a community eager for her arrival. Now, fourteen years later, it was her daughter who lay deathly ill while Cabby, her Down syndrome son, sixteen and with the mind of an eight-year-old, was vibrant and healthy.

"I'm sorry," she apologized, and the doctor nodded, understanding. "What time did you say the tests were going to be run?"

"We'd like to start as close to 2:00 p.m. as possible, and it will take the better part of the rest of the day. Would that work for you?"

He waited for her assent while she mentally calculated what it was going to take to alter her schedule. When she nodded, he continued, "How about if we take a quick look at her last results." He motioned to an office adjacent to where they were standing and added, "I can bring them up on the screen here, it will only take a couple minutes, and then I'll have you give me a few signatures that we need, answer any questions you might have, and get you on your way."

She glanced once more at Cabby, but he was still busy,

focused on the photos. He seemed oblivious to anything that was happening, humming to himself while making exaggerated motions with his arms and hands as if conducting an orchestra visible to only the most prescient. Usually one of the many young hospital volunteers would help keep an eye on him, but none had arrived yet.

The charts, signatures, questions, and explanations took longer than Molly anticipated, and time passed quickly. She finally allowed herself to ask the most difficult question, steeling herself in anticipation of the answer.

"Can you tell me what Lindsay's real chances are? I mean, thank you for taking the time to explain all of this to me…again, but what are her chances?"

He reached out and touched her arm. "I'm sorry, Ms. Perkins, but we simply don't know. Realistically, without a bone marrow transplant, the chances are less than 50 percent. Lindsay has responded to the chemo, but, as you know, it's been arduous and extremely wearing on her. She's a fighter and sometimes that makes all the difference. We will continue to run the tests and regroup."

It was in that moment that Molly remembered how long it had been since she had checked on Cabby. She glanced at the wall clock. Almost twenty minutes, which was too long. *Oh no*, she thought as she quickly excused herself, hurriedly promising the doctor that she'd be there the next day.

As she feared, Cabby had disappeared, taking with him his album of photographs but leaving behind an empty bag that had contained goldfish-shaped crackers, a snack they had not brought to the hospital. She glanced at the clock. If only Maggie was working, but her shift had ended and she was probably already at home. Maggie was a seasoned registered nurse who worked on-call shifts in Doernbecher's

Oncology/Hematology Department. They shared a house together and she was Molly's best friend.

First stop, down the hallway and into the ward in the direction of room 9, Lindsay's room. Her daughter was fast asleep and there was no sign of Cabby. After a couple of brief conversations she established that he had not come this direction, so back she exited to the main hall. Two choices at this point: back toward the clinic or in the other direction, toward the elevators. Knowing how his mind worked, she headed for the elevators. He was always pushing buttons, hers mostly, she thought to herself and couldn't help a weak but worried grin.

Hide-and-seek was his all-time favorite game, and because of it Molly and Cabby were on a first-name basis with the local law enforcement, which she occasionally called to help track him down. On more than one occasion he had slipped out of their house and returned without her noticing. Weeks and sometimes months later Molly would discover an unfamiliar artifact or piece of equipment not belonging to either of them stashed in his room. He loved cameras and taking pictures, even though he was shy and avoided being in the photos himself. On one of his escapades he found an unlocked door at a neighbor's home, entered, removed a camera, returned home, and hid it under his bed. Two months later she found it concealed in his room, and when confronted, Cabby without hesitation took her to the neighbor's house where it was reunited with its proper owner, a man who simply thought he had misplaced it. She hoped Cabby wouldn't find the Radiology Department.

The trail of sightings led her across the skyway from the children's hospital and into the main building, where she found the family picture album, and finally into the elevators leading to ICU, the last place she wanted to look for him. Cabby had no sense of protocol or social boundaries. It was his goal in life to make a friend of every person, be they awake or unconscious, and with his love of lights and buttons, ICU was the perfect storm. Finally, with the help of more than a few nurses, volunteers, and staff, she narrowed the search to Neurological Sciences ICU and specifically to room 17. Somehow he had gotten past all the security precautions, probably tagging along on the heels of a visitor during a busy moment. Molly approached quietly. She didn't want to startle him or potentially disturb room 17's occupant or visitors.

Cabby had been inside the room for almost five minutes by the time Molly found him. It was dimly lit and quiet, and much to his joy gadgets were everywhere, each making a distinct beeping or whirring noise, oscillating to different rhythms and beats. He liked it in here. It was cooler than out there. After a few minutes of exploration, he was surprised to discover that he wasn't alone, that a man was asleep in the bed.

"Wake!" Cabby commanded and pushed the man's arm, with no response.

"Shhhhhh," whispered Cabby, as if others were in the room with him.

The man was sound asleep and Cabby noticed he had uncomfortable-looking tubes sticking out of his mouth. He tried to pull one out, but it was wedged in pretty tightly so he gave up, turning his attention instead to the array of machines connected to him. He watched the lights, fascinated by the alternating colors and waves of green that some produced, while others simply blinked on and off, off and on.

"Kikmahass!" He muttered his favorite epithet. There were lots of buttons and switches, and Cabby knew what to do with those. He was about to turn one of the big knobs when, on impulse, he leaned down and kissed the sleeping man on his forehead.

A loud voice exclaimed, "What the...?!"

Cabby froze, motionless except for his eyes, his hand hovering inches from the knob. He glanced down at the man, who was still unmoving in his sleep. There was someone else in here, but even though his eyes had adjusted, he couldn't see anyone. Slowly he brought his finger to his mouth and whispered as loud as he could, "Shhhh!"

At that moment the door opened.

"Cabby!"

She had found him. The game was over for now, and he was in her arms in a flash. He smiled broadly while Molly quietly apologized to those with her who had assisted in the search and rescue.

Tony was sliding. It felt warm and comforting, headfirst, facing up in pitch-black but enveloping darkness, and there was nothing to do but enjoy the sense of being carried, lifted, and finally deposited into a room that hummed and beeped with flashing lights.

He looked down and was shocked to see himself. He was not looking well.

"What the...?!" he exclaimed, trying to remember what had gotten him here. He had fallen asleep in Grandmother's mud living room, in front of a fire, with Jesus. What had she just said? Oh yeah, she had said it was time. And now here he was, looking at himself in a hospital room, attached to uncomfortable-looking tubes and all manner of high-tech mechanical paraphernalia.

He watched in the dim light as a chubby finger slowly rose to where his lips should have been.

"Shhhh!" someone whispered loudly.

Tony decided that was probably good advice, especially as a door swung open and a woman stood there looking at him, frazzled but relieved. He heard her exclaim, "Baby" or "Coffee," which made no sense whatsoever, but a wave of something wonderful cascaded over him and a tumbling sequence of jumbled images followed. A glimpse of the floor, some furniture and machines, and then flying straight at this strange woman and being enveloped in her arms. Instinctively, he had reached out, but felt only an empty pressure, and while he had a sense of his own body, there was nothing tangible to grip or with which to catch himself. He didn't need to. A force kept him upright and steady regardless of what was happening outside, as if he were caught and held inside a gyroscope. The only thing that seemed consistent was the window of sight in front of which he was suspended. It occasionally, and for only the briefest of instants, went dark. Even in the collision with the woman, he had not felt the impact, but could smell the sweetness of her perfume mingled with a little anxious perspiration.

Where in the world, he wondered, *am I now?*

8

WHAT IS THE SOUL OF A MAN?

I read the Bible often
I try to read it right
As far as I can understand
It's nothing but a burning light.
— Blind Willie McTell

Tony desperately tried to process the muddle of images, but he felt trapped on an emotional tilt-a-whirl at a cosmic carnival.

The woman leaned down and looked right at him, inches from his face. "Cabby, you have to stop playing hide-and-seek without telling me. Especially when we come to visit Lindsay, okay?"

She was stern but kind, and Tony found himself nodding along with Cabby, whoever he or she was. Soon he was gliding through hospital corridors, down an elevator and out toward a parking structure, where they buckled into an old-model Chevy Caprice.

Desperation car, thought Tony, a twinge of conscience

riding on the wave of his snap judgment. It was a habit and not one that was likely to change quickly.

As they descended a hill, Tony finally recognized where he was, on the winding road through the wooded area between the Oregon Health and Science University hospital and the city. It was almost as if this woman were heading toward his condo. But on Macadam they passed his buildings and continued toward the Sellwood Bridge where they crossed the Willamette, then on to McLoughlin Boulevard and into the backstreets by Milwaukie High School.

This much Tony had figured out. He was "inside" someone's head, someone named Cabby who was the son, maybe, of the woman driving this car.

He wasn't certain who could hear him if he said anything, so he quietly spoke. "Cabby?"

The head snapped up. "What?" came the slurred speech.

"I didn't say anything, honey!" came the voice from the front driver's seat. "We're almost home. Maggie's making supper tonight, and I have some root beer and 'nilla for you for dessert; would you like that?"

"'Kay!"

"Then it will be time for bed, okay? We've had a long day, and tomorrow I need to go back and visit Lindsay at the hospital, okay?"

"'Kay. Cnabby go!"

"Not tomorrow, sweet boy. You have school tomorrow, and Maggie-buddy wants to take you to church with her tomorrow evening. Would you like that? Go to church to see some of your friends?"

"'Kay."

So Tony now knew he was inside the head of a boy who was not the best communicator in the world. He also realized that even though he was peering out through Cabby's eyes, it was more like looking through a window. It was an odd sense, to maintain his own visual focus regardless of what Cabby was looking at, as long as Cabby had his eyes open. The flashes of darkness were blinks, and already Tony hardly noticed it.

Tony tried to catch a glimpse of Cabby's face in the rearview mirror, but it was enough out of the boy's range of sight that he couldn't make it work.

"Cabby, how old are you?" Tony asked.

"Sicktheen," Cabby instantly responded, and then began to look around for the voice.

"Yes, you are, Cabby, sixteen. You are my big boy. Who loves you, Cabby?" came the soft words from the front seat, words that carried comfort and normalcy. Tony could feel Cabby relax.

"Mommy!"

"Right again! And always will, Cabby. Mommy will always love you. You are my sunshine!"

He nodded while still looking around the backseat for whoever was hiding.

They arrived at a modest four-bedroom in a modest neighborhood and pulled into the driveway. A newer sedan was parked on the street, a dent prominent in the driver's-side rear quarter panel. They entered through a small mudroom where Cabby seemed to know the routine, doffing his coat and hanging it on one of the hooks along the wall, then taking his boots off after undoing the Velcro straps. He placed them perfectly in their spot, repositioned a couple of other pairs, and followed his mom into the kitchen where another woman was bent over a pot of something that smelled wonderful, steaming on the stovetop.

"Maggie-buddy!" shouted Cabby and threw himself at her, a well-framed, well-apportioned black woman, an apron protecting her hospital scrubs.

"Well, who might you be, you handsome man?" She beamed at him, holding him at arm's length.

"Cnabby!" he announced, and Tony could feel the unabashed affection this young boy had for her. It was not only that he was seeing through his eyes; he could feel the emotions tumbling through the boy's inside world, his soul, and everything screamed trust regarding this woman.

"Well, if it isn't Cabby, my very own favorite Carsten Oliver Perkins. Not-too-shabby Cabby. Do you have one of your special hugs for me?"

They engulfed each other. Cabby tilted his head back and laughed. "Hungrey!"

"I bet you are, after a hard day's work. Why don't you go and wash up while I pour you a bowl of your favorite mushroom-and-peas-made-from-scratch noodle soup."

"'Kay!" Cabby raced to the bathroom where he reached for the soap and turned on the faucet. Tony looked in the mirror and for the first time saw the young man in whose mind he was intruding. One look and it was obvious to Tony that Cabby was a boy with Down syndrome. That explained the communication issues, as well as his inter-actions with those around him. Cabby leaned closer and smiled at Tony, as if he could see him, a full-faced beautiful smile that lit him up, inside and out.

Tony had never known a "retarded" person. He wasn't even sure if that is what you called them; maybe it was "mentally handicapped" or something else these days. His opinions on most nonbusiness matters may not have been founded on evidence or experience, but he was sure of them. People like Cabby were an unproductive drain on the resources of society; they were valuable only to their families. He believed they were tolerated because of liberal persuasions, not because such people had any intrinsic worth. Tony could recall himself spouting such views at cocktail parties without the slightest stab of conscience. It is easy to create a category of persons, like retarded or handicapped, and then pass judgment on the group as a whole. He wondered if that was not the heart of all prejudice. It was so much easier than considering each as an individual, loved and loving.

When it came time to eat, the three held hands around the small table and Molly turned to Cabby.

"Cabby, who are we thankful for today?"

What followed was a list of people who, whether they knew it or not, had found a place inside the grateful hearts of these three. It included one another, Jesus, Lindsay, the doctors and the nurses at the hospital, the farmer who grew the vegetables that were in the soup, the people at the dairy who milked the cows for the butter and milk and especially the ice cream, Ted, friends at school, people who made root beer, and a host of others who participated in expression of God's affection. Tony almost laughed out loud when Cabby snuck a piece of bread during the expressions of gratitude.

During the meal, he listened and experienced. As Cabby ate, Tony could literally feel the flavors in the soup and fresh bread, and how everything resonated inside Cabby, especially the 'nilla (vanilla ice cream) and root beer. By watching through his eyes the unspoken or truncated sentences that passed between Maggie and the mom, Molly, he learned that Lindsay was Cabby's younger sister and very sick up at Doernbecher, one of two children's hospitals on the OHSU campus. Molly had already made arrangements with work to take the next day off, and Maggie, who shared this house with her and the kids, would oversee Cabby, picking him up from school and probably taking him with her to church in the evening.

When Cabby had to pee before bedtime, Tony self-consciously averted his eyes, but felt the sense of relief he had taken for granted all his life. Such little things that make up everyday routines, largely unheeded and unnoticed, but quite essential. Cabby donned Spider-Man pajamas, brushed his teeth, and climbed into bed.

"Ready," he yelled, and a few moments later Molly entered the bedroom, switching on the ladybug night-light on the bedside stand and switching off the overhead one. She sat down on the bed next to where he lay, and for a second bent over, her face in her hands. Tony could feel Cabby reaching out to her emotionally, trying to tell her something. The best he could do was touch her, patting her on the back.

"'Kay, Mommy! 'Kay?"

She took a deep breath. "Yeah, Cabby, I'm okay. I have you, and Lindsay, and Maggie, and Jesus. It's just been a long day and Mommy is tired, that's all."

And then she leaned down and laid her head on Cabby's chest and began singing something that Tony hadn't heard since...when? Not since he was a little boy. Now in this woman's voice he could hear his own mother's song, and suddenly he was deeply sad. He felt tears sliding down his face as this mother sang, "Jesus loves me, this I know."

Cabby sang, in a slow, halting monotone, "DJE-SUS LUB MME." Tony tried to sing but couldn't remember the words, his emotions toppling in a cascade of memory and longing.

"Cabby, honey, why are you crying?" Molly was brushing tears from her son's face.

"Sad!" Cabby tapped his heart with his fingers. "Sad!"

ℰ∞✝ ⚡∞✳︎⑤⑱

Tony woke, tears collecting in his ears. He sat up and took a deep breath. Grandmother was tapping his chest to wake him, and handed him a cup of what looked like coffee but smelled like tea.

"Here, blow your nose!" she directed, handing him a clean cloth. "We should give you a good Indian name, One-Who-Cries-a-Lot."

"Whatever," was all he could think to respond. He was still caught in the aftermath of unexpected emotions, and the remnants were not quickly dissipating.

Finally, he collected his thoughts enough to ask, "How was any of that possible?"

She grinned. "Powerful stuff, quantum fire." She continued, "Just think about who is asking the question—a guy in a coma in Portland, Oregon, asking a Lakota woman inside his own soul about how he could end up inside the eyes of a very special boy in Portland, Oregon. Seems to me," she said with a chuckle, "it is all self-explanatory."

"Of course it is," and this time it was Tony who was grinning, but then he grew somber. "So all of that is actually happening? Lindsay is really sick, and Cabby, you know, and his mother and Maggie?"

"Real time," responded Grandmother.

"And this is not real time?" asked Tony.

"Different real time," she grunted. "More in-between time. Don't ask, just drink this."

He did, careful at first, but whatever disgusting thing he had braced himself for was immediately proved false as the flavors of this liquid dropped into his chest, warming him thoroughly and leaving a sensation of complete gratification.

"I am not going to answer that either," she said, anticipating his question. "Trust me, you don't wanna know. And don't go tellin' me I could make a lot of money if I sold this stuff."

He looked at her sideways but didn't pursue it. Instead, he asked, "So, why was I there, and why am I back?"

"There are lots of reasons why you are there," she began. "Papa never does anything for just one purpose, and most of these you will never understand or even know. All part of the weaving."

"So will you tell me one of the reasons?" he asked.

"One reason, dearest, was to hear your mother sing to you. If nothing else, that was enough." She threw another log onto the open fire and pushed wood around until satisfied that all was perfectly situated. Tony was lost in her response and for a time afraid to attempt to speak, the emotions too immediate.

"I agree," he finally offered. "That was reason enough, but very painful."

"You are welcome, Anthony."

They were quiet for a time. Tony looked into the fire. Grandmother scooted her stool closer until she was touching him.

"And why am I here now, and not there?"

"Cabby is sleeping, and he preferred that you not be inside his dreaming," she said, as if it were a most logical explanation.

"He preferred?" He looked at Grandmother, who kept

looking into the fire. "What do you mean, he preferred? Did he know I was there?"

"His spirit knew."

Tony didn't respond but just sat there waiting, his eyebrows raised in the question he knew she knew he was asking.

"Trying to explain a human being," she began, "a being who is a unity, one, and yet comprising spirit, soul, and body, is like trying to explain God: Spirit, Father, and Son. The understanding is in the experience and relationship."

He waited, not even knowing how to ask the next questions.

She continued, "Cabby, like you, is a spirit interpenetrating a soul interpenetrating a body. But it is not simply interpenetration. It is dance and participation."

"Thanks." He sat back and took another mouthful, swallowing slowly to allow himself to savor the liquid's descent. "That's very helpful, Grandmother."

"Sarcasm originated in God. Just sayin'!" she enjoined.

Tony smiled at that while she kept a stony visage, more, he thought, for effect than anything. It worked. "Okay, so try me again. You said he preferred?"

"Anthony, like you, Cabby's body is broken and his soul is crushed and bent, yet his spirit is alive and well. But even though alive and well, his spirit is submitted in relationship to the broken and crushed parts of his person, his soul and body. Words are very inadequate to communicate sometimes. When I tell you 'his body' or 'his soul' or 'his spirit,' it sounds like each is some thing or piece that you own. It is more accurate if you comprehend that you 'are' your body, and you 'are' your soul, and you 'are' your spirit. You are an interpenetrated and interpenetrating whole, a unity of diversity but essentially a oneness."

"That doesn't make a lot of sense to me. I believe you; I just don't know what exactly I'm believing. I think I perceive what you are saying more than I am able to understand." He paused. "I just feel so bad for him."

"Cabby? He said the same thing about you."

Tony looked up, surprised.

"Yeah, don't go feelin' bad for him. His brokenness is just more obvious than yours. He wears it on the outside for all to see, while you have kept yours all locked away and hidden as best you know how. Cabby has internal sensitivities and receptors that are significantly more developed than yours. He can see things that you are blind to, can pick up on the good and the danger in people quicker than you, and his perception is much keener. It is just housed in an inability to communicate, a broken body and soul reflective of a broken world.

"Now don't you go all comparin' yourself and feelin' bad," Grandmother continued. "You and Cabby are on different journeys because you are each uniquely your own person. Life was never meant to be about comparing or competing."

Tony took a deep breath. "So, then, what is a soul, exactly?" he queried.

"Ah, now there is a deep question. To which there is no exact answer. Like I said, it is not a possession, it is a living. It is the Cabby-who-remembers, it is the Cabby-who-imagines, it is the Cabby-who-creates, who dreams, who emotes, who wills, who loves, who thinks. But Cabby as soul is housed inside the dimensions limited by who Cabby is as a damaged body."

"It just doesn't seem fair."

"Fair?" Grandmother mumbled, "That's a good one. Anthony, there is nothin' fair in a broken world full of broken people. Justice tries to be fair, but fails at every turn. There is never anything fair about grace or forgiveness. Punishment never restores fair. Confession doesn't make things fair. Life is not about granting the fair reward for the right performance. Contracts, lawyers, disease, power, none of these care about fair. Better to take dead words out of your languages, maybe focus on living words like *mercy* and *kindness* and *forgiveness* and *grace*. You might stop being so concerned about your rights and what you think is fair." She looked up from her rant. "Just sayin'..."

They were silent for a time, again watching the fire burn down.

"So why don't you fix him?" Tony asked quietly.

Grandmother was equally soft in her response. "Anthony, Cabby is not a broken toy, a thing to be fixed. He is not a piece of property to be renovated. He is a human being, a living being who will forever exist. When Molly and Teddy chose to conceive..."

"Teddy?" he interjected.

"Yes, Teddy, Ted, Theodore, Molly's ex-boyfriend, Cabby's father, and yes, he did abandon Molly and his own son." Tony looked at Grandmother, tight lips silently communicating his disapproval and verdict.

"Anthony, you barely know anything about this man, only what you assume from a snippet of a conversation. Where you think scumbag, I think lost sheep, lost coin, lost son, or"—she nodded toward him—"lost grandson."

She let him sit inside his own judgment, wrestling with the implications of how he looked at everything, and everyone. It made him feel sick inside. He was internally facing another massive darkness that he had long treasured, and it grew as he rationally scrambled to justify himself. No matter the mental gymnastics or how he tried to mask it, his first inclination to pass judgment emerged more hideous and terrifying, a threat that might destroy anything within him that could ever have been considered good.

He felt a hand on his shoulder and it was enough to snap him out of the dark place. Grandmother's face was pressed to his, and he felt himself slowly calming.

"This is not a time for self-loathing, Anthony," she said gently. "It is important that you realize you needed the skill to judge in order to survive as a child. It helped keep you and your brother safe. You and he are alive today partly because the ability to judge was in your toolbox. However, such tools eventually become debilitating and damaging."

"But I saw it. It's so ugly. How do I stop?" He was almost begging.

"You will, dearest, when you trust something else more."

The dark wave had receded, but he knew it wasn't gone, just a monster in waiting, lurking for another opportunity. For the moment it was tamed by the presence of this woman. This was no longer only a game or lighthearted adventure. This was war, and it seemed that the battlefield was in his own heart and mind; something old and hurt was in conflict with something that was beginning to emerge.

Grandmother brought him another drink, this time earthy and hearty. He could feel it tumble down his throat and spread throughout his body, even reaching his fingertips and toes. A prickly sensation went up and down his spine and she smiled, satisfied.

"Don't ask, won't tell, won't sell," she grunted.

He laughed. "Weren't we in the middle of something, something about Cabby?" he asked.

"Later," she replied. "Right now it is time for you to go back."

"Back? Like, back into Cabby?" he asked and she nodded.

"Don't you need to, you know, do something?" he asked.

"Quantum fire?" She grinned her big, wide-hearted grin. "That was just child's play, just a little"—and she shook her hips—"razzle-dazzle! Nope, I don't need anything. One more thing, Anthony: when you find yourself in a difficult spot, and you will recognize it when it happens, just turn."

"Turn?" he asked, puzzled.

"Yeah, turn, you know...," and Grandmother hopped off her feet, slightly spinning, just enough to do a quarter turn. "Like one of those line-dance things."

"Can you do it one more time, just so I'll remember it right?" He was teasing her.

"Nope," she said and smirked. "Once is more than enough. And don't expect to see it again either."

They both laughed.

"Now go!" It was almost a command.

And he was gone.

9

A STORM OF CONGREGATION

A woman is the only thing I am afraid of that
will not hurt me.
—Abraham Lincoln

Tony arrived just as breakfast was ending, and from the scraps that remained on Cabby's plate it appeared he had enjoyed a burrito with chicken, beans, and cheese. From the contented feeling of satisfaction that had settled over him, it was obviously a Cabby favorite.

"Cabby, you have about twenty minutes to play before I take you to school. Maggie is going to pick you up 'cause I have to go up and visit Lindsay, and she is going to take you to church with her tonight, sound good?"

"'Kay."

"And guess what? Maggie-buddy is going to make a chicken for supper, and she's going to let you pick the meat off the bones for her, okay?"

Cabby was thrilled and held up his hand until his mom stopped long enough to give him a high five. Pleased with the world, he two foot trotted to his bedroom and shut the door. Reaching under his bed he pulled out a guitar case and opened it. Inside were a small red toy guitar and an expensive-looking compact camera. Satisfied that all was well, he closed the case, snapped the clips, and hid it again under his bed. Looking around, he spotted a favorite picture book and began leafing through its pages. Touching under each animal in turn, he grunted something intelligible enough that Tony could tell Cabby knew what each was. But one animal either stumped him or he didn't know how to pronounce its name, and he sat there tapping under its picture.

Tony couldn't help himself. "Wol-ver-ine." Tony said it without thinking and then froze.

So, too, did Cabby. He snapped the book shut and sat for almost ten seconds, absolutely still, only his eyes darting around the room in search of the origin of the voice. Finally, he slowly opened the book again and tapped repeatedly under the picture.

"Wolverine," said Tony in a resigned fashion, knowing that the beans had been spilled.

"Kikmahass!" squealed Cabby, rocking back and forth and putting his hand over his mouth.

"Cabby?!" came his mother's voice from the other room. "What have I told you about saying that? Don't say that word, okay?"

"'Kay!" he yelled back, and doubled over, smothering his laughter and delight in his pillow. "Kikmahass!" he whispered.

Sitting back up, he opened the book again and this time tapped the picture slowly and deliberately. Each time he did, Tony said, "Wolverine!" and Cabby would disappear once again into his pillow in a fit of giggles.

He rolled off his bed and onto the floor, taking a quick look under it to make sure no one was hiding there.

He checked his closet, which besides all his usual stuff was empty. He even peeked hesitantly behind his dresser. Finally, he stood in the middle of the room and said loudly, "Gen."

"You need something, Cabby?" came his mother's voice.

"Cabby, I'll do it again, but shhhhh," said Tony.

"Nuh!" yelled Cabby to his mom and then whispered, "Kikmahass!" and doubled over again.

Tony was laughing, too, caught up in the boy's sheer delight at this unusual adventure.

Cabby stifled as best he could his giggling and lifted up his shirt in search of the mystery voice. He examined his belly button and was about to lower his pants when Tony spoke.

"Cabby, stop. I'm not in your pants. I'm in…" He paused, trying to find the words. "I'm in your heart, and I can see through your eyes and I can talk to you in your ears."

Cabby covered his eyes. "Okay, now I can't see," responded Tony. Again and again, Cabby covered, then uncovered his eyes, Tony reporting each time the current state of visibility. It seemed the game might never end when Cabby stopped and walked over to his dresser mirror. He looked close into his own eyes, as if he might see the voice. Pursing his lips and with a sense of determination he pulled back, looked into the mirror at himself, put both hands on his chest, and announced, "Cnabby."

"Cabby," started Tony, "my name is To-ny! To-ny!"

"Tah-Ny." It didn't come out clear or distinct, but he knew. And then came the unexpected, catching Tony off guard. A brilliant and broad grin erupted on Cabby's face, and he put both hands over his heart and said softly, "Tah-Ny…frund!"

"Yes, Cabby," came the voice, tender and kind. "Tony and Cabby are friends."

"Yessss!" announced the boy and put his hand in the air for a high five, but then realizing no one was there, swatted the invisible hand of the invisible voice.

Then came the next unexpected; looking back into the mirror, Cabby asked in a halting attempt to form the words, "Tah-Ny lob Cnabby?"

Tony was caught, suddenly trapped by the three-word question. Cabby made the effort and had the will to ask, but Tony didn't have what it took to answer. Did he love Cabby? He didn't really know him. Did he know how to love anyone? Had he ever known what love was? And if he didn't, how would he recognize it if he ever found it?

The boy was waiting, upturned face, for a response.

"Yes, I love you, Cabby," he lied. Immediately Tony could feel Cabby's disappointment.

Somehow, Cabby knew. The gaze dropped, but the sadness lasted only a couple of seconds. He looked up again. "Sun-dy," he said.

Sun-dy... Sunday? Tony wondered. Was he saying Sunday or ... someday? And then it dawned on him. Cabby was saying "someday" ... someday Tony would love him. He hoped it might be true. Perhaps Cabby knew things that he didn't.

꧁ ∞ 𝄢 ✦ ∞ ❄ ᘒ 𐂷

They arrived at the supported academic classroom where Cabby, and therefore Tony, would spend the better part of the day. The learning area for the developmentally delayed, which served about a dozen young adults in all, shared a campus with a local high school full of typically developing peers but was separated from the main building. Activity was constant, and Tony was repeatedly amazed by the skills that Cabby had mastered despite his disabilities. His reading level was only prekindergarten, but he could do simple math. Cabby especially excelled in the use of a calculator, stashing two away in his backpack that he had secretly appropriated during the course of the morning. He also had considerable skill in writing words, almost as if they were drawings, which he adeptly copied from the whiteboard into one of many notebooks already filled with them.

Tony stayed quiet, trying not to draw attention to either himself or Cabby. The young man clearly understood the shared secret, but at every opportunity during the day he would find a mirror, lean close to it, and whisper, "Tah-Ny?"

"Yes, Cabby, I'm still here."

Cabby would grin, make one sharp nod, and off they would be running again.

The kindness and patience of the teachers and staff, along with some of the high school students who dropped in to help, surprised Tony. How many people, he wondered, put time and care into the lives of others every day?

For lunch, Cabby ate reheated leftover burritos from breakfast, a cheese stick, and some Fig Newtons. Each one seemed his favorite food ever. Gym class was a combination of dance and a comedy of errors, but everyone survived. Tony was unaccustomed and captive to this world, but felt a grounding reality in each experience. This was life, ordinary yet extraordinary and unexpected. Where had he been all these years? *Hiding* was the answer that came to mind. It might not be the whole truth of it, but it certainly was a part.

Spending time with these children was both unexpected delight and difficult, his failures as a parent painfully obvious. He had tried diligently for a time, even read books on fathering and given it his best business try, but after Gabriel…he had left such matters to Loree and returned to the safer world of performance and production and property. Any pang of regret that surfaced throughout the day, he would push back into the closets and corners of his soul where they could be better ignored.

Maggie arrived on time, still dressed in hospital scrubs. When she entered she lit up the room, her carriage professional and her personality gregarious. After she carted them home in her dented car, she busied herself cleaning a chicken, preparing some fixings, and tossing them into the oven to bake. Cabby, a little peeved that neither of his two new calculators had made it through final school checkout, occupied himself with puzzles, some coloring, and an extended battle on *Zelda*, a video game he had mastered. Every few minutes he would whisper "Tay-Ny?" just to check in, and when Tony responded, he was always rewarded with a grin.

When the chicken had cooled enough, Cabby washed up and quickly and efficiently removed the meat from the bones. His hands were a greasy mess, as was his chin and his mouth, into which scraps of favorite pieces had mysteriously found their way. Supper was simply the addition of mashed potatoes and a few cooked carrots.

"Cabby, do you need help picking out some clothes for church?" asked Maggie.

"I'll help you," whispered Tony, as if Maggie could hear him.

"Nah," whispered Cabby, grinning as he headed to his room.

The two explored Cabby's closet and drawers until they agreed on just the right outfit: jeans, belt, a long-sleeved shirt that had snaps instead of buttons, and a pair of black Velcro sneakers. It took time dressing and the belt was a particular challenge, but finally finished, Cabby bustled back to the kitchen to present himself to Maggie.

"Look at you," exclaimed Maggie. "You are such a handsome young man and you picked out all this by yourself?"

"Tay...," Cabby began.

"Shhhhh!" hushed Tony.

"Shhhhh!" whispered Cabby, his finger to his lips.

"What do you mean, 'Shhhhh!'?" Maggie laughed. "There is no way I am going to shush about how handsome and grown-up my Cabby is. I think I will announce it to the whole world. You go run along and play for a few minutes while I get ready for church."

Church, thought Tony. He hadn't set foot inside one of those since his last foster family had been religious. He and Jake had been required to sit silently for what seemed hours, on hard wooden pews that seemed built to torment. Despite the discomfort they often managed to fall asleep, lulled into unconsciousness by the monotone monologue of the preacher. He smiled to himself, remembering how he and Jake had schemed together and "gone forward" one night at church, thinking it would win them points with the family, which it did. The attention their conversions garnered was initially rewarding, but it soon became clear that "asking Jesus into your heart" dramatically increased expectations for strict obedience to a host of rules they hadn't anticipated. He soon became a "backslider," in a category, he discovered, that was profoundly worse than being pagan in the first place. It was difficult enough surviving as a foster child. A foster child who had fallen from grace was magnitudes worse.

But both Maggie and Cabby seemed excited to attend, and Tony was curious. Perhaps things had changed during the years of his absence.

Maggie, a zaftig looker of a woman, applied a reasonably visible layer of makeup, donned a comely dress that enhanced her most fetching features, and put on red high heels that matched her clutch. She gave herself the once-over in the mirror, smoothing out a few wrinkles while sucking in ever so slightly, before she nodded approval, gathered her coat, and took Cabby by the hand.

It didn't take them long to reach the parking lot of Maranatha Holy Ghost Church of God in Christ, the good-sized city church that Maggie attended and Cabby often visited. It was midweek service and also youth night, so the place was full of hustle and bustle, the young and old in a mixing bowl of enthusiasm and holy intention. Tony was impressed at the blend of race and age, the financially secure rubbing shoulders with the less so. The ease of interactions was surprising, as was the general sense of kindness and community. This was different than he remembered.

Along their way toward the children's classrooms, Maggie stopped and chatted with this or that person, her personality magnetic and charming. She was engrossed in one of these conversations when Tony heard Cabby whisper, "Tah-Ny?"

"I'm here, Cabby. What is it?" he asked.

"See?" He was pointing across the room at a young couple, a pair of teenagers enamored only with each other. They were oblivious to the world around them, holding hands and whispering harmless nonsense. Their universe was just to be near each other. Inwardly, Tony smiled. It had been a long time since he had stopped to notice innocent love. When, he wondered, had he forgotten that it even existed.

Cabby, however, seemed a bit agitated, as if he were tugging at Tony's arm.

"What is it, Cabby? Are you okay?" he asked.

"Grl-frund," Cabby mumbled.

"Cabby," responded Tony, thinking that he understood. "That girl? You like her?"

"Ya...no." He shook his head. "Cnabby want..."

Cabby wanted. Tony understood. He felt the raw, passionate aching in Cabby and sensed the single hot tear that climbed slowly from the corner of Cabby's eye and rolled silently down his face. This young man somehow knew that a sweetness lay outside his power to have or hold, and he was sharing this longing with him. Cabby would never experience a gift that Tony had treated with callous disdain—the love of a girl. Cabby treasured what he had handled with reckless contempt. Again Tony realized how shallow were his assumptions regarding the maturity of this sixteen-year-old's heart. It was not a painful, shaming self-judgment, but an exposure and uncomfortable. It seemed Tony was growing a conscience, and he wasn't sure he wanted one.

I'm such an ass, Tony thought.

"I am really sorry, Cabby," he barely whispered.

Cabby nodded, still watching the two. "Sun-dy," he whispered back.

Maggie, tugging on his hand, continued their walk, Tony silent and shaken. They reached the designated room, and as she signed Cabby into his class, Tony heard a couple of boys snickering, one of them loud enough to be heard, "There's that 'tard!"

Cabby heard, too, and turned to face the boys. Through Cabby's eyes, Tony saw a pair of gawky junior high boys snickering and pointing in his direction. Cabby did his best to come up with the appropriate response, but gave them the wrong finger—his index finger, straight up with arm bent at the elbow—not quite remembering what he had been taught by his schoolmates.

"Wrong finger, Cabby, use the middle one," Tony suggested. Cabby looked at his hand, trying to decide which was the middle one, and quickly gave up, raising both hands and wriggling all his fingers in their direction.

"Ha!" Tony laughed. "That's it, give them all the fingers! Well done!"

Cabby looked down with a grin, delighted with the praise, but it made him self-conscious. He held up one hand, waving it slightly. "Stop," he said, embarrassed.

"Oh, pay those boys no mind, Cabby," encouraged Maggie. "They weren't brought up properly. They're not even smart enough to know what sort of ignoramuses they are. Anyway, I've got you all signed in, and I'll be back in about an hour to fetch you home. Lots of your friends are here and Miss Alisa. You remember Miss Alisa, don't you?"

He nodded his approval and was about to head into class when inexplicably he turned into the corner near the doorjamb and whispered, "Bye, Tah-Ny!" Tony was caught off guard and before he could say anything, Cabby turned and buried himself into Maggie's arms, giving her a huge hug.

"My goodness," expressed Maggie. "Cabby, are you okay?"

He looked up and nodded, smiling with his wide heart-filled grin.

"Good!" said Maggie. "Now, if you need me, someone will come get me, but I'll be back regardless in a little while."

"'Kay!" he acknowledged, and then he waited.

As Maggie had done a thousand times before, she leaned down and let Cabby kiss her forehead. This time she felt a breeze sweep through her body. *Wow,* she thought.

Holy Spirit, I will have more of that, please! and after giving Cabby another squeeze, headed toward the service.

Tony was sliding again.

🜂 ∽ 🜂 ⚶ ∽ ❋ 🜍 🜖

He knew instantly what had happened, but only now figured out the jump's catalyst. It was the kiss that allowed him to slide. It felt exactly the same as before, face up and back, warm and embracing, and then he was viewing the world through Maggie's eyes. The childlike wonder and simple colors—bright reds and greens and blues—of Cabby's soul had been exchanged for an older, more crafted environment, with deep textures and patterns, complexity, along with a breadth of space and maturity.

Maggie, oblivious to the intrusion, decided to stop off at the powder room on her way to the sanctuary. She nodded hellos and greeted many of the other women before she checked herself out in the mirror, made a last-minute adjustment to her dress, and was about to leave when she decided she had better pee. One never knew for certain how long these services might last, and once started she didn't want to miss anything.

Tony panicked. Maggie was just about to undo the necessities when he yelled, "Stop!" He did not know what else to do.

That is exactly what Ms. Maggie Saunders did. She stopped—stopped breathing, stopped moving, stopped unbuttoning, stopped everything, for almost five seconds. Then she screamed at the top of her voice, "Man! There's a man in here!"

Like a cannon blast full of confetti, the women exploded out of the ladies' room in individual and corporate disarray.

Somehow in the exiting wave, Maggie successfully buttoned up. Gesticulating and hyperventilating, she attempted to explain to a cluster of women who stood outside the door and to the three ushers who had come running because of the commotion. They calmed her down somewhat, got her story, and approached the bathroom with considerable caution. What followed was a careful search of every stall, including the mop closet at the back of the room, turning up nothing. She made them look again, reiterating that a man had certainly spoken to her, even though none of the other women had heard anything, excepting Georgia Jones, who was ever hopeful a man would talk to her.

After confirming there was no man in the women's restroom, the ushers gathered around Maggie.

"Maybe it was the Lord, Ms. Maggie?" offered one of the ushers, trying to be helpful. "We looked everywhere, and there is no way for a man to get outta there without being seen."

"I am so sorry," she apologized. "I really don't know what to say, but I did hear a man in there and he did say, 'Stop,' I'm sure of it."

Since there was nothing else that could be done, the group began to disperse. None of the women who had exited, however, were inclined to reenter the ladies' room. None except Maggie. Thoroughly embarrassed, she was determined to go back in there and see for herself. If Tony could have banged his head against a wall, he would have. What was with this woman?

Her careful exploration of the entire restroom confirmed there was no man in there. Finally she gave up and ran some water to cool her face and calm herself. Glancing in the mirror to ensure no one snuck up behind her, she took deep breaths and began to ease herself from the grip of adrenaline. As her body relaxed, she remembered what she had been doing before the uproar and reopened one of the stalls, preparing again to unbutton her personals.

"For crying out loud, Maggie, stop!"

Maranatha Holy Ghost Church of God in Christ is sedate and civilized compared to folks down the road at the Full Gospel Redeemer Fellowship, who had a reputation as authentic Holy Rollers. So nobody in the sanctuary filled with people quietly meditating on the holiness of the Almighty was prepared when Ms. Maggie erupted a second time from the ladies' room like a crazed woman, arms waving and purse flying. They had certainly witnessed the activity of the Holy Ghost many a time, and a few regulars were predictably slain in the Spirit. But while they could whip up a presence when led, they were only moderately active and always polite, making sure that if a woman went down under the power she was properly covered, especially if the youth group full of gawking teenage boys was in the service.

But no one had ever, even when they snuck down to Full Gospel Redeemer, seen the Spirit take hold like this. Like a small atomic bomb, Ms. Maggie Saunders burst into the sanctuary during the second chorus of "Oh Happy Day," and tore down the center aisle shrieking, "I'm possessed! I'm possessed!"

Some later said they thought it mighty coincidental that she went flying down the aisle aimed right at Elder Clarence Walker, the most eligible bachelor in the congregation, a veritable saint and pillar of the church.

Elder Walker stood, as all good elders should, when he heard the ruckus, but made the mistake of stepping into the center aisle to better see the problem. Once there, he froze as the rushing torrent of woman came at him like a train off its tracks. Just as she reached maximum velocity, one of her heels snapped off, launching her unceremoniously through the air and into the open arms of Elder Clarence. Though he had a few inches on her, she had a few pounds on him, and down they went in a tumbling heap, decorum and sanctification spilling everywhere. Clarence had the breath completely knocked out of him and there she sat straddling him, shaking his shoulders, and screaming, "I'm possessed," into his face.

The choir was completely baffled, although a few of them tried to continue the third chorus of "Oh Happy Day." It happened so fast that at least half those present only heard something but didn't actually see it, and most of those were not sure whether to shout amen or wave hankies in acknowledgment of the work of the Holy Ghost. A few in the back rows went down on their knees, believing a revival had started. Ushers and a few congregants seated nearby descended quickly on the entangled pair, hoping to help, some praying in tongues and reaching out their hands. It was pandemonium.

One bruiser of a young man clamped a firm hand over Maggie's mouth until she quit screaming, and with the help of two others separated her from the barely breathing Elder Clarence. Both were promptly escorted to the side prayer room, as the quick-thinking music director started the choir and congregation in a calming rendition of "Amazing Grace."

Maggie finally settled down enough to sip some water, while a couple of women patted her hand and repeatedly uttered, "Bless God" and "Praise Jesus." She was utterly mortified. Maggie had heard the man's voice—twice. But it didn't matter. All she wanted now was to move immediately back to Texas with her distant relatives, to live in obscurity and die unremembered.

Tony was both horrified for what he had caused and experiencing sheer glee at the unexpected turn of events. He could still hear the touching chords of "Amazing Grace" from behind the shut door, but for the first time, he was ready to hoot and howl in church. The second adrenaline rush that had blown through Maggie had lit him on fire, and he was giddy in its aftermath. *If this is church*, he thought, *I'll have to go more often.*

Elder Clarence slowly regained his breath and composure, and once recovered enough to speak without wheezing, sat in front of Maggie and took her hands. She couldn't look at him. They had known each other for some time, and this behavior was totally inconsistent with the woman for whom he held undeniable affection, albeit platonic and reserved.

"Maggie…" He paused. What he wanted to say was, "Maggie, what the hell is going on?" but he spoke quietly and in a fatherly manner. "Maggie," he began again, "can you explain to me, to us, what happened?"

Maggie wanted to die. She had once hoped for something more with this man, but she had killed all hope, body-slammed it to the carpet in the main sanctuary in front of God and everyone. She took a deep breath, and with abject humiliation, keeping her eyes glued to the floor, she said she had been in the bathroom and a man had spoken to her and then the ushers had searched it finding no one, and how one of the ushers thought it might have been God… She offered this last bit hoping it might be an option that Clarence would bite on, but he ignored it. *It would have been a lie anyway*, she thought, probably not the best idea at the moment. So she continued, how after searching and finding nothing, she had gone back in and the voice spoke to her again.

"Clarence… I mean, Elder Walker, it had to be a demon."

She finally looked up at him, pleading with her eyes to have him believe her, or at least offer some plausible explanation. "What else...?"

"Shhh, calm down, Maggie." He was still calling her by her first name; at least that was something. "What did this voice say to you?"

Maggie thought back. It was all a blur and she wasn't sure. "I think he said, 'Christ is outside. Stop, Maggie!' That's what I remember, but it happened so fast."

Clarence looked at her, wishing he could think of something that might help or comfort, but he was drawing a complete blank.

Knowing he was at a loss for words, she tried to prompt something. "Elder Walker, why would Christ be outside? And why do I have to be stopped?"

Clarence shook his head, stalling while praying silently for some wisdom, but nothing was coming. He thought he might try another tack. "So you really think it was a demon?"

"I don't know. It's just what popped into my head. Wouldn't a demon do that, pop a thought like that into your head? Do you think I have a demon, Clarence, uh, I mean, Elder Walker?"

"I am not a demon!" Tony interjected emphatically. "I'm not sure what a demon is, but I am not one of those."

"Oh my God." Maggie swooned, her eyes growing big as saucers. "It's talking to me!"

"Who?" asked Clarence.

"The demon," answered Maggie. Anger rose and flushed her face. "Don't you be talking to me, you demon from the pit o' hell... Sorry, not you, Brother Clarence; I was talking to the demon." She averted her eyes to an empty space behind the elder and where none of the others were standing. Where else could she look? "In the name of Jesus—"

"Maggie," interrupted Clarence. "What did he say?"

She looked back at him. "He said he wasn't a demon. Wouldn't you just expect that is what a demon would say, that he wasn't a demon?"

"My name is Tony," added Tony to be helpful, but enjoying this immensely more than he probably should.

Maggie put her hand over her mouth and added through clenched fingers, "He says his name is Tony."

Clarence tried not to laugh out loud. "You have a demon who says he's not a demon, whose name is Tony?"

She nodded.

He bit the inside of his mouth, but then asked, "Maggie, does your demon have a last name?"

"*My* demon?" The insinuation stung. "He is not *my* demon, and if I got a demon, I got him in *your* church." She instantly regretted what she had said and quickly attempted to recover. "Of course he doesn't have a last name. Everyone knows that demons don't have last..."

"Sure I do," volunteered Tony. "My last name is..."

"Shush," muttered Maggie. "Don't you be telling me you have a last name, you lying demon from the pit o' hell."

"Maggie," continued Tony, "I know you are friends with Molly, and I know about Lindsay and Cabby."

"Oh my God." She gripped Clarence's hand tighter. "It's a familiar spirit. He just told me he knows all about Molly and Cabby and..."

"Maggie, listen to me," said Clarence, gently removing his hand from hers. "I think I need to pray for you right now...uh, we all do. You know that we love you. I don't understand the kind of pressure that you're going through right now, but I want you to know that we are here for you. Whatever you or Molly or Lindsay and Cabby need, all you have to do is ask."

And with that Maggie knew that Clarence and the others were not going to ever believe her about the demon who was talking to her. The more she said, the worse it was getting. It was time to shut up before they called in professionals.

They all gathered around her, and she let them anoint her with some sweet-smelling oil from the Holy Land. They then had a lengthy time of prayer, the kindness of people trying to find the right words to assist God with this strange event. And it did help. Maggie felt something, a quiet that came over her and a peace that everything was going to be better somehow, as impossible as that seemed in the moment.

"Oh my, look at the time. I really must be getting Cabby before it gets any later," she said as they all stood. A few hugged her while others tried not to look as though they feared being contaminated by whatever she had. Maggie tried to look an apology at Clarence, who was gracious as he smiled and hugged her back. She held him a second longer than she probably ought to, but she figured it was likely their last and wanted something to remember. "Thanks, everyone, for your prayers and support." *But not for understanding*, she thought. She didn't even understand herself. Someday this would be a good story, but for the moment she didn't want to see another living person, except Cabby and Molly. Molly was going to flip.

10

DOUBLE-MINDED

*Tragedy is a tool for the living to gain wisdom, not
a guide by which to live.*
—Robert Kennedy

Maggie and Cabby arrived home to Molly waiting at the front door. She raised an eyebrow inquisitively as Maggie hobbled in on two flat red slippers. It had been too cold to walk barefoot to the car, and rather than hobble on one heel she had deliberately broken off the other heel to match. A little duct tape from the maintenance closet had replaced the broken shoe's strap. Her dress was torn in a couple of places, and her hair was still frazzled.

"Wow! A service I shouldn't have missed?" inferred Molly.

"Girl," Maggie began, laughing and shaking her head while she took off both shoes and walked in stocking feet to the trash can and unceremoniously dropped them in, "you have noooo idea! It'll take an act of God to ever get me in that place again. I've pretty much used C-4 to blow up my bridges there."

"What happened?" Molly was incredulous.

"I'm not even sure myself, but after what I did, I just wanna dig a big ol' hole about the size of Texas and drop in it."

"Maggs, it can't be that bad. It'll work out, really; things always have a way. So tell me what happened. I don't understand what you're saying."

"Molly," Maggie began as she looked up at her friend, her mascara and makeup obviously not waterproof, "you shoulda seen their faces when I came yelling down the aisle, in the middle of 'Oh Happy Day,' screaming that I had a demon, people scattering and praying in the Spirit and pleading the name of Jesus, and then my damn shoe, pardon my French, broke and I almost killed Brother Clarence." She sat down and began to cry, while Molly stood with her mouth open.

"What have I done?" she moaned. "I scared the living crap outta Clarence...cute, Jesus-lovin' Clarence. I am now declaring that I have agoraphobia. I can't leave my own home. That'll be me from now on. I am from now on a shut-in. Just tell people I have a social disease so nobody can come visit."

"Maggs," Molly said as she hugged her tight and handed her a paper towel to wipe some of the mess from her face, "why don't you go and clean up, maybe put your pajamas on, and I'll make you a lemon-drop. It sounds like a lemon-drop kind of night. And then you can tell me all about it."

"That sounds good." She sighed, slowly getting up. "I've had to pee for over an hour anyway, another reason I'm glad to be home. Believe me, there is nothin' like peeing in your own pot."

Here we go again, thought Tony.

Maggie hugged her friend one more time. "Molly, my dear, I don't know what I'd do without you, and Cabby and Lindsay. Bet you didn't know you were going to be living with Hurricane Katrina and now I've made a mell-of-a-hess. You think the folk over at your white church will mind if a slightly large but very sedate, genteel, and quiet black woman sneaks in to sing a few songs? I promise to even clap on the on-beat."

"Anytime, Maggs," Molly said, laughing. "We could use a little life in that place."

Maggie headed for her bedroom and separate bathroom, but was met in the hallway by Cabby, already dressed as Spider-Man. He stood with both hands raised. "Stop!" he commanded.

She did, especially because this was uncharacteristic of Cabby. "What is it, Cabby? Everything okay?" she asked.

He patted her chest and looked at her intensely. "Tah-Ny!" He patted her again. "Tah-Ny."

"I'm sorry, little man, it takes me a while to get things sometimes. I'm a little slow that way. Can you sign?"

Cabby thought for a second, grinned, and reached down and took off one of his socks. He wiggled his foot in the air.

"Your foot? Something's wrong with your foot?"

He shook his head, sat down, and covered all his toes with his hand until only his big toe was showing, and then raised it up toward her. "Tah!" he declared.

"Toe?" she asked.

He nodded his one sharp nod for yes, grinned, and stood up pointing to his leg. He raised his leg and toe in the air, dancing in a circle like a dog that couldn't find a wall fast enough.

She wasn't getting it. He stopped, pursed his lips together as he thought, and then reached out, took her hand, and placed it on his knee. "Knee?" she responded correctly, and he wriggled his big toe. "Knee-toe, neet-o?" And then she got it. "Tony! Tony?" she slowly repeated.

Cabby was elated. "Tah-Ny!" he exclaimed and nodded repeatedly. He then reached up and tapped her chest. "Frund."

"Tony is your friend?" she said slowly, astounded.

Cabby did his once nod and then tapped his own chest. "Frund." With that he hugged her and, mission accomplished, skipped toward the kitchen, leaving Maggie leaning against the wall.

She would unravel the mystery while she peed.

Tony, who witnessed the entire interchange with Cabby, was even more astounded than Maggie. Who was this boy, and how could he possibly know the things he did? But now he was faced with the original dilemma that had generated the disturbance in the first place. Who would have thought a simple pee would have such unexpected consequences?

It was then Tony remembered Grandmother had said that in a difficult situation he should "turn." Mentally he tried to do it, but nothing happened. *The little dance*, he thought. He had to recall the line-dance hop thingy. And he did. Tony discovered he could "turn," spinning so that he was looking into the darkness and away from the window of the person's eyes.

It took a few moments to adjust to the dimness, but once it happened he was surprised to realize he was standing in what appeared to be a large room, almost as if his back were to a window looking out onto constantly changing scenes. Someone had once told him that the eyes were the windows of the soul, and maybe it was true; perhaps they actually were. Now he was looking from those eyes into Maggie's soul. The light of the bathroom behind him cast vague shadows on a far wall, filled with what appeared to be photographs and pictures but distant enough not to be distinctive.

Later he might take a closer look, but for now he could sense she had finished and he hop-turned back.

Maggie decided to first take off what was left of her

makeup, and she went on autopilot to accomplish the woman's routine of examinations and wipes and more inspections and finally the relief that comes from removal of oils and colors.

Next, she took off her necklace and teardrop pendant, and her rings, all five of them, which she placed in the drawer of the dressing table at which she sat. Each in its place. She noticed an earring missing, one of a matched set of inexpensive diamonds her mother had given her, a personal treasure from a woman who lived a life without means. It was probably lost in the carpet at the church. She would call first thing in the morning and ask them to keep an eye out for it. She might have to offer to check the vacuum cleaners. Well, there was nothing she could do about it at the moment; the church was closed and locked. She stood, exited the bathroom, and headed toward the kitchen, anticipating her lemon-drop.

Molly had it ready, topped by the thin coating of sugar on the rim that took some of the bite out of the first sip. It went down slow and smooth. Maggie snuggled into the big easy chair that faced the kitchen while Molly slid another next to hers, sitting down with her cup of nightly tea, the tea bag still steeping. Cabby was already falling asleep, snug in his own bed.

"So," Molly said, grinning mischievously, "tell me all about it, all the gory details." And Maggie did, until the two of them were whooping and hollering like a couple of schoolgirls and their sides ached from laughter's exertions. Molly was on her third tea while Maggie nursed her original lemon-drop. She liked the taste of alcohol, but her family had been damaged severely by this beast, and she had no intentions of ever giving it anything but a passing nod.

"Maggs, what I don't understand...," admitted Molly, "is the Tony part. Any idea who this Tony is?"

Maggie shook her head. "You mean the demon? I was hoping you might be able to help me with that piece. Cabby says that Tony is his friend?"

"His friend?" Molly thought for a minute. "I can't think of any Tonys who are friends with Cabby." She glanced back at her companion, who had frozen midsip with a wide-eyed look of surprise and fear.

"Maggie, you okay?" she asked, reaching over and taking the glass from her hand. "You look like you just saw a ghost!"

"Molly," she whispered. "He just said something to me!"

"Who?" Molly whispered back. "And why are we whispering?"

"The guy I thought was a demon, that's who," came the response through gritted teeth and lips that were barely moving. "He just told me his name is…it's…Tony!"

"Tony? Oh, you mean, 'the' Tony?" She leaned back, starting to laugh. "Maggs, you had me going for a second…" But Maggie wasn't moving, and when Molly looked back she could tell this was no joke.

"Sorry, Maggie, I didn't hear anything, and I thought you were just pulling my leg." Maggie sat transfixed, staring into the distance as if preoccupied. "So what did he say, your Tony?" Molly inquired, leaning a little closer.

Maggie snapped back to attention. "First, he is 'not' *my* Tony, and second"—she paused—"he hasn't stopped talking, and I can't get in a word edgew—Tony?" She put her hand up to her ear as if she were talking through a loudspeaker. "Tony? Tony, can you hear me?…You can, good, then shut up for a minute. Thank you! That's better…Yes, I'll explain it to Molly. Uh-huh. Tony? Okay, then, thank you. Yes, I'll talk to you in a second.

"Molly!" Her eyes widened even more. "You are not going

to believe this. Actually, I don't believe this. Maybe I am losing my mind…No, Tony, I am calm…just let me work this out for myself. Yes, uh-huh. Tony? Shut up! Yes, I know you got lots to say, but how long have you been doing this? Give me a break. I just now found out about it, so please, how about giving me at least a minute or two. It would be nice to figure out what the crap is going on! Do you know what a mess you got me into?…No, please, don't start apologizing. I don't even want to go there. Just shush your blabbering for just a minute and let me talk to Molly, okay? Okay then, thank you!"

She turned back to Molly. "I'm talking to an idiot," she whispered. "Oh, you heard that? Can I say anything without you hearing, snoop?

"I can't? My worst nightmare—no privacy."

She turned her attention back to Molly, who was staring at her wide-eyed, one hand to her mouth. Maggie leaned forward and spewed her irritation. "I know I told God I wanted a man in my life, but this isn't what I meant. I was thinkin'"—she looked upward as if offering a prayer—"more along the lines of Elder Clarence, thank you, Jesus."

She paused for only a second, cocked her head to one side, and demanded, "So, tell me this, are you black or white? Whaddya mean, black or white? You know…skin color, are you a black man or a white man?"

"Oh my God!" She turned back to Molly. "Molly, I got a white man living inside my head. Tony, you just hang on there…What do you mean you think you might have a little black in you? Everybody's got a little black in them, what with the whole Africa thing an' all…or some Indian? Are we talking like Tonto Indian or the faraway Indian, like the telemarketer Indian? *You* think *you're* confused? What? You have a grandmother who's an Indian? Well, then, yes, I would say that you have Indian in you, but…what? She's not your biological grandmother? This is not helpful information, Tony. Let's go back to you shutting up and me talking to Molly, okay? Shush! Shhhhhhhh! Thank you."

She slumped back into her chair, blowing away a strand of hair that had fallen down, looked at Molly, and asked, "So, how was your day?"

Molly played along, still unsure about what was going on. "Oh, the usual; nothing much out of the ordinary. Went up to the hospital to be with Lindsay during her tests. Nance and Sarah are up with Lindsay this evening. I forgot to tell you, when I was up there yesterday Cabby decided to play hide 'n' seek, and I found him over at OHSU in Neuro ICU, about to unplug an almost dead guy...no big deal. You?" She took a sip of her tea.

"Oh, like you, nothing much; just made a freak-out fool of myself in front of the whole universe because I thought I was demon possessed, but it was nothing to worry about, just a white guy who decided to crawl inside my head, you know, same ol', same ol'."

They sat quiet for a moment and then it registered what Molly had been saying. "Molly, I am so sorry! With all this Tony stuff, I didn't even ask how Lindsay is doing. I've been making everything about me."

Before Molly could answer, Maggie continued, "Tony, you still there? Uh-huh, I was afraid of that. Anyway, Tony, Molly has a darling little girl. Her name is Lindsay and she is the sweetest baby in the whole world, even if she is fourteen. About a year ago"—she paused, looking at Molly, who nodded—"she started getting sick, and then about six months ago Lindsay was diagnosed with AML, acute myelogenous leukemia, and she's been having a real tough go of it lately. So while you and I were at church playing Kill the Romance, Molly was up at Doernbecher with Lindsay.

You got all that? Good . . . yeah, we are all sorry, but it is what it is. If you know how to pray, you might start."

She turned back to Molly. "You were saying, before I so rudely interrupted? This feels like I'm having a conversation and on the phone with another party at the same time, and I can't conference you in, sorry!"

Molly waved it off. "Not a problem, not that I understand any of it." She paused to change her focus. "Lindsay is doing the best she knows how. They expect that all the counts will be zero in the next day or two, then we'll ramp up for the next round of chemo. I keep asking for a prognosis, but you're a nurse, you understand; no one wants to offer too much, false hope and all. I wish I could just talk to the Wizard behind the curtain of all the deferring."

"I do understand, honey, and I know it's not much of a comfort, but she is in the best place with some of the most brilliant and kind people in the world. They'll figure it out. I wish I could be involved directly, but you know I can't. Us living together is a bit of a touchy issue up there as it is, HIPAA and all. We just need to keep trustin' that God is right here, in the middle of the mess."

"I'm trying, Maggie, but some days just seem so much harder than other days, and some days I start to think that God is off doing more important things for more important people, or that I've done something wrong and he's punishing me, or . . ."

The ever-near tears began to fall as Molly dropped her head. Maggie gently took her cup and set it on the nearby table, enfolding her friend into an embrace that held her pieces together, letting her voice her sadness.

"I don't even know what to pray anymore," Molly stammered between her sobs. "I go up there, and in room after room, there are fathers and mothers who are just waiting,

waiting to smile again, waiting to laugh, waiting to live. We are all just holding our breaths, waiting for a miracle. And I feel so selfish, praying that God would heal my baby, that somehow I could get his attention or if he would just tell me what I needed to do, and everyone else is praying, too, for their babies, and I don't get it and it's too hard. Why does it have to be Lindsay? She's never hurt a ladybug. She's good and beautiful and fragile, and there are people out there who hurt other people and they're healthy while my Lindsay…" A torrent of anger and despair that she had been holding back became a river of tears.

Maggie said nothing. She just held her friend, stroking her hair and handing her tissues. Sometimes silence speaks loudest and presence brings the most comfort.

Tony, witness to the entire conversation and meltdown and emotionally captive to Maggie's compassion for her friend, still found a way to withdraw, as if turning and walking to the back of the room. Sure, he felt for the woman. If anyone knew what she was going through, he did. But he didn't know her or her daughter, and like she said, there were lots of other families in the same situation, dealing with the same or even worse tragedies. It was of no real concern to him. He had a bigger and more important plan for his one opportunity to heal, and it didn't include Lindsay. It even made him a little angry that God would manipulate him like this, putting him in the middle of a situation that might tempt him to deviate from that purpose.

"Thank you, Maggs," Molly said, the pressure she had felt released for the moment. It would return, she knew, but that would wait for another day. She blew her nose one more time and changed the subject.

"So tell me more about your new friend." She smiled through swollen and red eyes.

"My new friend, huh!" muttered Maggie as she sat back in her chair. "I suppose you mean Tony? He's no friend of mine." Then she laughed, a deep and rich laugh and slapped her knee. "But I gotta admit, it's going to make a fine story." Maggie continued as if talking to herself, "So, Tony, who are you and why are you here and how does Cabby know you and how did he know you were inside of me?"

Tony would explain and Maggie would relay back to Molly the answers, and in this disjointed conversation the stories slowly merged. There were more than a few surprises. Tony told them about his collapse and coma and briefly how he had found himself in conversations with Jesus and the Holy Spirit and how they had asked him to be part of a journey that landed him inside the middle of Maggie's and Molly's worlds.

"So you were inside Cabby's head before you were inside mine and that is how Cabby knew?" asked Maggie.

"That's the only thing that makes sense to me," answered Tony. He explained how Cabby had played hide-and-seek and ended up in his room, that he was the "almost dead guy" in the coma in Neuro ICU, and that was when he had slid into Molly's son. He went on to describe the day he had spent with, or in, Cabby at school.

"Cabby's a remarkable young man. Do you know he has someone's camera in a toy guitar case under his bed?"

Molly laughed when Maggie reported to her what Tony had said, but she was on another track.

"But how did you get into him and from him to Maggie?" she pressed.

"I really don't know," he responded. "There is a lot about this that is a mystery to me." Tony wasn't sure why he lied about the kiss. Perhaps information was advantage and he was not ready to trust even these two. Maybe it was something deeper. Whatever, he shrugged it off as he had many times before.

"Hmmm," mumbled Maggie, not convinced. "So why are you here, in our worlds?"

"I really don't know," he answered, which was mostly true. "I suppose we will have to trust God with that." In his mouth his words sounded plastic and fake, and he winced, but it was an easy way to avoid the question. "So, Maggie, how did you two meet?" he asked, changing the subject.

Maggie explained that she was employed as an on-call practicing registered nurse, referred to as a resource RN, at OHSU and Doernbecher. She had to work a set number of minimum hours per month to maintain her contract, but she usually worked substantially more. Portland had been the end of a long migration west after the hurricane had decimated her family in New Orleans. The few distant relatives who were left planted new roots in Texas, but she wanted something different and greener and took jobs along the Pacific until she landed in the big hospital on the hill.

"Is that where you got your accent?" asked Tony.

"I don't have an accent," retorted Maggie. "I have a history."

"We all have histories," added Molly. "Everyone is a story. It was Cabby that brought the two of us together; this was a while back, before Lindsay got sick. I found this house but couldn't swing the expenses on my own..."

"And I had been in town for a while and was looking for a place to settle," interjected Maggie.

"So one day," continued Molly, "Cabby and I are at Trader Joe's not far from my apartment, and he runs a shopping cart into this pyramid of cantaloupe. Maggie 'happened' to be there and helped me clean up. She couldn't stop laughing and turned a mess into a new possibility. She was an answer to prayer, and that's what Maggie is. God's kiss of grace."

Maggie smiled. "I would say the same thing about Molly and the kids. After my 'history,' home is not as much about a place you belong as people you belong to. I belong here." Tony knew it was true. He could feel it as she spoke, and he suddenly felt lonely. He quickly changed the subject again.

In the course of the next hour Tony tried to explain what it was like to be inside someone's head, to see with their eyes, how he could look at something other than what they were looking at as long as it was in their field of vision. Maggie made him demonstrate until she was convinced. To answer her concerns about propriety, he explained how he could hop-turn until he was looking away, allowing privacy, but he neglected to mention what he could see when he did. He avoided any mention of the gift to heal and nothing about the barren wasteland of his own heart and soul. Jack, who was still a mystery to him, also did not make it into the exchange.

They had question after question about Jesus, and couldn't believe he was serious when he told them Grandmother, the Holy Spirit, was an old Native American woman.

"I don't believe this is happening!" said Molly at one point. "Maggie, I'm talking to a man who's living inside your mind. It is a great story, but we can't tell anyone. They'd think we're nuts! I'm thinking we're nuts!"

It was well past midnight when Maggie and Molly discussed the schedule for the coming couple of days to make sure all bases were covered.

"Now don't stay up all night visiting, you two," Molly said and snickered, dismissing herself and heading for her room, stopping as she always did to check on Cabby.

Maggie sat thinking in silence for a few moments. "Well," she finally stated, "this is awkward!"

"You think?" Tony responded.

"Can you read my mind? I mean, do you know what I'm thinking?"

"Nope! I have no clue what you're thinking."

"Whew!" She breathed a deep sigh of relief. "Thank God for small favors. If you knew what I was thinkin', we'd a got a divorce already."

"Been there, done that," he revealed.

"Well, you can tell me about all that another time. I'm tired and I want to go to bed, just not sure how to do that with you, you know, roaming around."

"If it helps, I don't think I'll be in your head all the time," he explained. "I wasn't in Cabby's every minute. Somehow he told God that he didn't want me in his dreams and so I wasn't. I was back with Jesus and Grandmother."

"Dear God, I do not want this man in my dreams. Amen!... You still here?"

"Yeah, sorry! I don't know what to tell you."

"Well, you figure it out and let me know. I will be right here sitting in this chair waiting." With that Maggie reached over and pulled a fleece blanket from the couch and draped it over her legs, settling in for what could be the night.

"Maggie?" Tony hesitated.

"Tony?" she responded.

"May I ask you a favor?"

"Maybe. Depends."

"I would like to go up to OHSU tomorrow and, you know, visit myself."

"That's your favor? You want me to take you up to the hospital so you can see yourself in a coma?"

"Yeah, it probably sounds silly, but it's just something I need to do."

Maggie thought for a couple of moments. "Actually, I'm

not sure that I can do that, even if you are still here tomorrow. Neuro ICU is not where I work, and they have a closed area, you know; only relatives and people on a short list can visit, and even then only two at a time, which in your case is not the problem. Cabby gettin' in there was nothing short of a miracle, and I'm sure they are not too happy about it. You got any next of kin that I can contact and go in on their coattails?"

"No, I don't, wel—no, not really." He hesitated and Maggie waited, her eyebrows raised in question.

"Well, I have a brother, Jacob, but I don't know where he is. We haven't talked in a few years. He's really all I have and I don't really have him."

"No other family?"

"Ex-wife on the East Coast and a daughter that lives close to her who hates her father."

"Hmmm, you always had such a positive effect on people?"

"Yeah, pretty much," Tony admitted. "I've tended to be the cross other people have had to bear."

"Well," Maggie noted, "I am prayin' right now that God would remove one particular cross from me. That's what I'm prayin', just so you know, but if you are still here tomorrow, I'll try and figure out a way so you can go and visit yourself." She shook her head, incredulous at her situation.

"Thanks, Maggie. By the way, I think you can go to bed, because I think I am leaving..."

He didn't know how, but he sensed it coming this time, and as quickly as he wondered about it, he was gone, again asleep, in between.

11

BETWIXT AND BETWEEN

*What one regards as interruptions are
precisely one's life.*
—C. S. Lewis

Tony woke with a start, a little groggy and uncertain of his whereabouts. Stumbling out of bed, he drew back the curtain and to his surprise realized he was back in the bedroom of the ramshackle ranch where Jesus supposedly lived. But it was larger and better appointed. His bed was solid and crafted, a significant improvement over the springs and old mattress he had first experienced. Hardwood had replaced part of the plywood floors, and at least one of the windows was now airtight and double-paned.

He heard a knock at the door, like before, three taps, but when he opened it expecting to find Jesus, it was Jack holding a tray of breakfast and coffee and sporting a big grin.

"Oh, hi, Jack-from-Ireland!" exclaimed Tony. "I wondered if I would ever see you again after our first little encounter."

"It is a delight and gift to see you again, Anthony." Jack

smiled and Tony stood aside, letting the man and his bur-
dens into the room where he set them down carefully on
an end table and proceeded to pour a black, aromatic liquid into a larger than normal mug. He turned, handing the
drink to Tony.

"Black coffee, if I remember. As far as I am concerned,
you can never get a cup of tea big enough."

Tony nodded his thanks and took the first sip, smooth
and sliding like silk.

"And I am pleased to let you know," added Jack as he
took the cover off a plate of eggs over easy, some steamed
vegetables, and a buttered scone, "that you and I are des-
tined to see a great deal of each other, in time as it were."

"I'm not sure if I should even ask what that might look
like," muttered Tony, enjoying his first bite of food.

"No matter," sighed Jack, pulling up a cushioned chair
and plopping himself down. "This moment contains all
moments anyway, no need to be anywhere other than now."

"Whatever," Tony acquiesced. He had become more at
ease with his own lack of comprehension, even for words
spoken in his own language. "Let me ask you this, Jack, if I
may…" He waved his fork in a spiral motion in the man's
direction, as if to make his question more pertinent. "This
place, this in-between-time place where you and I are right
now, is this the afterlife?"

"Oh, heaven's no!" asserted Jack, shaking his head. "This
is more the inner-life, not that it is independent of what you
consider the afterlife, which you should know is more accu-
rately the life-after."

Tony still held his fork in midair, frozen as he tried to
follow.

"You are caught, as it were, in between life-before and

life-after, and the bridge that is connecting the two is inner-life, the life of your own soul."

"So where do *you* live?"

"Well, I live wherever I am, but my dwelling is in life-after. Dear boy, I am only visiting you here, in between."

Tony chewed his food but hardly tasted it, his mind awhirl. "So this afterlife, I mean, this life-after, what is it like?"

"Ah, now there is a question." Jack sat back into the chair pondering, absentmindedly pulled out his pipe, still lit, from his jacket pocket, slowly inhaled, and returned it to its nest before returning his gaze to the man across from him. He let the smoke emerge from between his lips as he spoke.

"You are asking me something where the knowing is in the experiencing. What words exist that truly communicate the sensations of a first love, or an unexpected sunset; the smell of jasmine, gardenia, or oriental lilac; or the first time a mother holds her baby; or the moments you are surprised by joy; or a piece of music that is transcendent; or standing for the first time on a mountain you have conquered; or a first taste of honey from the comb...Throughout history we have been searching for words that link what we know to what we long for, and all we get are glimpses through a glass darkly."

He scanned the room. "Here, let me give you an example." Jack walked to the dresser by the window, on which, among other items, rested a garden pot. In it bloomed a stunning multicolored tulip. He brought it back and sat down. Carefully he began to break away the dirt, gently so as not to injure the plant, until he revealed the bulb, the stem, and flower above.

"This is a classical parrot tulip," he explained, "grown

right in your own backyard. Notice"—he leaned in so Tony could look closely—"these extraordinary petals. They are feathery and twisted, fringes of scalloped edges that curl around a variety of colors, gold and apricot and bluish-purple. Look, there are even ravines of green that run through the yellows. Magnificent!

"Now look here, Tony, at the bulb that produced this wondrous flower. It looks like an old piece of wood or clod of dirt, something that one would discard if one didn't know better. It really is nothing to look at, nothing that would draw your attention, utterly common. This root, Tony..." Jack was animated, now carefully replanting it in the pot, moving and packing the soil with tender care. "This root is the life-before, everything you know and experience rippled as it is with foretastes of something else, something more. And within what you know and experience, all part of the root, you find hints of the flower—in music and art and story and family and laughter and discovery and innovation and work and presence. But having seen the root only, could you begin to imagine such a wonder as the flower? There will be a moment, Tony, when you finally see the flower, and in that moment everything about the root will make utter and complete sense. That moment is the life-after."

Tony sat and stared at this beautifully simple but complex flower, stunned as if he were in the presence of something painfully holy. Again he wondered, *Where have I been all these years?* He had never really lived, as far as he could remember. But along with that thought came others, small remembrances of mystery that had penetrated his rush and agenda, bits of light and love and wonder and moments of joy that had whispered to him in his pleasures but screamed for attention in his pain. He had never been one to sit, to listen, to look, to see, to breathe, to wonder...and it had cost him, of that he was now certain. He felt, in this moment, like a waste, expressed in the damage of the land outside this window.

"Tony, you are a root," Jack said, interrupting his spiral, "and only God knows what the flower will be. Don't get lost castigating yourself for being a root. Without the root, the flower can never be. The flower is an expression of what now appears so lowly and unimportant, a waste."

"It's the melody," exclaimed Tony, finally understanding, even if only a little.

Jack smiled and nodded. "That is exactly right. It is the melody."

"Will I know you, Jack? In the life-after, will I know you?" Tony hoped he would and needed to ask.

"Completely! In flower-ways that you cannot begin to comprehend looking as a root at a root."

Tony thought he understood but waited for more, which Jack was kind enough to give.

"The way you see me right now, Anthony, is the best that your recollections can conjure up, a composite of memory and imagination of how your mind thinks I should look to you. You are a root looking at a root."

"And if I saw you in the life-after?"

"Well, this might sound like sheer self-aggrandizement to you, but it would be true for anyone you encountered in the life-after. If from where you sit now you saw me as I truly am, you would probably fall on your face in reverence and worship. The root would see the flower and it would undo you."

"Wow!" exclaimed Tony, surprised at the answer. "You're right, that does sound like you are full of yourself."

"In life-after, I am everything that I was intended to be, more human than I ever succeeded in being on earth, and fully dwelt within by everything God is. You have barely heard one note of a symphony, seen one color of a sunset, heard one drop of a waterfall. You are rooted in your life and grasping after anything that will bring you a sense of transcendence, even turning other roots into the imagination of flowers."

Tony stood up and began pacing the room. "Jack," he confessed, "my life that I defined as a success is actually a total shambles, and yet you're suggesting that underneath it all, there is an unimaginable beauty? Are you telling me that I matter? That even though I am this ugly, ordinary-looking root, that I was designed and intended to express a unique and extraordinary flower? That's what you are telling me...right?"

Jack nodded, again removing his pipe for a puff.

"And I assume," Tony continued, "this is true about every human being, each person born—"

"Conceived!" interrupted Jack.

"Each person 'conceived' on the planet, each one living in life-before, each one is a root in which a flower is waiting? Right?"

Again Jack nodded, and now Tony walked over and positioned himself directly in front of this man, leaned forward and put a hand on each shoulder until their faces were inches apart. Through gritted teeth came the next words, biting and desperate: "So why all the crap, Jack? Why all the pain and disease and war and loss and hate and unforgiveness and cruelty and brutality and ignorance and stupidity and..." The litany of evils came spewing out, a list terrible in their speaking. "You know what we do with roots, Jack. We burn them, we use and abuse them, we destroy them, we sell them, we treat them like the disgusting pieces of detritus we think we are ourselves!" With that pronouncement he pushed himself back and away from Jack, who had listened kindly to the tirade, never changing his expression.

Tony walked over to the window and looked out, seeing nothing in particular, and combed his hand through his hair. The silence, hanging thick and almost separating like a curtain, was brushed aside by Jack.

"The problem of pain," he said softly, "is a root issue."

Tony heard the answer behind him and dropped his head, looking at the floor.

"I don't know, Jack," he revealed. "I don't know if I can face all my stuff. The pile is awful and high."

"No worries, dear boy," responded Jack kindly. "You will cross that road when you come to it. You must remember, Tony, that there is not one good thing, or memory, or act of kindness, not one thing that is true and noble and right and just, that will be lost."

"And what about all the bad, the cruel, the wrong?"

"Ah, there's the real miracle." Jack must have gotten up from his chair because Tony now felt a firm, meaty grip on his shoulder. "Somehow the pain, the losses, the hurt, the bad, God is able to transform these into something they could have never been, icons and monuments of grace and love. It is the deep mystery how wounds and scars can become precious, or a ravaging and terrifying cross the essential symbol of relentless affection."

"Is it worth it?" whispered Tony.

"Wrong question, son. There is no 'it.' The question is and has always been, 'Are *you* worth it?' and the answer is and always, 'Yes!'"

The statement hung in the air like the last note of a cello, lingering while fading. Tony felt a tightening of the grip, friendly and encouraging, loving even, and Jack offered, "Would you like to go for a hike? See the property?

Meet some of your neighbors? You should probably put some clothes on."

"I have neighbors?" inquired Tony.

"Well, not neighbors exactly. More like squatters. But I'm here to take you to meet them, if you would like. Up to you. I am going to be right outside while you decide."

With that he exited, leaving Tony to a fluster of thoughts and emotions and even more questions, but the curiosity of meeting someone else in this place was intriguing so he quickly dressed, splashed some water on his face, smiled and shook his head at his image in the mirror, and headed for the door.

ξ ∽ ⬥ ⚡ ∽ ❋ ⑤ ⬥

The morning was crisp, with that bite and shiver reflective of a change in weather. A few clouds had begun to form a colloquy on the horizon, not yet ominous but portentous.

"Here, take this." Jack handed Tony a jacket as he stepped from his room. It was a familiar Columbia soft-shell windbreaker and Tony put it on, grateful that it wasn't tweed. Jack was dressed as always, but carried a knobbed walking stick and wore an old tweed fisherman's hat that begged a remark.

"Nice hat!" acknowledged Tony.

"Oh, this old thing? Well, thank you. I keep losing it and it keeps turning up. Not sure what else to do when it does but put it back on till it disappears again."

As he stood and scanned the property, Tony was surprised that it seemed somewhat improved, as though a breath of order might have been blown into its former chaos but not much more than an innuendo. On a darker note, breaches in some of the distant walls were clearly visible that he had not remembered being there earlier. *Probably just not paying attention*, he thought as Jack pointed down a path and toward a clump of trees, beyond which were barely visible smoke curls rising in a cluster.

"Neighbors?" he asked.

Jack smiled and shrugged, as if he were reluctant to say more.

As they walked Tony asked, "Jack, is this place, this in-between place that I know somehow is me...Was I brought here to be confronted with what I have done wrong?"

"No, my dear boy, quite the reverse," Jack assured. "The in-between and the life-after is centered and built upon everything you got right, not what you got wrong. And it's not that what you got wrong is inconsequential or just disappears; much of it is all around you as you can see, but the focus is on the rebuilding, not on the tearing down."

"Yes, but—" Tony began, only to have Jack raise a hand to stop him.

"Yes, the old must be torn down for the new to be raised; to have a resurrection you must have a crucifixion, but God wastes nothing, not even the wrong we have imagined into existence. In every building torn down there is much that remains that was once true and right and good, and that gets woven into the new; in fact, the new could not be what it is without the old. It is the refurbishing of the soul. You are from Oregon so you should understand recycling, aye?"

Jack chuckled, and it made Tony smile.

"Well," responded Tony, "I like the building part. It's the tearing-down part that I'm not a big fan of."

"Ah...," sighed Jack. "And there's the rub, isn't it. There has to be a tearing down for the real and right and good and true to be built. There has to be a judgment and a dismantling. It is not only important, it is essential. However, the kindness of God will not do the tearing down without your participation. Much of the time, God has to do very little. We are masters at building up facades, only to tear them down ourselves. In our independence we are very destructive creatures, first creating houses of cards and then knocking them down with our own hands. Addiction of every imagined sort, the will to power, the security of lies, the need for notoriety, the grasping of reputation, the trading in human souls...all houses of cards that we try and keep together by holding our breath. But, thanks to the grace of God, we must someday breathe, and when we do, the breath of God joins ours and everything collapses."

Their pace had slowed as the path narrowed and became more erratic, small boulders and tree roots haphazardly strewn over what once was probably a smooth and easy trail. A noxious odor, subtle at first but growing as they proceeded, finally became a stench and Tony wrinkled up his nose.

"Whew, what is that smell? It smells like..."

"Garbage? Yes, that is what it is," returned Jack. "Your neighbors are not the tidiest, and they waste no time cleaning up after themselves. They refuse to burn their own refuse." He winked at Tony, pleased with both puns. "Look!"

About a hundred yards down the path, two large figures were slowly approaching. Jack held his hand up and Tony stopped.

"It's time for you and me to part company, Anthony. I am not sure that I will again see you in the in-between, but assuredly, we will have many occasions in the life-after."

"You're leaving? But what about the neighbors? I thought you were going to introduce them to me."

"I told you that I was going to take you to meet them.

Introductions are not necessary." His words were kind and gentle, and with a bit of a sly grin he added, "I am not one of their favorite people, and our presence together would cause more confusion than yours alone."

"It's me that's confused, as usual," confessed Tony. "I don't understand."

"You don't need to, dear boy. Just remember, you are never alone. You have everything that you need for the moment."

Turning, Jack gave Tony a huge hug and then tenderly, with barely a brush, kissed him on the cheek, as a father would his precious son.

Tony slid.

12

A Thickening of Plots

True friends stab you in the front.
—Oscar Wilde

"Oh, my gawd!" Tony was looking through Maggie's eyes, looking through the kitchen window at two men getting out of a Lincoln town car in front of the house.

"Maggie?" Tony interjected. "What's the matter?"

"Tony?" squealed Maggie. "Thank the Lord Almighty you're here. Where have you been? Never mind that now; we have a crisis of magnanimous proportions. Do you see who is getting out of that car out there; do you see?"

Tony could feel her agitation flooding him like a sneaker wave, but he focused on the two outside who were in a conversation, glancing in the direction of her house. Suddenly, Tony recognized one of them. "Elder Clarence is a cop? You didn't tell me he was a cop."

"Clarence is a police officer. Why would I think to tell you? Why are your tights all twisty—have you done something illegal?"

"No!" asserted Tony. "It's just unexpected."

"Please," exclaimed Maggie, "you—talking to me about unexpected? Oh, my gawd, they're coming here! Quick, do something!"

Tony had no idea what that meant. In a normal situation and by her tone he would have looked for somewhere to hide, which in light of the current circumstances was absurd and laughable, and he started giggling. Maggie tore down the hallway and in a panic began applying lipstick and makeup. Tony, not able to keep from howling in glee, advised her where to apply it. Finally he calmed down, trying his best not to grunt or snort as another wave of snickering would start. Maggie glared at the mirror. If looks could kill, there would be a dead white guy in her head.

The doorbell rang. "What are you so freaked out about?" asked Tony.

Maggie whispered into the mirror, tidying one last bit of hair. "That's Clarence out there, about the last person I ever wanted to see today, excepting for that other guy that's with him."

"The older white guy? Who is he?"

"The guy with the big Bible, that's Associate Pastor Horace Skor, that's who. If I remember, I'll tell you about him later," she added with a slight grin, which Tony was relieved to see.

The doorbell chimed a second time. "You better get that. They probably saw you at the window and your car is parked right outside. By the way, how'd you get that dent..."

"Not the time, Tony," she snapped. "Grrrrr, you can be so irritating."

She got up, smoothed her dress one more time, and headed for the door.

"Well, if it isn't Pastor Skor. What a wonderful surprise.

And Elder Walker, so good to see you so soon...after...um, I was just getting ready to leave."

"Well," began the elderly man, "we need to talk to you."

"...But if you would like a cup of coffee or tea, I have a few minutes. Come right on in."

She stood aside as the man entered, followed by Clarence, his eyes an apology even though a barely visible grin played at the corners of his mouth. Maggie was flustered but smiled her best and directed them to the living room, where elder and associate pastor situated themselves, the former rigid and erect, the officer at ease and comfortable.

"Well, old Harry's a bit pompous!" observed Tony. Maggie cleared her throat, more a warning to Tony than anything.

"I am so sorry, where are my manners? Can I serve either of you two gentlemen a cup of coffee or tea?"

"Nothing for me," answered the pastor stiffly.

"I would love a glass of water, Maggie, if that wouldn't be too much trouble?" The pastor glanced sideways at the elder as if communicating this was a formal time, not one where personal address was appropriate.

"No trouble at all. Just give me a second." Maggie turned and entered the kitchen. She whispered, "Tony, you are going to have to shut up...way too distracting. And the man's name is Horace. Pastor Skor to you!"

"But he's an..."

"Shhhhhh! Not a word out of you, got that?"

"Yes, ma'am! Got it, loud and clear. Tony signing off, over and out."

"Thank you!"

She returned to the living room, interrupting a whispered conversation, and handed the glass to the elder, who nodded his thanks. She seated herself facing what felt like inquisitors.

"Mrs. Saunders," began the pastor.

"Ms. Saunders, actually," corrected Maggie. "I'm not married." She couldn't help but smile at Clarence and then wanted to kick herself for doing so.

"Of course. Ms. Saunders, as you know I am Pastor Skor, one of the lead pastors of the church that you have been attending for, how long now? Six, seven months?"

"Two and a half years," answered Maggie.

"My, really? How time flies," recovered the pastor. "Well, I am sorry that we haven't met before, or under better circumstances, but after last night's...uh, events, well..."

"Oh, about that..." Maggie reached over and started to pat the pastor on the knee. He immediately shifted himself in the chair out of her reach, as if she was contagious. "That was a huge misunderstanding. You see, I have been under a lot of stress, you know, with what is going on with Lindsay, and last night it sort of all came out and I am so sorry..." She knew she was stumbling through her apology but couldn't stop herself until Pastor Skor raised a hand. She halted midsentence.

"Lindsay is your daughter?" he asked, almost with an air of concern.

"My daughter? No!" Maggie was a little shocked and glancing at Clarence saw him shake his head slightly, almost as if warning her not to go there. She turned back to the pastor. "You don't know who Lindsay is, do you?"

"No, I am sorry I do not, but be that as it may, what is important is that you understand I have certain responsibilities at the church and among them I oversee spiritual life, the spiritual life of the members of the church."

"Hee-haw!" brayed Tony.

Maggie slapped her leg and then rubbed it as if bitten by a mosquito, trying to warn Tony to keep quiet and not attract question. She smiled, which the pastor took as encouragement to continue.

"In light of last night's...uh...events, I find it incumbent upon me to help shepherd and educate our people in areas where we have become entirely lax, and I take full blame and responsibility for that. God knows he has convicted my heart deeply, and I did not hardly sleep a wink last night confessing and repenting of the sinful and lazy attitudes I have had toward the Word, toward essential doctrines and the order of church polity and member behavior. Ms. Saunders, I am truly in your debt. You have done our congregation and I a huge service by bringing to light our backslidden condition. So I am really here this morning to thank you!"

With that he sat back, as did Maggie and Clarence, the latter two stunned and the pastor satisfied.

"Uh, you're welcome, I guess?" was all Maggie could think to respond.

"It's a trick!" Tony couldn't help himself. "I smell a rat in the manger. I'm thinking one of the wise men is on the take!"

Maggie slapped her leg again and was about to stand when the pastor leaned forward.

"Ms. Saunders, we have a healthy and vibrant religious community. We are open to the move and work of the Holy Ghost. We allow women to fully participate in the worship and even to occasionally bring a word of prophecy to the congregation, as long as the leadership first hears and then allows it, of course. Women teach our children, and there is no greater responsibility in the world than the teaching of our young boys and girls. They are the future of our church. We are committed to the truth that before God, we, men and women, are all equal..."

"But?" Tony whispered. "I hear a 'but' coming...Wait for it..."

Maggie slapped and rubbed.

"Both men and women are able to express the gifts of the Holy Ghost; both men and women are essential to the life and growth of the church..."

"Wait for it..." The leg slap was a little firmer and more pronounced, but the pastor paid no attention.

"...And we affirm the Word, which declares there is no longer male or female, but..." And now he grew even more somber, moving forward slightly before he looked deep into her eyes.

"Ta-da!" Tony said, gloating. "Didn't I see that one coming...This pompous dork sounds just like...me actually."

"But the Word is speaking of how God sees us, not about how we function in the church, and we must always remember that God is a God of order. It is vital that each person play their part, and as long as they stay within the roles God has mandated, the church functions as it was meant to and the health of the body is maintained and even celebrated.

"Now, Ms. Saunders, I would like to show you a passage in my Bible," and with that he produced a well-worn and aged King James Version, opening it directly to a place that had been marked in preparation for this meeting. Clarence sat forward in his chair, his attention riveted on the pastor and his Bible.

"Now it says, right here in First Corinthians, chapter 14; let me read this for you, Ms. Saunders, and you can follow along if you like, starting right here at verse 34: 'Let your women keep silence in the churches: for it is not permitted unto them to speak; but they are commanded to be under obedience, as also saith the law. And if they will learn any thing, let them ask their husbands at home: for it is a shame for women to speak in the church.'"

Having emphasized four words in the reading—*commanded, obedience, law,* and *husband*—he closed the book and sat back, nodding to himself in an entirely sanctified manner. "Now, Ms. Saunders, as it has now come to light that you are not married and therefore have no husband, and as it says here you are to ask your 'husband,' then the church male leadership stands in place of your husband as your head and covering; and if you have any questions, I would like to make myself available to you personally for counsel and encouragement in all matters spiritual."

The silence that descended in that moment was not holy. It was awkward. Even Tony was speechless. Maggie had no idea what she was supposed to do with this invitation.

"It's sarcasm!" Maggie and the pastor both turned to Clarence, who had spoken in a tone firm and sure.

"Excuse me?" The interruption caught Skor by surprise, but he recovered professionally. "Elder Walker, I asked you along because you know Ms. Saunders and I thought your presence might be helpful, but as we discussed earlier, you are not here to speak but to be a witness."

"It is sarcasm," Clarence stated a second time, clearly and slowly. If he was upset, he covered it well behind a stone face, focused and intent.

"What are you talking about, Brother Walker? Do you think I am being sarcastic?" There was an edge of challenge in Skor's voice, which Clarence expertly deflected.

"No, sir, not you. The apostle Paul. I believe that the

apostle Paul was being sarcastic when he wrote what you read."

"Well, Clarence, did you go to a Bible school or seminary that I didn't know about?" The tone now was clearly condescending. "Have you suddenly gotten ordained so that you understand all mysteries? Do you not believe that the Holy Ghost leads us into all truth?"

There was more than a challenge now, and still Clarence didn't bite.

"I do, sir, believe that the Holy Spirit leads us into truth, but sometimes we can't see the building for the underbrush, and sometimes it takes time for our eyes to heal."

Skor whipped out his Bible again, for a second time turning to the marked passage, and stuck it out in Clarence's direction. "So show me. And remember, I have been to Bible school and seminary, and I know the Greek pretty well."

Clarence took the Bible from the older man's hands and held it so both of them could see. "Here," he said and pointed. "Look at this next verse. It begins with 'What?' which is the first of three questions. None of these three questions make any sense whatsoever unless Paul is being sarcastic, that the point he is actually making is the opposite of what you just told Maggie. He is quoting a letter that these folk sent him with questions, and he is in total disagreement with what they have written to him."

"That's utter nonsense. Let me see that!" And he grabbed his Bible from the hands of the elder. A moment of silence passed as the pastor read and reread the passage.

Maggie, her eyes like saucers, hardly dared breathe.

"What about the law Paul was quoting?" challenged Skor.

"Show it to me," returned Clarence.

"Show you what?"

"Show me the law that Paul was quoting."

Skor was flustered in the presence of a man undeterred, and as often happens when someone is caught inside their own assumptions, he changed the argument to something more personal. "You, young man, are contradicting centuries of church history, of theological minds much smarter and wiser than either of ours, and they agree with me. This has now become more than a situation where a woman has created an uproar by drawing unholy attention to herself..."

"Excuse me?" sputtered Maggie.

"I think you should hold your tongue, sir!" advised Clarence, but the pastor was beyond that ability.

"As an authority in the church and one to whom you answer, Clarence, you need to submit yourself and embrace what the Scriptures say."

"I'm sorry, sir, but I don't answer to you. I am a Portland police officer. I answer to God, and I answer to the people in my community."

"Well! Then you have chosen your place alongside this...this...this jezebel." Skor instantly regretted his loss of control, as both Maggie and Clarence rose from their chairs. Clarence towered over the man. "It's best you apologize, sir! That was way outta line!"

"You're right," the pastor acquiesced. "I apologize for my lack of control. I am sorry," he stated to Maggie, turning his attention back to Clarence, anger visibly rising above his shirt collar, starched and imprisoning. "But you, young man, along with this woman, are no longer welcome at my church. I expect your letter of resignation from the Elder Board as soon as you can get it to me."

"You do whatever you need to do, Mr. Skor, but I refuse to send you any such thing, and I would also suggest that you leave this house. Now!" His tone was measured and sure, but there was no doubt of the intent and strength behind it.

"I love this guy!" exclaimed Tony, and Maggie allowed the slightest of grins to dance on her lips, which she was biting.

Without any further conversation Pastor Skor quickly vacated the premises, slammed the door of his automobile, and slowly drove down the street under the watchful eye of the police officer.

"Lord, save us from those who haven't been caught yet," he sighed mostly to himself. Then on his radio he called the precinct before turning back to Maggie. "I checked in and they're sending over a cruiser in a few minutes to pick me up. I'm so sorry, Maggie," he apologized. "I don't think Horace is a bad man, he just doesn't know any better. I had no idea what was coming down, and I'm embarrassed that I was any part of it."

"Are you kidding?" hooted Tony. "Apart from last night, that was the most fun I've had since I can remember."

"Uh...about last night...," she began, but he didn't let her finish.

"Oh, I almost forgot," he exclaimed, reaching into his coat pocket and holding up a small ziplock. "The real reason I came with Horace was to return this. I think it belongs to you. I don't often find a woman's earring embedded in my clothes."

Maggie was more elated than embarrassed. "Oh, Clarence, thank you! This is one of a pair that's all I have from my mom and it means a lot to me. What can I say?"

And before Tony could scream, "Don't kiss him!" she

turned, embraced her hero, and planted a big one right on
his cheek.

"Crap!" Tony groaned as he started to slide.

ξ ∞ ℘ ⚡ ∞ ❄ ⑤ ⑯

As he emerged from the darkness, he found himself looking directly at Maggie. If kindness and affection were colors with attached emotions, he knew that is what he was
feeling, right before the familiar wave of adrenaline picked
him up.

Clarence pulled back and reached for his gun. "Maggie,"
he whispered, "is there a man here?"

"Oops!" uttered Tony, and Clarence spun around to
look behind him.

Maggie knew instantly what had happened.

"Uh, Clarence?" He turned back, hypervigilant and
looking past her into the rest of the house. "Clarence, look
at me!" she commanded.

"What!" he whispered, but seeing no movement finally
locked his eyes on Maggie.

"We need to talk, quickly, because your police buddies
are coming and there are things you need to know before
they get here. Come and sit down."

Clarence chose a chair where his back would be against
a wall and sat down slowly, his senses still on alert. Only
then did he turn his attention back to Maggie.

"Maggie, I swear I heard a man say, 'Crap,'" he asserted.

"Well, you probably did..." Clarence looked right at her,
confused. "But the man isn't in my house, he's in your head."

"What? Maggie, you're not making any sense right now.
What do you mean, he's in my head?" He began to get up,

but Maggie put her hand on his shoulder, looking him right in the eyes.

"Tony! Say something. Don't just leave me here hangin' like this," she demanded.

"Uh, hi, Clarence. Nice uniform?"

Clarence's eyes swelled and Maggie could see an edge of fright dancing in their corners, probably not something that happened often.

"Clarence, stay with me," urged Maggie. "I can explain." She actually had no idea of how, but she knew she first needed to keep him calm.

"Maggie," whispered Clarence, "are you talking about your demon, the one named Tony, from last night? Are you saying he is in my head now?"

"I am not a demon!" stormed Tony.

"He's not a demon," stated Maggie.

"Then how come I can hear him talk to me?...Oh," he said as the truth dawned on him. "Then you really could hear him talking to you last night?" Clarence wasn't sure whether to be relieved or freaked out.

"What? You didn't believe me?" Maggie was enjoying the moment but a little perturbed. "Tony, how come you didn't tell me that if I kissed someone you would move?"

"Who were you kissing?" asked Clarence, concerned.

"Cabby, she kissed Cabby," answered Tony.

"I kissed Cabby," confirmed Maggie.

"Tony says he didn't think it was important at the time," reported Clarence. "He says he was afraid you would go looking for his ex-wife and kiss her...and he's sorry." Clarence looked sideways. "I can't believe I am doing this! Maggie," he pleaded, "what is going on?"

"Okay, listen." She leaned forward. "Tony is an older white—"

"He says he's not that old," interrupted Clarence.

"Ignore him…Tony, shut up. Anyway, he's a Portland businessman who doesn't really believe in God, but he was in an accident and ended up at OHSU where he's in a coma, and he met God, who sent him on a mission of sorts, which no one seems to understand, and Cabby was playing hide 'n' seek and he ended up in Cabby and then last night I kissed Cabby and got infected and thought it was a demon when he talked to me and today I kissed you and now he's yours."

"For real?"

She nodded.

Clarence sat, shocked. This was so utterly bizarre that it might be true. *Occam's razor*, he thought, the principle that other things being equal, a simpler explanation is better than a more complex one. And while this might be simple, was it even possible?

"I'm not sure I want to share you with a white guy," was all he could think to say.

Maggie folded her arms and hunched her shoulders in a look of question. "Really? I tell you this unbelievable story, and all you are concerned about is me and you?" And then it dawned on her what he had said.

They grinned and nodded.

"So, what's his full name?" asked Clarence finally, looking straight at Maggie.

"Uh, I'm right here and can answer for myself, thank you very much!" began Tony.

"Tony…Anthony Spencer," answered Maggie.

"Tony?" Clarence was asking loudly, as if Tony were in the other room. "Wait, are you Anthony Sebastian Spencer?"

"Uh, yeah," responded Tony, "and you don't need to yell…just talk normal. Anyway, how do you know my middle name? No one knows my middle name."

"I'm a cop, remember. We pulled your case. It looked a little suspicious, so we searched your condo, the one with blood on the doorjamb. Yours I presume?"

"Yeah! I think it was...I was really sick and that's where I fell...don't remember much. By the way, how did you get into my condo?"

Clarence smiled. "Sorry, busted down the door. Couldn't find anyone with the key code, so we entered the old-fashioned way."

Just then a black-and-white pulled up and the officer driving honked the horn. Clarence walked to the door and held up a hand, motioning for another five minutes. The policeman in the car grinned and nodded, giving him the thumbs-up sign. "Great!" muttered Clarence to himself. How was he going to explain this?

Turning back so as not to appear to be talking to himself, he asked, "Tony, we found a lot of surveillance stuff at your place, pretty high-end tech... You know about that?"

"Yeah," Tony admitted. "It's mine. I was getting a little paranoid, but I promise, there weren't any cameras in the bathroom or bedrooms." He suddenly felt guilty. Probably just being in the presence of a police officer was enough to cause that.

"Yeah, we noticed that. We did try and backtrace the signal but got nowhere. It totally shut down on us. Were you recording somewhere?"

Tony groaned inwardly but didn't let a sound escape. This meant that all the codes would automatically reset, which was a problem.

"Office downtown," he offered. It was a lie, but he was not about to divulge his secret place.

"Hmmm," Clarence grunted and turned to Maggie.

"So, Maggie, what do we do?"

"I got an idea," piped up Tony, trying to sound helpful but effectively changing the course of the conversation.

"Uh, Tony says he has an idea, Maggie. He says..." Clarence grinned before he said it. "He said I should kiss you again."

"Really? He said that? How do I know he said that or you're not just making this up in order to sneak a little sugar?"

"You don't," agreed Clarence, "but I personally consider his plan to be entirely reasonable and with merit. At least we should try it. Best thing that could happen right now is that you get him back."

"The best thing?" Maggie tilted her head and raised her eyebrows.

"Well, other than the kiss itself, I mean." Clarence chuckled.

And they kissed again, not a slight peck on the cheek this time, but a for-real-I've-been-waiting-a-long-time-for-this sort of kiss. Thankfully, Tony could feel himself sliding again, back into a familiar place, looking into the eyes of the man Maggie loved.

"Enough!" exclaimed Tony. "Something about this is entirely wrong and it's giving me the willies!"

"He's back, Clarence." Maggie smiled. "But don't kiss me again. I have no idea if it would work again, and trust me, you don't want him trying to help you solve cases."

"Well," Clarence said as he gave her a tender hug, "I gotta say you are the most interesting and strangest woman I have ever known. Is he, you know, Tony, is he here all the time?"

"Nope. He comes and goes. I have no control it seems. A God-thing as strange as that is, mysterious ways and all. I'll call you when I can... when he's gone," she whispered.

"I heard that," said Tony.

Suddenly Maggie thought of something and grabbed the officer's arm as he turned to leave. "Hey, Clarence, when you were doing your cop thing, background and all on Sebastian here..."

"It's Tony, please, leave Sebastian outta this," he begged.

She continued, "...Did you find any next of kin?"

"Yeah, we tracked down his brother, Jeffrey or Jerald..."

"Jacob?" Tony was stunned, and Maggie repeated the question. "Jacob?"

"Yeah, Jacob. He's living right here in town. Why do you ask?"

"I need to talk to him. Can you make that happen?"

Clarence hesitated before answering, "Let me see what I can do. Not like any of this is normal anyway." He shook his head.

Maggie caught herself just as she started to kiss Clarence good-bye, giving him another hug instead, and watched him walk to the car without looking back, all business. She couldn't see how difficult it was for him to suppress the grin that threatened to interfere with his professional demeanor.

Tony was speechless, awash in memories and emotions that almost foundered him.

13

THE WAR WITHIN

*The apostle tells us that "God is love"; and therefore,
seeing he is an infinite being, it follows that he is an
infinite fountain of love. Seeing he is an all-sufficient
being, it follows that he is a full and overflowing,
and inexhaustible fountain of love. And in that
he is an unchangeable and eternal being, he is an
unchangeable and eternal fountain of love.*
—Jonathan Edwards

Hello?"

The voice on the phone surprised Maggie, not completely unlike Tony's, but softer and with a tenderness that bordered on resignation. She hesitated.

"Hello? Is anyone there?"

"Yes, so sorry, is this Jacob Spencer?"

"Yes, ma'am, it is. Who's asking?"

"Hi, Mr. Spencer, my name is Maggie, Maggie Saunders, and... I'm a friend of your brother, Tony?"

"We're friends now?" Tony piped in. "Not a painless process, being your friend."

She raised her hand to quiet him.

"Didn't know my brother had any of those. Do you know him well?"

"Intimately." It was the wrong word and she knew it as soon as it inadvertently slipped out. "I mean, not intimately, like…you know…not intimately…" She rolled her eyes. "We never dated or anything, just friends. You hang around him for a while and he sort of gets in your head." Through the receiver, she heard a gracious chuckle.

"Yeah, that's the Tony I remember. So, Ms. Saunders, what can I do for you?"

"Maggie, please…Of course, you're aware that Tony is in a coma up at OHSU…Have you been up to visit him?"

Another pause. "No, I only found out yesterday when the police contacted me. I've been hesitating. Not sure why, since he wouldn't even know I was there, but…our relationship is sort of complicated and we sort of had a falling-out. Anyway, I probably will at some point…maybe."

"I have a huge favor to ask of you, Mr. Spencer…"

"Please, call me Jake. You need a favor, from me?"

"I am an RN and work up at the hospital but in an unrelated department. I would really like to check in on Tony once in a while and make sure he is being looked after, but because I am not family I don't have any access. I was wondering if…"

"I apologize in advance for this question," Jake began, "but I feel that I need to know for sure that you know him. Can't be too careful these days. Can you tell me what his ex-wife's name is? His parents' names?"

He asked his questions and Tony gave Maggie all the right answers, which seemed to satisfy Jake.

"Maggie, may I ask you one more question?"

"Sure, Jake, what is it?"

"Did Tony ever…I mean, did he…" His voice began to break a little, and Maggie heard a younger brother seeking, almost begging. "Did he ever, you know, talk to you about me? Did he mention me?"

Tony was silent, and Maggie was momentarily lost for words. "Jake, I wish I could tell you something different, but Tony didn't talk about family much. He kept that to himself."

"Yeah, yeah…I understand." Jake sounded defeated. "I was just wondering, that's all." He cleared his throat. "So, Maggie, as soon as I hang up I will call the hospital and have them put you on the list, and thank you! I don't know what you mean to him, but I am grateful that there's someone in his life that cares about him…so thank you!"

"You're welcome, Jake." A thought occurred to her. "Jake, where do you live? Maybe…" But the phone went dead.

"Tony?" Maggie turned her attention inward, a demand hidden in her question.

"Don't want to talk about it," came the curt reply.

"Well, when you are ready, I'll be right here," she added.

Tony did not respond, and she felt an emptiness. "Tony?" Still nothing. She knew he had gone to wherever it was that he went. "Dear God," she prayed, her voice hushed, "I don't have any idea what you are up to, but I pray you heal these boys' broken hearts."

᠁ ∞ 🜂 ∞ 🜍 ∞

Tony stood alone and watched two figures slowly and carefully approach via the incline. For all the time he had just spent with Maggie, Clarence, and Horace Skor, it appeared that none had elapsed here. *In-between time?* he wondered as he struggled to reorient himself. Jack was indeed gone, and the pair of large figures was approaching and within a hundred yards.

Tony was now in no mood to meet anyone, especially neighbors. He was caught in the immediate turmoil and upheaval of his inner world. Listening to Maggie's conversation with Jake had dismantled him, filling him with more self-loathing and tapping into a rush of uncomfortable memories he'd concealed inside well-constructed internal compartments. He didn't understand why, but he felt his guard collapsing. He could no longer stuff his feelings into private vaults and bury them. He stood and waited, not disposed to extend hospitality.

As they approached, Tony felt deep and increasing isolation and loneliness, as if their impending presence was pushing him into a corner. Strangely, the duo, who appeared huge at a distance, seemed to diminish in stature as they advanced. They stopped, jostling with each other for position, and stared at him from less than ten feet away, an odor of decay permeating the space between. Neither was more than four feet tall.

As odd as they looked, their demeanor was vaguely familiar. The taller and slimmer of the two was dressed in a three-piece Italian silk suit that had lost much of its sheen, attire barely appropriate for a business power lunch. The other hardly fit inside an outfit sewn together in haphazard chaos from a smattering of materials in out-of-sorts colors. Both were completely out of place in these barren surroundings. If not for a lingering sense of anxiety and tension that accompanied them, the juxtaposition would have been almost laughable.

"So who might you two be?" asked Tony, not taking a step toward them.

The shorter, squatter one immediately began to respond, his voice high-pitched and wheezy, "Well, my name is..."

The other cuffed him up the back of his head, leaned down and growled in a deep baritone as if Tony were entirely absent. "We don't just give him our names, you idiot. Are you trying to get us in deeper trouble?" He then smiled at Tony, a beaming almost creepy grimace, and waved his hand as if it were a wand. "My deepest apologies, sir, for my friend here who doesn't seem to know his place. You can call us Bill"—he pointed a thumb toward his companion—"and Sam," he finished, bowing ever so slightly to indicate he was the latter.

"Bill and Sam?" exclaimed the shorter, squatter one. "That's the best you can do? Bill and Sam?" Bill cringed as Sam raised his hand to buffet him a second time.

Thinking better of it, Sam refrained from striking Bill again and turned back to Tony with an air of being large and in charge.

"Okay, then...*Sam*," emphasized Tony, "what are you two doing here?"

"Well, sir," he said, rolling his eyes as if to indicate that the question was almost beneath a response. "We...are the keepers of the walls, that is what we be!" He stated it as if it were an announcement of utmost importance and brushed an invisible something off his lapel.

"Yes," jumped in Bill, "that is what we be...yes, sir, keepers of the walls. All the walls, and we are very skilled keepers, too, we are, every one of us busy keeping the walls and good at what we do, we are..." His voice trailed off as if he were looking for a way to end the sentence.

"And we are gardeners," interjected Sam. "We do the weeding around here."

"You do the weeding? All I've seen are weeds."

"No, you haven't…Sir, beg your pardon, but we are good at what we do…keep walls and weeding." Sam was looking around as he spoke and spotted something that made him brighten. "You see, right there, sir?" He pointed a stubby little finger and walked a few steps off the path and pulled something from under a boulder overhang. Satisfied, he held up a beautiful wild rose, which appeared to be dying by his very touch, if not because it had been torn out by its root.

"That's a flower!" exclaimed Tony.

Sam looked at it carefully before turning back. "No, it's not! It's a weed. See, it has color, so it's a weed. And it's covered in all these nasty, prickly…uh…"

"Thorns," offered Bill.

"Yes, that's it, thorns. Why would a flower have a thorn? This is a weed! And we pull them and burn them so they don't spread. That's what we do, and we are very skilled at it, we are."

"Well," Tony said, indignant, "this is my land, and I am telling you that you are no longer allowed to pull up and burn flow—weeds, even weeds with thorns on them. Is that clear?"

The two looked like they had been caught stealing from a cookie jar.

"Are you sure?" asked Sam. "What if those weeds start taking over the land with all their nasty colors and thorns…"

"Yes, I am sure! No more weed pulling. Clear?"

"Yes, sir," mumbled Bill. "But I'm not telling the others; no, I'm not."

"Others?" asked Tony. "How many of you are there?"

"Hundreds!" responded Bill immediately. He looked up at Sam, perhaps for permission or support, but getting neither, continued, "All right, thousands; there are thousands of us." He paused as if thinking. "To be honest, there are millions of us, pulling weeds and keeping the walls 'cause that is what we do...keep walls, millions and millions of us, weed pulling, wall-keepers."

"Well, I would like to meet them," asserted Tony.

"You can't do that," responded Sam, his smile smarmy and plastic.

"Why not?"

"Be-cause...," Bill began, looking for a satisfactory answer. "Because we are all invisible, that's why. Invisible! Millions of invisible weeding wall-keepers."

"But I can see you," Tony observed.

"Oh, that," began Bill. "We didn't have a lot of choice. When they send you to do a job, you better do what they say, or else..."

Sam gave Bill another cuff to the back of the head and to Tony another manufactured grin.

"Who is 'they'?" demanded Tony.

"Well," returned Sam, "in every successful organization there is a chain of command who establish and encourage order. These..." He looked to Bill as if this had become some sort of training exercise.

"Benefactors," inserted Bill.

"Exactly," continued Sam. "These *benefactors* have asked us to fulfill the role assigned to us by our organization, to meet..." He looked again at his partner, who was nodding along as if to a script.

"...The demands of duty and responsibility," offered Bill.

"Exactly," Sam said with a nod. "To meet the demands of duty and responsibility by coming to meet you and explain the importance of your staying away from us, for your own good, of course."

"Keep away from you?" retorted Tony. "I want to meet your benefactors."

"Oh, that is not possible," sputtered Bill, shaking his head.

"And why not?"

"Because...you'll explode, that's why not, into millions and millions of pieces. Little tiny bits of bone and flesh and disgusting stuff flying in a million directions...not pretty, well, maybe mildly pretty in a repulsive sort of way." Bill had become quite animated, while Sam nodded knowingly, his eyes almost remorseful, his lower lip slightly aquiver.

"I'll explode?" exclaimed Tony. "You actually expect me to believe that nonsense? I think it is time you told me your real names."

The smaller looked up at the less small. "Do we have to, Swagger? I mean, tell him our real names?"

With a look of disgust the other retorted, "You just did, you idiot! You never learn, do you?" Turning to Tony, a note of haughty superiority in his tone, he continued, "So, now you know, I am Swagger." He bowed again ever so slightly, maintaining his arrogant air. "And this fool," he said, tilting his head toward his companion, "is Bluster. He once was named Bluff, but he was recently demoted, and..." He leaned forward a little toward Tony as if including him in a secret before continuing, "and you can certainly understand why."

"Your names are Bluster and Swagger?" Tony repeated, incredulous. "That's the silliest thing I have ever heard. Where did you get such ridiculous names?"

"Well, from you, of course," blurted out Bluster and promptly received another cuff on the head.

"Shut up, you dolt," snarled Swagger. "You just can't keep

your yap shut, can you? Ego is going to eat you for lunch, and that will be the end of…"

"Quiet!" demanded Tony, and surprisingly they went completely silent, turning in unison to face him. Tony saw a hint of fear had replaced some of their conceited attitude. They avoided direct eye contact and glanced at the ground or one side to another. "Bluster, what do you mean that I gave you those names?"

Bluster now shifted nervously from one foot to the other, as if pressure were building up inside him. Finally it seemed he could no longer contain himself. "You don't recognize us, do you?"

"Why should I? You are a ridiculous pair."

"But you named us, or rather, we were named after your behaviors and choices? We belong to you. We, you see, are *your* Bluster and *your* Swagger."

"It is true, Tony," came the voice of Grandmother, who had suddenly appeared next to him. "They are here because you gave them a voice and a place in your soul. You thought you needed them to become successful."

The two were totally unaware of her presence and seemed unable to hear Grandmother when she spoke, but their nervous agitation increased. "Squatters!" stated Tony, an admission to Grandmother that he now was beginning to understand.

"Squatters?" squealed Swagger. "We are not squatters. We live here. We have a right to be here!"

"This is my land, my property," asserted Tony, "and I don't…"

"What?" howled Bluster, attempting to look larger and ferocious. "Who told you this was your property? I've had enough of your insolence. I've got a good mind to walk right over there and…"

"And do what, exactly?" Tony demanded.

"Well...nothing really, I was just thinking..." Bluster seemed to shrink even shorter and smaller in the face of being challenged.

"That's what I thought. You two are just bad breath, a waste of space, an imagination of something I thought I needed to succeed."

"But it worked, didn't it? Weren't you successful?" offered Swagger, for an instant looking up. "I mean, we did win, you and us. You owe us!" he whined, withering quickly under Tony's gaze.

"I owe you?" asked Tony, distraught at what he now realized. "What was winning, especially if I had to use Bluster and Swagger to succeed? If you exist because I thought I needed you, I am a greater fool than both of you put together. I didn't need you, I needed honesty and integrity and..."

"Weeds!" suggested Swagger.

"What?"

"Weeds. Honesty and integrity, them are weeds, all full of colors and thorns, wicked things."

"Meet the others," encouraged Grandmother, who had remained next to him.

"I demand you take me to the others," Tony commanded the pair, "and don't tell me any more nonsense about exploding."

"Just one small request," groveled the less short one, barely a swagger left in his demeanor. "Would you tell Ego that you made us take you to him, that we had no choice?"

"Ego? That's your *benefactor*?" He waited until they nodded. "Ego is your boss, then?"

"Yeah," admitted Bluster. "He's stronger than we are and tells us what to do. He is not going to be happy about us bringing you to meet him. He reports direct to the big boss...Oops." He grimaced, waiting for another hit alongside the head, but Swagger had withdrawn in resigned caution.

"And who is that big boss?" asked Tony.

A sly grin passed across Bluster's face. "Why, you are. Mr. Anthony Spencer, the sorry owner of this excuse for a piece of land, you are the big boss here. I'd watch myself around you, I would. Heartless and conniving, that one."

Tony couldn't tell if this creature was insulting him directly or not, but it didn't matter. He was done with this conversation and waved them back toward the place they had come from, following with Grandmother at his side.

As they descended, the path became increasingly rocky and unkempt, the passing made difficult by fallen trees and boulders that looked as if they had been sown indiscriminately by some giant hand. The trail branched and Tony glanced to his right down the path the two had not taken, spotting a distant building standing alone. It was a thick windowless block almost indiscernible against the rock wall into which it appeared embedded.

"Hey, what's that place?" He stopped, pointing in its direction.

"Oh, Mr. Spencer, you don't want nothing to do with that place," proclaimed Swagger, continuing his pace. "Best you keep away from there. Bad enough we are taking you to meet the boss."

"Just tell me what it is," demanded Tony.

"It's a temple," stated Bluster over his shoulder, and then laughed as if heckling. "You should know, you should. You built it. You worship there."

"That's enough," growled Swagger as he quickened his stride down the path the two had chosen.

"How odd...a temple?" mused Tony. Whatever it was, it would have to wait, and he soon caught up to the short-legged duo. The smell that had wrinkled his nose earlier now became a stench of rotting eggs, and Tony breathed through his mouth to keep from gagging. Along with the stagnant reek, his sense of isolation and desolation grew with each step and he was grateful for Grandmother's presence. She silently walked beside him and seemed unfazed by any of these strange events.

Rounding a bend in the trail, Tony stopped, stunned. Not fifty yards from where he stood huddled a cluster of buildings of various quality and miscalculated dimensions. A couple of hundred yards beyond these rose the base of the towering rock walls marking the farthest boundary of the property that until now he had seen only from a distance. He had paid little attention to the stone edifice when he first entered, but now he was close enough to appreciate how the enclosure was constructed. It appeared fashioned from gigantic boulders fitted together with care and precision, impenetrable and rising hundreds of feet into the air before disappearing into a bank of accumulating low-lying clouds.

A tall, thin fellow emerged from one of the structures. He looked odd, as if he were built disproportionately. Something was off, and Tony almost wanted to look at him sideways to see him better. It was his head, considerably larger than it should have been in relation to the rest of his body, his eyes a little too small and his mouth a little too wide. A thick layer of makeup, like flesh-colored paste, had been applied to his face.

"Mr. Spencer, good of you to come to my ever-humble abode. I am forever your servant." He grinned obsequiously, his voice decadent and smooth like chocolate syrup. As he spoke, the makeup on his face drooped, hanging loosely but not quite falling off. In the spaces that separated, Tony could see what looked to be ugly dark bruises. Tony felt a rush of sickening arrogance, as if he were standing in the presence of someone totally self-absorbed.

"You must be Ego," stated Tony.

"You know my name? Well, then, I am Ego, at your service, I'm sure." He bowed deeply. "I am rather surprised to see you here." He shot a look of barely masked contempt toward the duo who had escorted Tony. "I'll *reward* you two later," he growled.

They both cowered, seeming to shrink even shorter. Not much swagger or bluster remained in the presence of their superior. Nearly a dozen odd-looking creatures gathered in tangled clusters near the buildings, watching him.

"Why do you exist?" asked Tony, more a demand than a question.

"Why, to help you make decisions," responded Ego, a look of cunning sliding across his broken face. "I remind you of how important you are, how necessary you are for the success of those who feed off you, how much they are in your debt. I help you keep score of the ways they have offended you and the mistakes they have made that cost you. It is my job to whisper in your ear that it is you who counts in the world. Mr. Spencer, you are a very important man, and everyone loves, admires, and respects you."

"That isn't true," snapped Tony. "And I don't really deserve their respect or admiration."

"Oh, Mr. Spencer, it pains me to hear you say such nonsense. You deserve all that, and more. Look at all you have done for those people; the least they could do for you is to acknowledge your efforts on their behalf. They owe you that much, at least. You're not asking for the world. Just a little recognition, that's all. Your employees would be out of a job if it were not for you. Your partners would be working manual labor if it were not for your superior skills. And still they talk behind your back and plot ways to wrest your authority away from you. They don't understand you. They don't see you as the gift that you are. It hurts me to even think about it!" He put his hand to his immense forehead, as if mortally wounded, a look pitiable and sad.

Tony had voiced these thoughts only to himself. They contained a self-fueling logic, tapping into resentments and bitterness that he now recognized lay behind many of his actions. Confrontation with his own damaged ego was ugly and distorted. "I don't want to be like that anymore!"

"Mr. Spencer, *there* is exactly a perfect example why you are such a great man. Listen to the authenticity of your confession. Well done! God must truly be pleased with a follower like you who is so humble and contrite, so willing to lay down self and choose a different path. I am honored to be your friend, to call you brother."

"You are not my brother!" Tony exclaimed curtly. Tony struggled for words. Wasn't Ego right? Didn't God want Tony to change? To repent? But Ego's words had a hint of ugly and wrong, almost like Tony's old agenda was being replaced with a newer one, perhaps shinier, prettier, and more self-righteous. But underneath there was always an expectation, sometimes obvious, often hidden, but always still an agenda, the same performance-based agenda.

"I know what you are," Tony declared. "You are just some uglier and maybe even more honest form of myself!"

"Mr. Spencer, you are right as usual. You must die to yourself, put others and their concerns and issues in place of your own needs and desires and wants. Selfless love, that is the utmost and most beautiful sacrifice and one that

God would be greatly pleased with. You must crucify the self, die to self, and put God on the throne of your life. You must decrease so that he"—he pointed up with a skinny finger—"can increase."

"I suppose, I mean, that sounds right, I guess?" Doubt clouded Tony's thinking and his heart was unquiet. He glanced at Grandmother, who looked directly at him but remained stoic and silent. Her eyes were affectionate and assured him she would not abandon him, but her manner told him this was his fight. Tony was irritated by Grand- mother's lack of involvement. How could she just stand there and do nothing? He was hardly prepared to deal with this.

"Of course, you are right, Mr. Spencer, as you usually are. Look no further than the example that Jesus set. He gave his *self* a ransom for us all. He became nothing so you could become everything. Don't you see, that is what he wants, for you to become like he is, *free*." Ego yelled the word, and it echoed off the stone towering overhead. He danced in a slow circle, raising his arms slowly and drop- ping them while in a singsong voice he declared, "Free! Free to choose. Free to love and live and let live, free to pursue happiness, free from societal and family bonds, free to do whatever you want because you are free!"

"Stop!" bellowed Tony.

Ego froze, standing on one foot, arms akimbo.

"That's what I have been doing already, whatever I want, and it hasn't been freedom at all." Tony's anger surged. "All my 'freedom' did was hurt people and build walls around my heart until I couldn't feel anything anymore. Is that what you mean by freedom?"

"Well," Ego said as he lowered his arms and planted both feet firmly on the ground, "freedom always has its price." He held the last syllable and let it echo off the structures before continuing, "Mr. Spencer, look at history. Some people always have to die for some to be free. No government or state on your planet came into existence without the necessary shedding of blood. When war is needed and justified, it is peace that is the sin, and if that be true for the government, it must also hold true for you as an individual."

Tony didn't know exactly why, but he felt Ego's logic was sick and twisted. Ego saw his hesitation and quickly continued, "Look to Jesus, Mr. Spencer. Your freedom cost him everything! He gave his very life to set you free. This man went to God and cried..." Again Ego became theatrical, turning skyward with eyes closed as if in the deepest pleading and intercession toward heaven: "Dear God, pour out all your wrath, all the anger you feel toward this vile and wicked creation, for the myriads of disgusting activities of wretched humanity, pour out your just and holy fury, the bow of your wrath bent and the arrow made ready on the string, and justice bending the arrow at their hearts, pour your righteous wrath instead on me. Let me bear your cruelty, the just deserts of their wickedness. Burn me with your eternal fire instead of them, that your sword of divine justice that is brandished even now over their heads would fall instead upon me." And with that Ego bowed his head, as if a mighty edge would cleave his being in two.

His words rang into the distance. There was silence.

"So, then tell me," began Tony, his voice stronger but his tone soft. "Did it work?"

Ego snapped back to attention. He had not anticipated such a question. "What do you mean?"

"I mean, did it work? Did Jesus bear the wrath of God successfully? Did it work?"

"Of course, it worked, this is Jesus we are talking about." He didn't sound completely sure.

Tony pressed the point. "So God poured out *all* his wrath and anger on Jesus instead of human beings and his wrath and fury were forever satisfied? Is that what you are telling me?"

"Exactly…well, not *exactly*. Great question, though, Mr. Spencer, excellent question. You should be proud of yourself for thinking of such an ingenious question."

He was stalling and Tony knew it. "Well?"

Ego fidgeted, alternately putting weight on one foot, then the other. "Here is how you have to look at it, Mr. Spencer, and I wouldn't be explaining this to just anyone. It's rather hush-hush, you know, belonging to the category of assumptions better left unspoken, but it can be our little secret. You see, the truth is God is rather difficult to get along with. His creation"—he raised his palm, indicating Tony—"has disobeyed him grievously. As a result, the wrath of God is now a constant part of God's being, like an ever-burning fire, a necessary evil if you would; and it continues to burn with an eternal flame, consuming everyone and everything that does not accept and appropriate what Jesus did. Are you following?" He raised one eyebrow, which stood out starkly on his pasty face, looking to Tony for agreement. "Well, regardless, you must always remember that the one constant about God is his anger and righteous wrath, which he has already fully poured out on Jesus. So if you want to escape the wrath of God, you have to become like Jesus, surrender your life and live like Jesus did, holy and pure. Be ye perfect, even as I am perfect…That's in the Bible."

"So, then," Tony said as he looked at the dry and desolate ground at his feet, "there's no hope for someone like me; that's what you're saying. I don't have what it takes to live like that, like Jesus, holy and pure."

"No, no, that is not true, Mr. Spencer. There is always

hope, especially for someone who tries as hard as you, who is as special as you. There is just no certainty, that's all."

"Then you are telling me that relationship with God is only wishful thinking, nothing to really stand on, just a possibility?"

"Please, don't discount wishful thinking. Almost everything in your world was manufactured by wishful thinking, Mr. Spencer. Don't sell yourself short. In your wishful thinking, your hoping, you become very much like God."

"For God so loved the *world*...," challenged Tony. It was part of a verse that Tony remembered from somewhere.

Ego dropped his gaze dramatically to the ground. "That is so incredibly sad, isn't it?" he said and shook his head.

"Sad?" Tony refuted. "It isn't sad. If it's true, it's the most beautiful thing I have ever heard! God loves the world! That means God loves those of us in the world. God loves me!" The realization ignited his anger, which flashed bright, and he embraced it, spewing it on Ego. "You know what? I don't care what you want. You are liars and your lies are demonic..."

"Shush!" shrieked Ego, who regained control quickly and smiled broadly. "Mr. Spencer, we don't use that word around here. That is just old-school mythology. We are not those...those ugly, detestable, and miserable creatures! We are sent here to help. We are spirit messengers of God, guides of light and grace, commissioned to ease your way and lead you into the truth."

"A bunch of liars, that's what you are! What right do you have to be here, any of you? I demand to know, by whose authority have you claimed a right to be here?"

"Yours!" echoed a booming voice from inside another building, the grandest in the settlement. Startled, Tony took a step back as the door slowly opened and a huge man stepped out. An odor of pungent waste and sulfur emerged with him. Tony stood stupefied, face-to-face with…himself, except much bigger. The man towered over him, probably close to ten feet in height, but otherwise it was almost as if he were looking in a mirror. But as Tony looked closer, little details were off. This giant's hands and ears were slightly too large, while his eyes were a bit too small and unbalanced. The mouth was too wide and the grin was askew. He carried himself with authority and confidence.

"Sosho," muttered Grandmother to the giant, standing close to Tony's shoulder. "Wakipajan!" By her tone, the strange words were not compliments. Tony was grateful for her presence, glad she offset some of his intimidation.

"And who are you?" demanded Tony.

"Come, come, Mr. Spencer." He laughed, folding his arms across his expansive chest. "Surely you know me. I am your superior self, all that you had hoped and wished to be. It was you, with the help of a few of *your* benefactors, who empowered you to create me. You fed me and clothed me and over time I have grown stronger and more powerful than even you imagined, and it is now I who have been creating you. Birthed as I was in the deepest recesses of your need, you were first my creator, and I was in your debt, but I have been diligent and have repaid you many times over. I now no longer need you for my existence. I am stronger than you!"

"Then leave! If you no longer need me for your existence, pack up and leave…and take your cronies with you."

This amused the big Tony. "Oh, I cannot do that, Mr. Spencer. This is my territory; this is my life's work. You may have set the foundation, but it is we who have built upon it. Long ago you gave us our right to be here, sold to me your birthright in exchange for safety and certainty. It is you who now need us."

"Safety and certainty?" contradicted Tony. "Is this a sick joke? I've never known either one."

"Ah, Mr. Spencer, not the point," prompted the other, his voice almost hypnotic and monotone. "It was never whether you actually had any true safety or certainty; it only mattered that you believed you did. You have a magnificent power to create reality from suffering and dreams, hopes and despair, to call from within the god that you are. We simply guided you, whispering what you needed to hear so you could realize your potential and create an imagination from which you could manage your world. You survived this cruel and heartless world because of me."

"But—" Tony began.

"Anthony, if it weren't for me," the bigger Tony interrupted and took a step toward the smaller, "you would be dead. I saved your miserable life. When you wanted to snuff out your existence, it was me that talked you into living. I own you! Apart from me you can do nothing."

Tony felt his footing giving way, as if teetering on the edge of an invisible cliff. He turned toward Grandmother, but there remained only an outline of her presence; she was fading. A curtain was drawn across his sight, and everything clear and tangible over the last few days lost clarity and color. The ground leaked a dark visible poison, rising like loose marionette strings around him, constricting his ability to see clearly and think lucidly. A ravenous despair consumed the delicate pieces of his heart that had begun springing to life and sucked them into the well of deep loneliness that had always scarred his heart. Grandmother vanished. He was alone and blind.

Then he felt the breath on his face, kissing him with the sweetness of an intoxication. The fragrance pushed out and replaced the foul stench that had dominated. And then he heard the whisper, "You are utterly alone, Tony, just as you deserve to be. It would have been better if you had never been born."

It was true, he thought. He was alone and deserved it. He had killed the love of everyone who had offered it to him, and now he was nothing more than a dead man walking. The admission swept through him like the last crumbling walls of a stronghold. Fingers of icy dread slipped like bands around his chest, penetrating through the flesh, reaching for his heart to squeeze until it no longer beat. He froze, stone from the inside out, and nothing he could do would stop it.

And then he heard in the distance, but drawing near, the sound of a little girl's laughter and singing. He couldn't move and was barely able to breathe. She would never find him in this inky darkness. She wouldn't even know he was here. "God," he prayed, "please help her find me."

He saw a flicker of movement and light far away, but it grew, as did the singing, until she was standing directly in front of him, perhaps all of six years old, raven hair tied back from smooth olive skin by a wreath of tiny white flowers, a white trillium tucked behind one ear. She had stunning brown eyes and was all smiles.

So he wasn't alone. She could see him. The palpable sense of relief loosed some of the tension in his chest and he took a bit deeper breath. *I can't speak*, he thought.

That elicited a beaming grin. "I know that, Mr. Tony," she said, laughing, "but sometimes it's the thought that counts."

He felt himself smile. *Where am I?* he thought.

"We, Mr. Tony, where are we? We, Mr. Tony, we are not alone." And she twirled in her dress of flowered blues and greens as if onstage, finally taking a deep and slow-motion bow. Her presence was innocence and warmth, and he felt the icy weights ever so slightly lighten. If he could have laughed out loud he would have.

We, then… where are we? He again thought the question.

She ignored him. "Who are you, Mr. Tony?" she asked and cocked her head to one side in childlike inquiry, waiting for his answer.

A hopeless failure, he thought and felt his chest tighten with the attending despair.

"Is that what you are, Mr. Tony? A hopeless failure?"

A litany of successive images tumbled through his mind, all in support of his self-accusation, validations of the judgment against him.

"Oh, Mr. Tony!" she exclaimed without any sense of incrimination. "You are so much more than that!" It was an observation, not a value statement.

So who am I, then, he thought, *if more than just a hopeless failure?*

The little girl began to hop-skip around him, moving in and out of his view while touching her fingers in no particular order as if keeping a count. In a singsong voice, she declared, "Mr. Tony, you are also a mighty warrior, you are not alone, you are someone who learns, you are a universe of wonder, you are Grandmother's boy, you are adopted by Papa God, you are not powerful enough to change that, you are a beautiful mess, you are the melody…" And with each phrase the ice chains that seemed to bind him loosened and his breathing deepened. Thoughts arose that wanted to argue and deny each statement, but as he calmed, he chose to simply watch her dance and listen to her sing.

What did she know? She was just a little girl. Regardless, her words carried power, of that he was certain, and they seemed to resonate in his frozen core. Her presence was like springtime unfolding, the thaw that warmed and invited new things. She stood directly in front of him, leaned in, and softly kissed his cheek.

"What is your name?" He was finally able to find a whisper.

She beamed. "Hope! My name is Hope."

Any reserve he had left broke and tears splashed to the ground. Hope reached up and lifted his chin until he was looking deep into her incredible eyes. "Fight him, Mr. Tony," she whispered. "You do not fight alone."

"Fight who?"

"Your empty imaginations that raise themselves up against the knowing of the character of God. Fight them."

"How?"

"Get angry and tell the truth!"

"I thought anger was wrong."

"Wrong? I get angry all the time, at everything that is wrong."

"Who are you?" he finally asked.

"I am the one who relentlessly loves you," she said, beaming, and stepped back. "Mr. Tony, when you find your-self in the darkness, don't light your own fires, don't circle yourself with a blaze you have set. Darkness cannot change the character of God."

"I thought Grandmother left me...right in the middle of the battle."

"Never left. Your imagination hid her from view. You were lighting your own fires."

"I don't know how not to do that," confessed Tony.

"Trust, Mr. Tony. Trust. Regardless of what your rea-soning or emotions or imagination are telling you, trust."

"But I am so not good at that."

"We know. Trust that you are not alone, that you are not

hopeless." She smiled and kissed his cheek again. "Mr. Tony, simply trust your mother's word to you. Can you do that?"

"As best I know how, I will," admitted Tony, more to himself than the little girl.

"It only takes the smallest desire, Mr. Tony. Jesus is very good at trusting. He will make up the difference. Like most things that last, trusting is a process."

"How do you know so much?" asked Tony.

She grinned. "I am older than you think." A third time she waltzed her breeze-driven dances in a circle around him and a third time leaned in to kiss his other cheek. "Remember this, Mr. Tony, Talitha cumi." She stepped back, then leaned forward and touched her forehead to his, breathing deep. "Now go," she whispered, "and be angry."

And he felt it come, like the roll of an earthquake, the tremors coalescing to a roar as his anger tore a hole into the darkness and scattered it like a murder of startled crows. Tony had been dropped to his knees, and with a grunt he heaved himself back to his feet. Grandmother stood where he had last seen her, impassive except for a hint of a grin that lit the corners of her mouth.

"You are a liar!" roared Tony, pointing a finger up at the grotesque image of himself. "I don't need you anymore, and I revoke any right that I have ever given you, any right to have any say or authority in my life, and I revoke it now!"

For the first time he saw a break in the confidence of the other, larger Tony, who staggered and took a step back. "You can't do that!" he stormed back. "I am stronger than you are."

"That may be true," refuted Tony, "but you can go be stronger somewhere else. This is my property, this is my home, and this is my heart, and I don't want you here."

"I refuse!" The other stamped his foot adamantly. "You have no power to make me leave."

"I…" He hesitated, then plummeted headlong. "I don't stand here alone."

"You!" screamed the other, raising his fist. "You have always been alone… totally alone. I don't see anyone here, do you? Who would want to be with you? You are alone now and only worthy of being abandoned. I am all you have!"

"Liar!" yelled Tony with fury. "You have told me these lies all of my life, and it has produced nothing but heartache and hurt. I am finished with you!"

"You are alone," hissed the other. "Who would lower themselves to be with you?"

"Jesus!" It surprised Tony to hear himself say it, out loud. "Jesus!" He said it again and added, "And the Holy Spirit and the Father of Jesus."

"The Father of Jesus." The hulking creature spit the words. "You hate the Father of Jesus. He killed your parents; he crushed your mother." He took a step closer, gloating. "He murdered your only son, took him screaming and kicking into oblivion. He ignored every prayer you prayed. How can you trust such an evil being who would kill your innocent son like he did his own?"

"I don't!" bellowed Tony, and as he said it, he knew it was true.

A look of triumph crossed the monster's face.

Tony lowered his gaze, glancing quickly again at Grandmother, who still stood like a statue, unwavering. "I don't know him well enough to trust him, but Jesus trusts his Father, and that's good enough for me."

The false Tony, large and formidable, began to shrink. His features caved in on themselves, his clothing hanging loosely from his body, until he stood a mere shadow of his former self. He became a caricature.

Tony felt a sense of peace, like when he was in the presence of the little girl. "So do all these other wall-keepers answer to you?" he asked the pitiful shrinking man.

For a moment it appeared the shrunken Tony might argue, but instead he shrugged in acquiescence.

"Good!" declared Tony. "I want you to leave and take all your lying followers with you." The dozen odd-looking creatures who had gathered during the confrontation along with the few he had met glanced nervously in his direction. Most stared their hatred and contempt for their despised leader, now reduced to a sniveling excuse. As their chief had lost his power and authority, so, too, had each of them. Even Bluster and Swagger were flimsy representations of their former selves, and none too happy about it.

The motley crew wound down the path toward the nearest breach in the stone facade, a collection of muttering and grumbling malcontents who abhorred one another's company. As he and Grandmother walked behind, Tony could now see at their backs a filament of dark light that bound each to the other. During the short march one occasionally would yank his arm, causing another to stumble, much to the glee of the group.

Tony noticed the winding trail continued through a maze of fallen boulders and into the dark forest beyond the standing walls. "Where are they going?" Tony whispered to Grandmother.

"No concern of yours, Tony. They are being escorted."

"Escorted?" Tony was surprised. "But I don't see anyone."

"Just because you are not able to see something doesn't mean it isn't there." Grandmother chuckled.

"Touché," returned Tony with his own grin.

The two of them stopped and stood together at the perimeter of the looming walls, watching the now subdued company disappear down the footpath and into the first row of evergreens.

Grandmother reached up and put her hand on Tony's shoulder. "You fought well today, son. But even though these in particular have been defeated, you must be on guard for the echoes of their voices that still remain within the walls of your mind and heart. They will come to haunt you if you allow them."

Her touch felt empowering, and he understood her warning. "So, why are the walls still here? If the wall-keepers are gone, shouldn't the walls be gone, too? Why don't you just knock them down?"

They turned and walked back toward the careless bundle of vacated buildings.

"Because you built these facades," Grandmother began, "we will not tear them down without your participation. In one's hurry to knock walls down, one can cause them to fall on those they love. Freedom can become a new justification for disregard and a lack of compassion for the bondages of others. Roses have thorns."

"I don't understand. Why do roses have thorns?"

"So that you handle them carefully and gently."

He understood. "But they will come down then, someday? The walls?"

"Of course, someday. But creation wasn't spoken in a day, Anthony. Such walls aren't erected overnight either. They were built over time, and it takes time and process for them to come down. The good news is that without the help of all those 'friends' you just kicked off your property, it will be harder for you to keep the facades standing."

"Me?" Tony was surprised. "Why would I want to keep them standing?"

"You built these walls to keep you safe, or at least for the imagination of safe. They substitute for trust. You are beginning to understand that trusting is an arduous journey."

"So, I needed these walls?"

"When you believe that you alone are the only one who can be trusted, then yes, you need these walls. Self-protective measures, intended to keep evil out, often wall it in. What initially kept you safe can eventually destroy you."

"But don't I need walls? Aren't they good things?"

He felt the hug from behind. "You need boundaries," said the voice of Jesus, "but not walls. Walls divide while boundaries honor." Tony let himself relax into this tender embrace, his tears unexpectedly appearing and spilling softly onto the ground.

"Even in our material creation," continued Jesus, "boundaries mark the most beautiful of places, between the ocean and the shore, between the mountains and the plains, where the canyon meets the river. We will teach you how to thrill with us in the boundaries while you learn to trust us with your security and safety. One day you will no longer need walls."

Even as he spoke, Tony could sense more internal walls crumbling. Not disappearing, but tangibly impacted by an inner knowledge that he was utterly accepted, with all his flaws and losses, all his conditioning and pride. Was this love? Was this what it was like to be loved?

Grandmother spoke. "Okay, One-Who-Cries-a-Lot, you have more work to do, and the moment for you to leave is again approaching."

Jesus produced a bloodred handkerchief for Tony's nose and tears and then began brushing him off.

They arrived back at the loose aggregation of structures, so recently the habitation of deceivers. Curious about its construction, Tony reached up and touched the nearest building. It appeared solid and sturdy, but with barely a nudge, the edifice toppled into a pile of rubble and dust.

"Just facades," he stated out loud to himself. "Lies with so little substance."

Grandmother stood back, beaming. "It's good to hear the changes in your voice," she stated.

"What does that mean?" asked Tony.

"As healing happens in a person's soul, their voice changes, noticeable to anyone with ears to hear."

"Hmph," Tony grunted. It wasn't anything that he'd ever thought about, but it made sense.

"I have something for you, Tony," Jesus said, interrupting his thoughts. "You will want this soon."

He extended a large ring of keys, dozens of differing shapes, sizes, and textures.

"What are these?" Tony queried.

"They are keys," grunted Grandmother.

Tony grinned. "Yes, I know they are keys, but what are they for?"

"To open locks," she muttered.

He knew she was enjoying this. "What locks?"

"Doors."

"Which doors?"

"All kinds. Lotsa keys, lotsa doors."

"I give up." Tony laughed, turning back to Jesus. "What do you want me to do?"

"Simply choose one key. The one you choose will become important at some point."

Tony hesitated. "You want me to choose just one key? What if I choose the wrong one?"

"The one you choose will be the right one, Tony," encouraged Jesus.

"But…" Tony stalled. "Why don't you choose for me? You are divine and all, so you would know better than I do."

Jesus smiled, the wrinkles at the corners of his eyes only adding to their brilliance. "This is about participation, Tony, not about puppeteering."

"So, you…trust me with this choice?"

"Absolutely!" Both nodded.

Tony took the time to sort through the ring, carefully considering one and then another until finally he settled on a particular skeleton key. It looked older, as if from a bygone era, as if it belonged with an old oak door in some medieval castle in Europe.

"Good choice," agreed Grandmother. "Well done." From a pocket she pulled a string of blue light and slipped the key onto it. Then, reaching up, she put it around Tony's neck, tucked it into his shirt, looked deep into his eyes, and simply said, "Go!"

14

FACE-TO-FACE

What lies behind us and what lies before us are tiny matters compared to what lies within us.
—Ralph Waldo Emerson

M aggie?"

"Oh, nice of you to join me. Where have you been, anyway? Never mind, I still don't want to know."

"You wouldn't believe me if I tried to explain it. Nothing about my life at the moment makes a whole lot of sense, and yet, mysteriously, it does." Tony paused to look through her eyes. "I see we're heading up to the hospital." They were on Terwilliger, passing viewpoints that overlooked the Willamette River. Taking a right on Southwest Canyon, they climbed toward what Tony had always thought looked like Legoland for smart people, a massive array of buildings housing some of the brightest minds in medicine and student wannabes.

As they approached the Canyon Garage, Maggie finally asked, "Tony, why are we doing this? Why are you coming up here to look at yourself in a coma?"

"I'm not exactly sure," hedged Tony. "Just one of those things I have to do."

"Hmmm," grunted Maggie. "I don't have to read body language to know when someone isn't telling me the truth, at least not the whole truth, so-help-you-God kinda truth. Well, whatever it is, I hope it's worth it."

Tony didn't respond and Maggie let it go. Finally, he broke the silence. "Maggie, can I ask you a medical-type question?"

"Sure. I'll do my best."

"Do dead people bleed?"

"Well, that's an easy one. Dead people do not bleed. You have to have a beating heart to bleed. Why do you ask?"

"Just curious," Tony replied. "Something someone said to me a while back. Seems obvious now that you answered it."

"Nothin' is obvious if you don't know it," responded Maggie, pulling into a parking spot. She pulled a badge from her glove box and dropped it into her purse.

"What, don't rate your own parking pass?" teased Tony.

"Nope, there's a waiting list. Sometimes it takes years, so I don't expect a reserved parking spot anytime soon."

"And here I thought nurses existed to protect us from the doctors," he said and chuckled.

Maggie exited the car and headed for the nearest building, a huge white block-looking structure that sprawled across a skyway and connected to the tan-colored main hospital.

As they passed by the Eternal Flame monument and signage for Doernbecher OHSU, Tony asked, "Why are we going this way?"

"I'm stopping to visit Lindsay, that's why," Maggie muttered under her breath.

He knew better than to argue. She was his warden.

Two statues guarded the front entrance to Doernbecher

Children's Hospital, one of a dog balancing stones and another that looked like a cat and monkey perched on the head of a goat, a touch of humor at the introduction of what easily could be a grim place.

"Believe it or not, Tony," Maggie whispered, "as hard as moments can be here, this is one of the most uplifting and wonderful places I have ever worked. Best job I ever had."

"I'll take your word for it," he commented. He was surprised to see how open and airy the hospital lobby was, well lit and clean, children's playhouses on the left and even a Starbucks with its requisite line of thirsty addicts. Entering a full elevator, Maggie pressed the button for the tenth floor.

"Ten South, Pediatric Oncology," she announced to Tony, before realizing how it would look. A few glances and smiles in her direction and an uneasy quiet dominated the rest of the upward trip, the occupants seeming to exit as quickly as possible.

They emerged at Seahorse, each floor and area named for various animals and creatures. Passing by Intermediate Care, non-Oncology, they entered Sand Dollar, the clinic area, and then on to Hematology/Oncology, Starfish. Just before entering, Maggie whispered, "These are my friends. Play nice."

"Aye, aye," responded Tony. "Maggie," he said, his tone changed, "thank you!"

"Welcome," Maggie grunted and pushed open the door.

"Maggie!"

"Hey, Misty!"

Maggie made her way to the corner of the reception counter to be met and hugged by a taller brunette. She was careful not to kiss as was her custom. Things were complicated enough.

"Are you on today?"

"Nope, just stopping by to check in on Lindsay."

Various others in conversation, on telephones or otherwise preoccupied, still waved, smiled, or nodded their greetings.

"You might check with Heidi; she was just with her a few minutes ago. I've been busy directing traffic, same ol', same ol'. Oh, here she comes anyway."

Maggie turned again to be quickly embraced by a pert blonde with an easy smile. "Hey, Maggs, you here to see Lindsay?"

Maggie nodded and Heidi continued, "She played for a couple of hours today and wore herself out pretty good. Don't be surprised if she's sleeping by the time you get back to her room. Fighter, that one, and so adorable. I'd take her home if they'd let me."

"I'd love to take her home," agreed Maggie. Tony could feel the tug in her heart. "I'll just pop in and sit with her a couple minutes. I'm actually on my way over to Neuro."

"Anything I should be concerned about?" asked Heidi, raising her eyebrows.

"You sick?" Misty asked from around the corner.

"Oh, nah, just got another... friend over there. Makin' the rounds today."

"Gotcha," responded Heidi. "I've got to get back to rounds, too." Another hug. "Maggie, lots of us praying for Lindsay, just so you know."

"Thanks, darlin'," responded Maggie. "That is the best gift you can give us right now."

Tony hadn't spoken, absorbed in the emotions and tender flow of conversation. Maggie knew her way around here, and they soon headed down the hall toward room 9.

"Your friends are sweet," offered Tony, "and cute!"

"Ha!" Maggie chuckled under her breath. "The folks here are the best, but don't let those two fool you. The Pineapple Princess, that would be Misty, is this floor's guard dog, and if you try and sneak a sniffle past her HEPA filtering, she will take your head off and make you leave it at the reception desk so you don't contaminate anyone else. And don't trifle with the Chambermaid either; when they say blonde bombshell around here, the emphasis is on 'bomb.'" She laughed quietly again before adding, "And when you get well, don't you go hittin' on my friends. I googled you. Your rep with the women, not so complimentary."

They arrived and Maggie quietly opened the door, slipping inside. A fragile little girl lay fast asleep on the Sketcher bed, partially propped up for comfort, her bald head only adding to an aura of childlike beauty and innocence. One arm was wrapped around a stuffed dinosaur, a stegosaurus, judging by the dominant spiny protrusions from its back. She lay only half under her blanket, an adolescent gangly leg dangling over the near edge. Soft and gentle but labored breathing provided a rhythm to the room.

It was almost too much for Tony. He hadn't allowed himself this near a children's hospital room, since... It had been many years. He could feel himself withdrawing and fought it. Along with his own emotions came a mix of Maggie's deep and ferocious affection for this teenager, and it joined the battle within him. Slowly, she won. As if her compassion had grabbed his arm as he was going out the door and wouldn't let go, he looked again. He listened. He breathed in. All so terribly familiar.

"Not fair," he whispered, even though only she could hear him.

"True that," she whispered so as not to stir the sleeping child.

He hesitated to ask, knowing that the more information, the more personal the connection, and that could create a conflict of interest. He asked anyway.

"You said she was diagnosed with…?"

"AML, acute myelogenous leukemia."

"That's treatable, right?" he asked hopefully.

"Almost everything is treatable; problem is she is positive for Philadelphia chromosome, and that makes it all much more dicey."

"Philadelphia chromosome? What's that?"

"It's where one part of one chromosome becomes part of another. Let me try and explain it this way; Lindsay is sleeping here in room 9 and Philadelphia chromosome involves chromosome 9. It's like a bunch of furniture was taken out of room 22, crammed into room 9 and only some of the stuff from chromosome 9 gets put into room 22 and none of it belongs where it ends up. And here's an irony. If Lindsay had Down syndrome like Cabby, her chances would be better. Some things in this life just don't make any sense. The more you stare at them, the less sense they make."

"Prognosis?" he finally asked, not sure he actually wanted to know. Knowledge has its own burden, but perhaps sharing the burden might make it lighter for everyone.

"With bone marrow transplant, chemo, and such, about 50 percent, but the Philadelphia issue reduces the probability of recovery by quite a bit. On top of that, Lindsay's father was mixed race, which makes a match more difficult, and now he's nowhere to be found. They're talking about looking at a cord blood transplant, but that has its own set of challenges. Bottom line, we need a miracle."

They sat in silence, Maggie watching this child as though she were her own, silently praying, while Tony struggled with the dilemma that faced him. This hospital had many

Lindsays, and each one of them was the center of someone's life. How could he heal just one of them? Wouldn't it be better if he healed himself? He had connections and access to wealth that could really make a difference, in many lives, not just one. Look at everything that had changed for him, in him. Would Grandmother be angry if he made the choice for himself? She would understand.

It was a tug-of-war. He would almost succeed in stanching his ebbing resolve but then would watch this little human person, a lifetime of potential experiences in front of her cut short by a feud within her own body. There was no question what he would have done for his own son, but... this was not his child.

"Can we go?" he whispered.

"Yes." Maggie sounded tired and resigned. She stood and walked over to the girl, laying her hands gently on her head. "Dear Jesus, I have no power to fix my love, so I am asking you again for a miracle. Please heal her! But even if you choose to heal her by letting her go home to you, I trust you, I do." She leaned forward to kiss her.

"Don't!" Tony warned, and Maggie stopped, then turned and touched her cheek as light as a feather to Lindsay's bald and beautiful head.

ʁ ∞ 🐦 ⚡ ∞ ❋ ⑤ 🜛

They exited Hematology/Oncology and headed toward the elevators that would take them down a floor to the ninth, which connected the different complexes housing OHSU, Doernbecher, and the Portland VA Medical Center. From the sky-bridge walkway they could see the spiderweb structure of the tram that routinely delivered staff, patients, and visitors to and from down below off Macadam Avenue by the river.

Entering the OHSU complex, Maggie again went directly to the bank of elevators and pushed the Down button.

"Thank you, Tony," she mumbled, barely audible but clear and distinct to him. "I just needed to see her today."

"No problem," he responded. "She is precious."

"You have no idea," she stated. Maggie was right, but he did have a sense of it.

They exited on seven, walked past Trauma ICU, through the waiting area, down another hall and took a left toward Neuroscience ICU across the way from Intermediate Care. Maggie picked up the phone and informed the receptionist on the other side of the locked doors that she was there to visit Anthony Spencer. The doors swung open and she went directly to the receptionist.

"My name is Maggie Saunders and I am coming to visit Anthony Spencer."

"Don't I know you?" The young woman smiled. "You look familiar."

"Oh, you've probably just seen me around the buildings. I'm over at Doernbecher Hematology/Oncology."

"Yeah, that's probably it," she said and nodded, checking her computer screen. "Let's see, Maggie Saunders; yup, got you on the list. Not a relative, are you?"

"What was your first clue?" They both grinned. "But I've gotten to know him fairly well." She almost slipped and added, "Since he's been in a coma," but luckily caught herself. "His brother put me on the list."

"That would be Jacob Spencer?" Maggie nodded and she continued, "You know only two at a time in there, right?"

"Of course," responded Maggie. "But there probably isn't a line to get in." It came out a wee bit sarcastic, but she was nervous. The receptionist consulted her screen again.

"Actually, you are the fourth person on the list," she said and smiled again.

"The fourth?" queried Tony, surprised. "Who are the others?"

"The others would be the family, then?" offered Maggie.

"Yes, the list says Jacob Spencer, Loree Spencer, Angela Spencer, and then you, but no one is with him now. He's in room 17, if you want to go ahead and go back."

"Thank you," said Maggie, relieved, and turned to leave.

"Crap!" uttered Tony, his thoughts awhirl.

"Shush!" muttered Maggie under her breath. "We can talk about this in a minute."

They entered a well-lit room, the center of its focus a bed on which a man was hooked to a myriad of machines. The whoosh of a ventilator rhythmically signaled his breathing. Maggie walked over and positioned herself in a spot where she knew Tony could plainly see himself.

"I look terrible!" he exclaimed.

"Well, you are almost dead," chided Maggie, scanning the machines. "And by the looks of things, there isn't much activity in the attic either."

Tony ignored her, his thoughts still in turmoil.

"I can't believe my ex is here and Angela!"

"The Loree on the list, that's your ex-wife? How long were you married to her? And who's Angela?"

"Yeah, Loree's my ex-wife. She lives on the East Coast, and our daughter, Angela, lives near her, mostly to be away from me, I think, and how long were we married…uh, which time?"

"What do you mean, 'which time'? You were married

to her more than once?" Maggie couldn't believe it and put her hand over her mouth to keep from laughing out loud. "How come you never told me any of this?" She was talking through her cupped hand.

"Well," Tony began but hesitated, not sure how to answer in a way that wouldn't elicit a new barrage of questions. "It's true. I've been married twice in my life, both times to the same woman, and I'm rather ashamed of myself for the way I treated her and so... I haven't exactly been wanting to talk about it."

"And Angela? Your daughter?"

"I was a terrible father. The physical presence of a man in the house does not disprove the absence of the father. I was gone, in one sense or other, her whole life."

"Does she know?"

"Does who know what?"

"Your ex. Does she know that you feel bad; does she know?"

"I doubt it. I never told her. I didn't understand all that I had done and what an absolute ass... You know... and you've only had to put up with a bit of my less-than-admirable character... Sorry for that, by the way..."

"Tony," she replied, "I've never met anyone that was *all* bad. Mostly bad, yes, but never all bad. Everyone was once a child, and that gives me hope for people. They just end up bringing to the table what they have and they do what they do for a reason, even if they don't know themselves what it is. Takes time to find it sometimes, but there is always a reason."

"Yeah, I'm finding out about some of that," he stated. Maggie was kind not to pursue it further, and they watched and listened for a few moments, each lost in personal thoughts.

Maggie broke the silence. "So then...their visit is a surprise?"

"Everything is a surprise," he grunted. "I suppose you like surprises, too?"

"Hey, don't knock surprises. They remind you that you're not God."

"That's funny!" he responded. "Remind me sometime to tell you about a conversation I had...Never mind." She waited.

"Yeah, until Clarence told us, I had no idea Jake was even in this part of the country. Last I heard he was in Colorado someplace. Loree and Angela hate my guts, so them being here makes no sense, unless"—he paused, thinking through another option—"unless they all think I'm dying and are here to get in on the will."

"Well, that's rather harsh and a little paranoid, don't you think? They can't be here because they might actually care about you?"

Silence. He hadn't considered that.

"Tony? Don't you go off and leave me here!"

The conversation had taken Tony down a mental path that had been absolutely obscured in the events of recent days, and he was dumfounded. "Oh no!" he exclaimed, almost panic in his voice.

"Tony, hush!" He was so loud that Maggie was concerned others might actually hear him. "What's going on? What's happening?"

"It's my will!" If he could have started pacing, he would have. "Maggie, I changed my will just before the whole coma thing. I totally forgot about it until now. I can't believe it! What have I done?"

Maggie heard alarm in his tone. "Shush, Tony, calm

down. So you changed your will, what's the big deal? It's your will."

"Oh, Maggie, you don't understand. I was being a total jerk; I was paranoid and thought everyone was out to get me, had too much to drink, and I..."

"You what?"

"Maggie, you gotta understand, I wasn't in my right mind."

"And you are now?" She almost laughed out loud at the irony but controlled herself for Tony's sake. "So what did you do that's got your gig in a whirly?"

"I gave everything to cats!"

"You what?!" Maggie couldn't believe what she was hearing.

"Cats!" Tony confessed. "I made out a new will and gave it all to a charity for cats. I just googled it and it popped up first."

"Cats?" Maggie repeated, shaking her head. "Why cats?"

"Dumb reasons. I've always had an affinity for cats; you know, they are master manipulators and I identified with them. But the main reason was sheer spite. Loree hates them. It was going to be my way of giving everyone the finger from the other side of the grave. Not that I believed I would even know, but I thought it would let me die with a sense of satisfaction."

"Tony, I like cats, but that is still the stupidest thing I have ever heard and one of the meanest, cruelest things I could ever even imagine."

"Yeah, I know that now, believe me. I'm not now who I was, but..." He moaned. "I can't believe this. What a terrible mess I've made of everything."

"So Tony...," began Maggie, controlling her instinct

to just rage against this man. "Why are we really up here today? Why did you want to come here? It's not about just wanting to see your pretty face, is it?"

Tony wasn't sure about healing himself anymore. He wasn't sure he wanted this ability to decide that a sick person would live. Who was he to make a decision of this magnitude, even on his own behalf? Now that he was actually here, Tony realized that he hadn't thought this through. Jesus and Grandmother had told him he could heal anyone, but this gift was complicated and starting to feel like a curse. Face-to-face with the choice, he was lost. Images of televangelist healers and movie carnival showmen came to mind. How exactly do you heal someone? He hadn't thought to ask.

"Tony!" demanded Maggie.

"Sorry, Maggie. I'm trying to figure something out. Would you put your hand on my forehead?"

"Your forehead? How 'bout if I just kiss you and send you back to where you came from?" threatened Maggie.

"I probably deserve that, but would you please just do this?"

Without hesitation Maggie reached out and put her hand on Tony's forehead. Then she waited.

"Jesus!" he exclaimed, not knowing what to do. It seemed the choice was obvious. He had to live. He had to fix some things, not the least of which was his will.

"Is that a prayer or an exclamation?" asked Maggie.

"Probably a little of both," admitted Tony. He decided to make the hard choice and let her in. "Maggie, I am in the middle of a dilemma. I have been trying to work through a decision, and I don't know what to do."

"Mmm-hmm, let's hear it."

"Maggie, God told me that I could heal one person and

I came up here to heal myself. But I'm not sure it's the right deci—"

"What?!" Maggie pulled her hand off Tony's forehead as if she had been stung.

"I know, I know," Tony began, trying to find the words to explain himself.

There was a tap on the door and a woman in scrubs opened it quietly, peeking inside. She looked around as if expecting more than one visitor. Maggie, still in shock, was frozen with her hand raised above Tony's head, not a sight that eased the woman's concern.

"Is everything"—the nurse paused, one eyebrow raised in question—"all right?"

Maggie lowered her hand as calmly and naturally as possible.

"Absolutely! Everything is absolutely fine; we are all good here." Maggie smiled her best and took a step away from the bed, which seemed to slightly settle the disquiet. "We…" She paused to clear her throat. "I was here visiting my good friend, and you probably heard me…uh…praying for him?"

"We are now 'good' friends?" Tony couldn't help himself.

The nurse scanned the room a second time, making sure that everything was in its place, then smiled an I-feel-kinda-sorry-for-you sort of smile and nodded. "Well, are you almost done? There are some others who want to come in, and I'd like to tell them how soon."

"Oh," exclaimed Maggie, "I am finished here!"

"No, we're not!" interjected Tony.

"Yes, we are," Maggie retorted and then corrected herself apologetically to the nurse. "I mean, we…God and I, we are done with what he sent me to do. Prayers, you know, can be prayed anywhere anyway, so if there are others waiting, why don't I just go ahead and slip by you here so the others can have a visit. I'll just come back another time."

The nurse held the door for a moment as if deciding what to do, but acquiesced, opening it to let Maggie out.

Once past her, Maggie whispered through gritted teeth, "God forgive me, I just lied about praying."

"Ma'am?" It was Nurse Eagle Ears and she was silently walking behind Maggie, ostensibly to keep everyone else safe from this strange woman. Maggie rolled her eyes and turned to smile again at the woman.

"Praying…just praying," she offered in a whisper. "Habit. Well, thank you for all your help; I'll be going now."

She turned and began walking toward the entry reception area where the check-in staffer was talking to a couple, an attractive woman dressed in a formfitting suit and a man in the common northwestern look of jeans with layered fleece and windbreaker. Maggie was the topic of conversation as they were pointing in her direction.

"I can't believe it!" began Tony, apprehension evident in his voice. "That's Loree and that's Jake with her. It's been years since I've seen either of them. What are we going to do?"

"Maggie? Are you Maggie?" It was Jake moving toward her and enveloping Maggie in a tender hug. "I am so glad that I got a chance to meet you," he said as he stepped back and smiled.

It was an authentic and tender smile and Maggie responded easily. "Jake, so wonderful to meet you." She turned to the striking woman who had just joined them. "And you must be Loree. I must say…if Tony knew you had come to visit him, I am sure it would have been a big…and wonderful surprise."

"Puh-lease," groaned Tony.

Loree took Maggie's hand in both of hers and shook it gently, as if communicating gratitude.

Maggie instantly liked them both, Tony could tell.

"I'm doomed," he grumbled. Maggie ignored him.

"Well, you are probably right about that! The surprise part…" Loree laughed, her face bright and alive. "The only conversations we've had over the past few years have been through attorneys, which probably at least kept the dialogue civil. I'm sure he has told you some horror stories about me."

"Actually, he didn't," disclosed Maggie. "He isn't much for talking about family or personal stuff." She noticed Jake look down at the floor and quickly added, "I do know that lately he's been trying to change. He told me what a horrible person he's been, pushing everyone away, how badly he has treated people…"

"Okay," piped up Tony, "I think they get the idea."

Maggie continued, "Actually, as I think about it, maybe the brain tumor was partly responsible for him being such a jerk. I'm a nurse and know a little about all that. It can do strange things to a person's sense of self and others."

"If that were true," Loree said, a little sadness in the corners of her eyes, "then he had a tumor for a lot of years. No, actually I think it had much more to do with losing Gabriel."

"Gabriel?" asked Maggie.

A look of startled concern crossed Loree's face, followed by a shadow of resignation. "Oh, Tony didn't tell you about Gabe. I shouldn't be surprised really. That was a subject that 'never' was allowed."

"I'm sorry," Maggie said and reached out and took Loree's elbow. "No, I don't know anything about him, and if it's personal, please don't feel like you need to tell me."

"No, you should probably know. It was the most difficult

time of my life, our lives. Over time it has become something precious to me, but for Tony, I just think it was an abyss that he could never climb out of."

One tear made its way down her cheek, and she quickly brushed it away. "Gabe was our firstborn child, and he was the light of Tony's life. He had been complaining of stomach pains and had been throwing up, so the day after his fifth birthday we took him to the doctor, who decided to do some imaging and they found tumors in his liver. Turned out to be a rare hepatic cancer, hepatoblastoma. The tumors had already metastasized so there wasn't much that could be done, except wait and watch him fade away. It was awful, really, but you're a nurse, you know how it is."

"I do, honey," Maggie replied and took her into her arms. "I work in pediatric oncology, so I do. I am so sad with you."

Loree stood there a moment before stepping back, pulling a packet of tissues from her purse to wipe her eyes. She continued, "Anyway, I think Tony blamed himself, as silly as that seems now. Then he blamed me. Gabriel was born with low birth weight, which they think is sometimes a contributor and somehow that was my fault, and then he blamed the doctors and God, of course. So did I, for a while, blame God. But I discovered that when you blame God for evil, there is no one left to trust, and I couldn't live that way."

"Yeah." Maggie nodded understandingly. "I found that out, too. You can't trust someone who you don't believe loves you."

"Well," Loree said, taking a deep breath, "Tony and I had a horrible divorce, two of them actually, but I still remember the man I first fell in love with despite everything, so Angela and I caught the first flight out. It's been really hard on her, as you can imagine."

"Angela?"

"Yeah, her last conversation with her dad was a screaming match, and she told him that she wished he was dead. That was a phone call on his last trip east, just before he collapsed. She's actually out in the waiting room, but when we got up here, she decided she didn't want to see him yet. Maybe later."

"I am so sorry," Maggie offered. "If there is anything I can do, please let me know." She turned to Jake, who had been silently listening, a rough exterior of a hard life covering a tenderness of heart. "Jake, you do have my number, right?"

"I don't but would love to have it." They quickly exchanged information. "I'm living at a halfway house until I get my feet fully under me. Been there a few months, but I have a steady job now and hope to get my own place pretty soon. Loree rented a phone for me so that I can be reached easier."

"Thank you, Jake. I don't know much about your relationship with your brother, but I know enough to sense that he really cares for you."

He grinned broadly. "Thank you for that, Maggie; that means a lot to me. Tony was the winner, I was the loser, and for a while the distance just got wider. Coming back has been a long road for me and I just wish"—tears fought to the surface, hung for a moment, and then spilled over—"just wish he had known how hard I've been working at it. I think he might even have been proud." He quickly wiped his eyes. "Sorry," he said with a grin. "Been doing that a lot lately. For me it's a sign of healing."

Maggie again hugged him, breathing in a distant air of nicotine and cheap cologne. It didn't matter. This man had substance.

"Maggie?" asked Jake. "I need to ask you something. We've been talking to the doctors and people here, and do you know if Tony had a Do Not Resuscitate signed? They told us that he isn't in the POLST Registry, so we are wondering if he might have just had the form at his office or somewhere."

"A DNR? I don't know," Maggie replied, then added quickly, "but I might be able to find out if he did. He might also have a medical power of attorney somewhere, too. I'll see what I can dig up and let you know, okay?"

"That would be great. They are telling us that it's not looking too good."

"Well, you two go in and see him. We can all keep praying for a miracle until a decision has to be made."

They both thanked her and headed in the direction of his ICU room.

"You got anything to say?" Maggie grunted under her breath.

"No, I don't." The voice was husky and broken, and Maggie softened. They walked out and into the waiting room. Maggie stopped to survey the people, occupied in conversation or with magazines.

"That's her," stated Tony, still very subdued. "The beautiful brunette in the corner texting. I did think about trying to make it right, but I was usually drunk at the time and never followed through. Now I don't know what to say"—his voice again broke—"to her, or anyone anymore."

"Then Tony, you just sit tight and listen."

Maggie walked to the corner where a red-eyed but striking young woman sat working her fingers over her phone. She looked up, cocked her head to one side, and asked, "Yes?"

"Hi, my name is Maggie Saunders, and I work here at OHSU as a nurse. You are Angela Spencer, right?"

The young woman nodded. "Well, Ms. Spencer, I not only work here, but I also know your father personally."

"You do?" Angela sat up and dropped her phone into her purse. "How do you know my dad?"

Maggie hadn't prepared for this. "Well, we met at church."

"Wait!" Angela's head snapped back in surprise. "My dad? You met my dad at church? Are you sure we're talking about the same guy?"

"Yes, your dad is Anthony Spencer, right?"

"Yes, but..." She gave Maggie a once-over. "You don't seem, you know, his type."

Maggie laughed. "What, you mean slim, petite, and know my place?"

Angela grinned back. "No, sorry, I just meant...you sort of caught me off guard."

Maggie chuckled and sat down next to Angela. "Just so you know, your father and I are not an 'item,' just friends who ran into each other not long ago at church."

"I still can't believe my dad would ever go to a church. He has rather an unresolved history with religious places."

"Well, maybe that's why we connected. I got a little of that, too. Doesn't mean there isn't some real life and value there, but it sometimes gets a little lost behind all the order and politics and job security and stuff."

"I know what you mean," responded Angela.

"Ms. Spencer...," Maggie began.

"Please, call me Angela," encouraged the other with a smile.

"And I'm Maggie, great to meet you." They shook hands as if formally being introduced. "So, Angela, I was talking to your mom and she told me you and your dad are sort of on the outs right now."

Angela dropped her gaze, working to control her emotions. She looked back and into Maggie's eyes. "Yeah, did she tell you what I said to him the last time we talked? I was screaming actually. I told him that I wished he was dead and then a few days later we find out that he's in a coma and might die and I can't tell him that I'm sorry, and..."

Maggie put her hand on the girl's shoulder and handed her a tissue from her own purse, which Angela gratefully accepted. "Listen to me, Angela. This wasn't your fault. I probably don't need to say that, but I just wanted you to hear it out loud. It's all about timing, and we don't have any control of that. You can still tell him."

Angela looked up again. "What do you mean?"

I'm a nurse and I have seen lots of things, including people in comas who I know were able to hear what was going on. You can still tell him whatever you want to, and I believe he will hear you."

"You really think so?" There was a glimmer of hope and light in her eyes.

"I do," Maggie stated emphatically, "and if you need someone to be in there with you, I gave my contact info to Jake. Just call me and I'll come any time, day or night."

"Thank you, Maggie." Angela's tears flowed easily. "I don't even know you, but I am so thankful that you were here. I needed to hear this. I was afraid..."

Maggie enfolded Angela in her arms and Tony wept inside Maggie, his face pressed against the window of light through which he saw but could not be seen, his hands trying to reach his daughter who cried, so close but so far away. He sobbed for all the losses to which he couldn't even begin to speak, for all the damage he had done. The regret was crushing, but he embraced it.

"Forgive me." His words barely found voice, and he was gone.

15

NAOS

Our hearts of stone become hearts of flesh when
we learn where the outcast weeps.
—Brennan Manning

Tony found himself back near the encampment by the far wall where the battle had so recently been fought. He stood again at the point where the trail branched in two directions: one down to the left toward the group of buildings that had housed his inner lies; the other to the right, which led to the block building referred to as a temple.

He felt spent, as if the last of his energy were being drawn from his body by the events and emotions that still swirled about. The words *forgive me* still lingered on his lips and rang true to his heart. A feeling of loneliness blew like a wayward wind across his face. The liars may have been bad company, but at least they had been company. Perhaps true change increased the space in one's heart, creating openness that allowed for authentic community. Within all the regret and loss there blew a hint of expectancy, an anticipation of something more and coming.

But there still remained this place down the path to the right. He could make it out in the distance, like a block of granite sewn into the wall. If it had not been for the clearly carved and crafted edges, it could have been mistaken for a massive boulder that had fallen from higher in the edifice.

A temple? What would he have to do with a temple? Why would this place have any significance? He knew he was being drawn there; he could almost hear the beckoning of a promise. But there was more. Within the weaving of anticipation there was a thread of dread, of something not right, an uneasiness that seemed to have locked his feet in place and wouldn't let them loose.

Could this be the temple of God? The Father God? Probably not, he surmised. Grandmother had said something about God being outside the walls. This structure was inside the walls. He couldn't imagine God would want to live in a place like this, no windows or even doors visible on the exterior.

He knew he was stalling, as if continuing to ask questions was a reasonable substitute for experiencing what lay ahead. As Grandmother would say, "It was time." She and Jesus were undoubtedly here, but he now knew it was his own limitations that clouded his ability to see them.

"Have I got some questions for you," he muttered and then grinned to himself. Prayer, it seemed, was simply a conversation inside a relationship.

As Tony took the path to the right, a small lizard scuttled away between the rocks. It soon became evident he was traversing an old dried riverbed. Once deep waters had flowed through this place, and various spots were visibly muddy from moisture that still existed somewhere below his feet. The river would have traveled directly through the temple and run into the wall on its far side. Each step became increasingly difficult as the soft sand grabbed at his boots. The final hundred yards were painfully arduous, and his breathing labored until he stopped and leaned over to recover.

The physical exertion was not the worst. It was the emotional turmoil that accompanied each step. Everything in him screamed go back. Expectancy that had marked the start of the walk dissipated like vapor into a whirlwind of dust that now rose from the riverbed to obfuscate his vision.

A storm was howling by the time he finally reached the nearest wall of the temple. He was desperate to find something on its surface to cling to against the rising onslaught of breathtaking fury, but it was smooth and slippery as glass and he had to turn and lean into the wall to protect himself. As far as he could see and feel, there was no door, no way in. He was stymied.

Tony was certain of only one thing—he was supposed to be here. One of those fiends had said that this was where he worshipped, that he had built this place. If that was true, then he must know how to gain entrance. Bracing himself against the squall, he sheltered his face in the crook of his arm and tried to concentrate in spite of the stinging sand. Where in his inner world would a place like this exist? A place of worship! What was a place of worship? It had to be something that he had placed at the center of his life. Success? No, too intangible. Power? Again, not satisfying or essential.

"Jesus, please help me," he breathed. Whether an answer to his prayer or not, a thought instantly occurred to him. It was like the stillness of morning breaking in the distance and gradually unfolding, but with its clarity came deepening despair. In a moment he knew what this place was. It was the hungering weight at the very core of his existence. It was a tomb, a sepulchre, a grave memorializing the dead.

He lifted his face and pressed it against the wall, his sorrow spilling like a river from his deepest and most precious place. He put his lips against the smooth cold stone, kissed it, and whispered, "Gabriel!"

Lightning struck next to him, shattering the wall like brittle glass and knocking him off his feet, but the concussion had exhumed the entrance to a corridor and he crawled deeper into the darkness. Inside, the tempest evaporated quicker than it had risen. Standing easily, he groped along one wall, sliding his feet carefully for fear of empty space and falling. A couple of turns and only a short distance later he was at a gate. It had a latch similar to another he had felt days before upon his arrival at his soul's gate.

This door, too, opened without a sound, and as he entered he had to look away until his eyes adjusted to the light flooding the space.

Tony stood at the end of what appeared to be a small cathedral, its construction stunning, ornamented yet simple. Filtered rays captured dust and particles around its beams, lighting them afire and spreading them as if caught in a breath. But the odor clashed with the glory of the place, the smell antiseptic and sterile.

There were no chairs or pews, just empty space and a distant altar bathed in light so bright he could not make out details. He took a step and whispered, "I'm not alone." It echoed off the marble framing and floor. "I'm not alone," he stated loudly this time and began walking toward the brightness.

Suddenly he saw movement inside the light and froze, gripped in a terror of anticipation. "Gabriel?" He couldn't believe what he saw. What he had feared most and longed for deepest appeared in front of him. It was not an altar, but a hospital bed, surrounded by lights and equipment, and facing him was his five-year-old Gabriel. He ran toward the figure.

"Stop!" the boy commanded, a note of appeal resonating through the temple. "Daddy, you need to stop."

Tony did, ten feet from his son, who looked exactly like he remembered. His memory had frozen a healthy and vibrant son, at the beginning of his life's adventure, now standing only arm's lengths away and connected by tubes to a bed and attending machinery.

"Is it you? Gabriel, is this really you?" he pleaded, almost begging.

"Yes, Daddy, it's me, but you see me only as you remember me. You need to stop."

Tony was confused. It took everything in him not to rush and wrap this child in his arms. He was standing only feet away and Gabe was telling him to stop? It didn't make any sense. Panic began rising like a cresting flood.

"Gabriel, I can't lose you again. I can't!"

"Daddy, I'm not lost. It's you that's lost, not me."

"No," moaned Tony. "That can't be true. I had you. I had you in my arms and I was holding on to you, and you slipped away and there was nothing that I could do, and I'm so sorry." He dropped to his knees and buried his face in his hands. "Maybe," he began as he looked up, "maybe I can heal you. Maybe God can take me back in time and I can heal you…"

"Daddy, don't."

"But don't you see, Gabe, if God can take me outside of time and back to you and I could heal you and then my life wouldn't be such a wreck…"

"Daddy." Gabriel's tone was gentle but firm.

"And then I wouldn't have hurt your mom so much and been so hard on your sister, if only you…"

"Daddy." The voice was stronger.

"If only you hadn't...died. Why did you have to die? You were so small and weak and I tried to do everything I knew how. Gabriel, I told God to take me instead of you, but he didn't. I wasn't good enough. I'm so sorry, son."

"Daddy, stop!" commanded Gabriel. Tony looked up and tears were streaming down his son's face, a look of utter love for him written clearly on his features.

"Daddy, please, you've got to stop," whispered his son. "You've got to stop blaming yourself, blaming Mom, blaming God, blaming the world. Please, you have to let me go. You've kept me inside these walls with you for years, and it's time for us to leave."

"But Gabriel, I don't know how!" The lament came from the innermost deep, and it was the most honest cry of his heart. "How do I do that? How do I let you go? I don't want to, I don't..."

"Daddy, listen." And now Gabriel dropped to his own knees so he could look straight into the face of his father. "Listen, I don't exist here. You're the one who is stuck here, and it breaks my heart. It's time for you to leave, to be free, to let yourself feel again. It's okay, you know, to really laugh and enjoy life. It's okay."

"But how can I, Gabriel, without you? I don't know how to let go of you."

"Daddy, I can't explain it to you, but you are already with me; we are together. We aren't separated in the life-after. You are stuck in the broken part of the world, and it's time to be free."

"Then Gabriel," Tony said, pleading, "then why are you here? How come I can see you?"

"Because I asked Papa God for this gift, Daddy. I asked to be given the gift of coming here to help you put your pieces back together. I am here, Daddy, because I love you with all my heart, and I want you to be whole and be free."

"Oh, Gabriel, I am so sorry, to cause you more pain…"

"Stop, Daddy. Don't you understand? I am not sorry. I wanted to be here. This isn't about me, this is about you."

"So what am I supposed to do?" Tony could barely get the words out.

"You walk out of here, right through the walls you built, and you don't look back. You let yourself go, Daddy. Don't worry about me. I am better than you can imagine. I am a melody, too."

At that Tony laughed and wept. "Can I tell you," he said, struggling with the words, "that it's really good to see you? Is that okay if I tell you?"

"It's good to tell me, Daddy."

"And can I tell you that I love you and miss you terribly and there are times when all I can think about is you?"

"Yeah, that's good, too, but now it's time to tell me good-bye. It's good to tell me good-bye, too. It's time for you to go."

Tony climbed to his feet, tears still streaming. "You sound like Grandmother." He laughed in gasps.

Gabriel grinned and said, "I'll take that as a compliment." He shook his head. "If you only knew. It's okay, Daddy. I am good."

Tony stood looking at his five-year-old son for a minute. Finally, he took a deep breath and said, "Okay, good-bye, my son! I love you. Good-bye, my Gabriel."

"Good-bye, Daddy. I'll see you soon!"

Tony turned away, took a deep breath, and began walking toward the wall near where he had entered. With each step, the floor began to crack like stone striking crystal. He dared not look back, certain he would lose all resolve. The barrier in front of him shimmered, then turned translucent and then vanished altogether. He heard a rumble behind him and knew without looking that the temple was caving in on itself, that his soul was heaving with transformation. His steps were now sure and certain.

Tony looked up and saw a monstrous wall of water descending on him. It towered above him and he could do nothing except face it and wait for it to sweep him away. He stood and opened his arms wide. The river had returned.

16

A Piece of Pie

God enters by a private door, into every individual.
—Ralph Waldo Emerson

M aggie?"

"Hey!" squealed Maggie, dropping a cup of flour onto the kitchen counter. "Don't sneak up on me like that! You know you've been gone almost two days since you left me at the hospital with your daughter? Now look at the mess you made, scaring me half to death."

"Maggie?"

"What?"

"I'm really glad to see you. Maggie, have I told you lately how much I appreciate you? I am so grateful..."

"Tony, you okay? I don't know where you've been, but you're sounding a little sick, you know, not like yourself."

He laughed and it felt good. "Maybe, but it's the best I've ever been."

"Well, just so you know, the doctors might disagree with you. You are not doing so good. We need to talk. I'm going to make this apple pie while we figure things out. Lots has happened in the two days since you went AWOL, and we need to put together a plan."

"Apple pie? I love homemade apple pie. What's the occasion?"

Tony could tell that Maggie was trying not to grin, a unique combination of emotions rising inside her. "Oh, don't tell me. You're baking for the policeman, aren't you?"

She waved her hand and laughed. "Yup, he's heading over here after shift for a little dessert. We've been talking on the phone a lot since you left. He finds me"—she waved her hands like a debutante—"rather mysterious. Just so you know, if I end up kissing him, it will be by accident, and in the moment I will have forgotten about you. Just sayin'. I will truly try not to, but...you know."

"Great!" sighed Tony, wondering what it would be like to exist as a Ping-Pong ball bouncing between souls.

Maggie talked as she scraped the flour into the sink and then moved from place to place gathering essentials for her mother's apple pie. "I learned more about you in twenty minutes at the hospital than you told me in all the time you were around inside my head. I was really mad at you for a while, hurting your family like that. Your wife, your ex-wife, is a doll; and that daughter of yours, she's remarkable and despite everything she still loves you, behind all that fury. And Tony, I'm sorry about Gabriel, really sorry." She paused. "And what's with you and Jake? That's one piece I don't understand yet."

"Maggie, slow down," interrupted Tony. "I'll answer your questions at some point, but we need to talk about some other things first."

Maggie stopped her work and looked out the window. "You mean, like being able to heal someone? Tony, that burned me good, getting me to go up there, watching me love on my Lindsay just so you could get me to lay hands on your sorry…"

"Please forgive me for that, Maggie," entreated Tony. "But I didn't know what else to do, and I thought that if I could just get well I could help a lot of people and maybe even rebuild some of the damage I've caused. I know it was totally selfish—"

"Tony, stop!" She held up her hand. "It was me that was being selfish, thinking only about what was hurting in my life, what I wanted to have fixed. Not many years ago I lost some precious people in my life, and I just didn't want to lose another one. I have no right to expect you to use your gift to heal Lindsay. I was wrong, so please forgive me?"

"Uh, forgive you?" Tony was surprised and strangely comforted by her request.

"Yeah, we need to get up there, Tony, and pray the healing prayer over you before those machines run outta gas, and we need to do it sooner than later. Like I said, in the last couple days you've been slipping deeper and the doctors don't think you're coming back."

"I've been thinking a lot about this healing gift, Maggie—"

"Well, I'm sure you have. But you cannot leave your estate to cats!" She stopped fork-mixing her pie dough and picked up a wooden spoon. "Cats! Now that is one of the nuttiest things I have ever heard. A zebra maybe or a whale or those cute baby seals, but cats?" She shook her head. "Lord have mercy, givin' away hard-earned cash to cats."

"Yeah, pretty dumb," he agreed.

"Well, let's get you healed so you can fix that little dumbness." She was waving her spoon in the direction of the window as she spoke.

"I've been thinking, Maggie—"

"Tony, you have every right to heal yourself. God gave you that gift so God must trust you with it, and if you decide that healing yourself is the best way to go, I am here to support you 100 percent. Not my place to tell people how to run their lives. I already spend more than my share of energy just judging them...which," she continued as she waved her spoon again, now covered in flour and butter, "I am trying not to do so much, but it's a process, I know, and sometimes, I confess, I probably enjoy judging a little too much. I get feeling all superior and think there are certain people who could use a little judging and I just happen to be the one who might can do it best. See, Tony? We are all messes of one sort or another. I'm done with my preaching. What do you think?"

"You make me grin, that's what I think," answered Tony.

"Well, then my life is complete." Maggie chuckled. "Seriously, getting a wedding band from Clarence, then maybe my life would be complete, no offense."

"None taken." Tony laughed. "Maggie, I have an idea about how to fix the cat dumbness, but we're going to need some help. The fewer people the better, and I'm thinking Jake because I don't think we have a choice, and Clarence because he's a cop and he'll make sure we do it right."

"Tony, you're scaring me a bit. We pulling a heist or something? Those things never seem to go very well. I watch the movies."

"It's not a heist exactly."

"Exactly? I'm not feeling much better. Is it illegal?"

"Good question. Not sure, sorta gray I think. If I'm not dead yet, I don't think it's illegal."

"And you want to get my Clarence involved in all this?"

"It's the only way, Maggie."

"Honey, I don't want to get Clarence mixed up in this. I'd rather let the cats win."

"Maggie, we have to."

"You know I can walk outside and kiss some stray dog, or maybe a cat would be preferable, since you are so stupid for them."

"It's never really been about the cats, Maggie. It's about me. Please trust me on this. We need Clarence's help."

"Oh, Lord." Maggie lifted her face to the ceiling.

"Thanks, Maggie." Tony continued, "I have a couple issues that I still need to work out. The place we need to get into belongs to me, but no one knows it exists. I set it up for all my private stuff and the security is about as good as it gets. Problem is when the police tried to backtrace the cameras from my condo, my security logged everything off and reset the entry codes, and I can't get in without them."

"And why are you expecting any of this to make sense to me?" asked Maggie.

"Sorry. Just thinking out loud."

"Well, just don't forget, you thinking out loud is me thinking out loud, and right now what I'm thinking is that I'm confused."

"Okay, I have a secret place down by the river off Macadam Avenue, but the codes are all reset and there are only three places that I can get the new codes."

"So get them from one of those," suggested Maggie.

"It's a little more complicated than that. A letter with the new code goes to a bank for automatic deposit into a special holding account. That account can only be opened by authorization that is in a safety-deposit box. That box can only be opened if they have a certificate of death."

"Bummer!" she pointed out. "Not exactly a good option."

"Option two," he continued, "isn't much better. When a code resets like that, it generates automatically an express-mail letter that goes to Loree. She has no idea what it is or why it arrives; it just shows up with no explanation at all. It's sort of a backup of a backup. No one would think my ex-wife would have anything that mattered to me anyway."

"Wait!" Maggie interjected. "What does this code look like?"

"It's just a series of six one- or two-digit numbers, between one and ninety-nine, that are randomly generated," he explained.

"Like lottery numbers?" asked Maggie, washing her hands quickly in the sink.

"Yeah, I suppose so."

"Like these?" Maggie reached for her purse on the hallway hook and rummaged through it. Triumphantly, she produced an express-mail envelope and withdrew its contents. It was a single piece of paper containing six numbers, each in a different color.

"Maggie," Tony exclaimed, "that's it! How in the world did you..."

"From Loree! I went back up to the hospital to try and help her and Jake with potential arrangements, God rest your soul, and she handed this to me. She said it came just before they left to come here to see you and she stuffed it into her purse on the way out the door. The return address is for your office downtown, she said, but she thought it might mean something to me. I told her I had no idea, but she told me to keep it anyway. I was going to ask you about it, but it totally slipped my mind until you just mentioned it."

"Maggie, I could kiss you!" Tony yelled.

"Now that would be a little weird," she responded. "I wonder what would happen? So this is what you needed?"

"Yes! This is the entry code. Let me see the date stamp on the front. Yup, that's it. Wow, this'll save us a ton of time."

"You said there was a third way to get the codes?"

"Won't need that now. The code is sent electronically to a special keypad that is in my downtown office. Only I know the access code for that keypad, and I thought we might have to go visit the folks where I work under some pretense to sit at my desk. Given he's my brother, I was thinking that Jake might be allowed to be alone in there."

"Yeah, but that would have meant..."

"I know, you would have had to kiss him, and this all is pretty complicated already. Now we won't even have to involve Jake." He felt a rush of relief. "Which brings me to my second issue." He paused before asking, "What is your take on Jake?"

"Oh, you mean Jacob Aden Xavier Spencer, your brother?"

Tony was surprised, again. "How did you find out his full name?"

"Clarence pulled a sheet on him. He has a record, you know, not anything major, mostly breaking and entering to support a drug habit a bunch of years ago. Served a nickel in Texas..."

"Nickel? Who says 'nickel'?"

"Honey, you don't know my history either or my family heritage, so mind your p's and q's."

"My apologies. Please, go on," he encouraged, grinning again.

"Yesterday I spent a couple hours with Jake up at the hospital. He talked a lot about you. Don't know if you know this, but he worships the ground you walk on. He told me you were the only reason he's alive. You protected him growing up when everything went crazy. Then you got separated and he got in with a bad crowd, got hooked, and was too ashamed to contact you until he got clean. You are as close to any sense of father that he's ever known, and he is the loser brother, the failure, the addict."

Tony listened quietly, emotions again surfacing that he hadn't prepared for.

"Tony, he's clean. Got set up with NA and rehab and Jesus. He's been clean almost six years. Went back to school between part-time jobs and graduated with a degree from Warner Pacific College here in the city. He's been working for something called the Portland Leadership Foundation and saving money. Jake was waiting until he could afford his own place and trying to build up enough courage to contact you when the police called him. Tony, he cried. He wanted you to be proud of him, probably more than anything else in the world. He feels like he missed his chance to tell you. But we'll get you healed and he can tell you himself. He really needs to hear from you that he matters to you."

Tony waited in the silence, struggling to regain his composure. "So," he began, "Maggie, what I need to know is, do you trust him? Do you trust Jake? Do you think the changes in him are real?"

She could feel the weight of his questions, the sense of importance that he was giving them, and she thought carefully before speaking.

"I do, Tony. I do. Everything in me tells me that your brother is smart and solid, works hard, and I would trust him with Cabby and Lindsay, and that is saying everything, coming from me."

"That's all I needed to know, Maggie, 'cause I trust you, and if you trust Jake that is more than good enough for me. Thank you!"

She could hear in his voice that there was more to the

story but didn't push it. Tony would tell her when he was ready.

"It is an honor to be trusted, Tony."

"You are among the very first, for me," Tony added. "That means more than I can begin to tell you."

"Faith takes risk, Tony, and there is always risk in relationships, but bottom line? The world has no meaning apart from relationships. Some are just messier than others, some are seasonal, others are difficult, and a few are easy, but every one of them is important."

She slid her pie into the oven, doubled-checked the temperature, and turned to make a cup of tea.

"Just so you know, Tony, everybody has met everybody, your side and mine. Just thought you might like to know."

"Thank you, Maggie. Thanks for making that happen."

"You are welcome, Mr. Tony."

"Why'd you call me that...Mr. Tony?" he asked, surprised.

"Don't know," Maggie answered. "Just felt right. Why?"

"Nothing really. I met a little girl who called me that. It just reminded me of her, I guess."

"Children!" Maggie laughed. "They are able to sneak into places that we would never let others near."

"Isn't that the truth," agreed Tony.

While the pie baked the two bantered back and forth like an old married couple, the conversation light but meaningful.

Only moments after a perfect-looking apple pie was taken out of the oven, Molly and Cabby burst into the house, both in good spirits. Cabby rushed his Maggie-buddy and gave her a bear hug, then leaned into her heart and whispered, "Tah-ny...sun-dy!" and giggled before running down the hallway and into his room.

"That kid," commented Tony, "he's something else."

"Sure is," agreed Maggie. "What was that all about?"

"Just a conversation we had a while back. He knows when I'm here, you know?"

"That boy knows a lotta things."

Molly emerged from her bathroom, a smile on her face like the best colors of a sunset, and gave Maggie a big hug.

"Good news?" Maggie inquired.

"About Lindsay? Not really. Pretty much the same." She lowered her voice. "Is Tony here?"

Maggie nodded.

"Hey, Tony. Spent a bunch of time with your family today, especially Angela. We hit it off big-time, actually more like her and Cabby hit it off. She is an absolute gift, your girl."

"He says, 'Thank you,'" replied Maggie, even before Tony had said anything.

"And..." Molly grinned. "I am kinda liking getting to know your brother, Jake. He took me up to visit you today and I gotta say, Jake's the better looking of the two of you."

"He says it's because he's sick," Maggie translated.

"That must be it." Molly laughed as she opened the fridge to rummage for leftovers for her and Cabby.

"There's plenty of pie, Molly, for you and Cabby."

"Wonderful. We'll have it for dessert. I'll be right back. I promised Cabby that he could eat his supper in the backyard and I have it ready."

At that moment the doorbell rang, followed by three sharps raps. No one would have found it significant except Tony and it made him grin. It probably was neither Jack nor Jesus, he surmised.

It was Clarence, waiting with a warm smile and embrace for Maggie. The flood of contentment that enveloped her was enough to make Tony close his eyes for a moment and then breathe deeply. There was so much he had missed out on or lost because of his walls.

"I'm not kissin' you," whispered Maggie. "You know who's here."

Clarence laughed. "Well, you just let me know when he's gone and we'll make up for it."

"I've got you on speed dial," Maggie said and chuckled.

"Wow, what is that I smell?" exclaimed Clarence. "Fresh-baked apple pie, and it smells just like my momma used to make. You got any ice cream?"

"Of course, Tillamook 'nilla okay?"

"Perfect!" He sat at the table while Maggie prepared apple pie à la mode. "If I hang around you, I'm going to have to start working out double, but if it tastes like it smells, it'll be worth it."

Maggie handed him a dish with more than generous portions and a big spoon, and waited for him to take the first bite. Clarence was up to the challenge and responded in childlike delight. "Maggie, this is spectacular. I hate to admit it, but it might even be better than my momma's."

She beamed.

"You two are kinda makin' me sick," interjected Tony. "All this mushy-gushy...barf!"

Maggie grinned. "Tony says hi."

"Hey, Tony." Clarence, addressing Maggie, grinned back. He took another bite, chewing it more deliberately, savoring the flavors.

"Hi, Clarence." Molly returned from Cabby's picnic and gave the officer a hug, retrieving her plate from the counter and sitting down with the others. "What's going on?"

"Your timing is perfect," said Maggie, dishing up her own bowl of pie and ice cream. "We were just about to get into that."

Clarence turned again to Maggie and spoke in a more serious tone. "Tony I have a big favor to ask you."

"He says, 'Good,' 'cause he has a big favor to ask you, too."

"Maybe," Tony wondered aloud, "you should just kiss Clarence so that I can explain what I want without all the interpreting. Might make it easier."

"You kidding me?" retorted Maggie. "And leave me outta the loop? No way! As much as the idea of kissing Clarence appeals to me at the moment, I will wait, thank you. If you two are going to be scheming about stuff, I'm going to be in on it. Go ahead, Clarence."

Clarence began. "Tony, I really have no right to ask you what I am going to ask you, and I don't even know if it's in the realm of possibility, so before I tell you anything, please know that I don't have expectations that you will do this. The favor you want from me is in no way contingent on your doing anything for me. Are we clear?"

"He says, 'Crystal,' but you should probably wait and see what his favor is first."

"I don't really care what it is." Clarence continued, "If Maggie is in, I'm in." He paused again. "Is it illegal?"

"He doesn't think it is."

"He doesn't *think* it is?" interjected Molly.

"That's...comforting," sighed the officer. "So here is what I would like to ask, and again, you can say no and it will be okay."

The three watched as this strong man visibly struggled with his emotions, not anything that appeared usual or customary for him. Maggie reached over and took his nearest hand, which about did him in, but he found control somehow and after clearing his throat in a husky voice, continued.

"My mother has Alzheimer's. A few years ago we finally

had to move her to a home that provides round-the-clock care because we couldn't. It came on much faster than we had anticipated, than anyone anticipated, and I was across the country completing a training course when she lost touch with all of us."

"I'm really sorry, Clarence," offered Molly, reaching and taking his other hand.

He looked up, his eyes glistening. "I never had a last conversation with her, nothing. One day she knew who I was, and the next time I saw her there was nothing at all, just this emptiness in her eyes that I wanted to fill.

"Tony," he continued, "I can't stop thinking that if Maggie kissed her, you might be able to slide into her and find her for me and give her a message or something and let her know that we miss her, that I miss her. I know it sounds crazy, and I don't even know if it would work or..."

"He'll do it," announced Maggie.

"He will?" Clarence looked straight at Maggie, his face relaxing from the strain of emotion held back.

"Of course, he will," stated Molly. "You will, won't you, Tony?" She looked at Maggie.

"Yes, he'll do it," repeated Maggie. "But he's not sure if it will work. It's not like he's an expert at any of this."

"Tony, thank you for even considering it. I owe you big-time just for that."

"He says you don't owe him anything and that his request has no strings either. You can say no."

"Understood," replied Clarence.

"So," began Maggie, "let me try and put into words what Tony needs. He has this top secret spy office somewhere down by the river off Macadam Avenue. He's not a spy or anything, but he has this office no one knows about and some of his really important stuff is in there. Clarence, he wants to know if you know someone who does industrial shredding?" She raised her eyebrows as if to communicate, "Don't ask me, I'm only the messenger."

"Yeah, I got a good buddy named Kevin. He works for a big shredding company. I think they have the contract for the city, too. Why?"

"Some stuff needs to be destroyed—not accounting stuff or illegal stuff, just personal stuff," said Maggie for Tony. She stopped, then turned away slightly, as if speaking to herself. "Tony, why don't you just wait until you get better and then take care of it yourself?"

Concern showed on her face as she turned back to Clarence. "He says because he isn't absolutely certain that he's going to get better and he doesn't want to take any chances." She continued the translating. "Tony needs to get into his office. He has the codes and everything he needs to get what he wants out of there. He says that he needs you, Clarence, to make sure that we do it right without leaving any trace that we were there. You know how to do that?"

Clarence nodded.

"He says it's really very easy. Quick in and out. He has to open a safe that's in the floor and go through some of the documents. He'll make one pile to be shredded and grab maybe a couple other things and that will be all. Probably less than half an hour tops. No one will see us and no one can ever know we were there."

"Not illegal?" mused Clarence.

"He says nope, not as long as he's still alive. This is his place and he has all the codes, so it's not breaking and entering. He will be with us, and even though no one would believe you, you'll know he is with us."

Clarence thought for a moment

"Can you help us?"

Clarence nodded.

"Tony wants to know if we can do it this evening. Can we see your mom now?"

Again Clarence nodded, checking the kitchen clock. "We have plenty of time. I'll call ahead and make sure she's ready for us. Who all's coming?"

"I have to stay with Cabby, so I can't," stated Molly. "But I want to hear about everything, and I mean everything, that happens, okay?"

"I always tell you everything, darlin'. You take good care of Cabby while the three of us go play James Bond."

Clarence was already talking on his phone.

Maggie hugged Molly deeply and tenderly. "Tony says you have his blessing," she whispered.

"About what?" Molly asked.

"About his brother...if anything comes of it, you have his blessing."

Molly grinned. "You never know." She leaned back in. "Thank you, Tony, love you!"

Her words caught Tony by surprise, as did the emotions he felt in just hearing them. "Uh," he said, his voice thickening, "love you, too."

Maggie smiled. "He says he loves you, too."

17

LOCKED ROOMS

A person isn't who they are during the last conversation you had with them, they're who they've been throughout your whole relationship.
—Rainer Maria Rilke

Y our mother will be so glad to see you," the volunteer said, smiling as she led Maggie and Clarence down the hallway toward a private room.

Normally such a statement would have irritated Clarence, but not tonight. The anticipation was churning in his stomach, and the more real it became the more probable the disappointment. He wasn't sure how he would handle it. *Dear God,* he prayed silently, *you work in mysterious ways. Here's a perfect opportunity. Thank you for walking in this with me, and for Maggie, and especially, tonight, for Tony.*

"Clarence, you never told me about your father," said Maggie in a hushed voice.

"Good man. My dad passed about ten years ago. He was everything a father was supposed to be, but it was my mom who was the force in our world. His leaving wasn't as hard as this, this...whatever this is. He's gone, but she's stuck in between, and we can't get to her."

Tony listened. Clarence's use of "in between" made him smile, and he almost jumped into the flow of conversation but thought better and held his tongue. It wasn't the time.

Soft light filled the room they entered and an elderly elegant black woman sat dressed in comfortable reds and soft blacks. She was a handsome woman with high cheekbones and sparkling eyes that belied the absence of her presence within.

After the volunteer dismissed herself, Maggie reached up and kissed Clarence fully on the lips, lingering and tender. When you only had one kiss, you had to make it count. Tony slid back into a place he had briefly been before, ordered and spacious, and he was looking into Maggie's eyes, up close and personal.

"All right, enough already," he exclaimed. They both smiled as their lips parted.

Clarence walked to his mother and leaned down.

"Hello, Momma, it's Clarence. I'm your son."

"I'm sorry." She looked away, no recognition in her face. "Who are you?"

"Clarence, your son." And he leaned down and kissed her on her forehead. She smiled, and Tony slid a second time in as many minutes.

This place was different from anywhere he had been, the light somehow muted and visibility masked. He was now looking into Clarence's face, etched with hopeful anticipation.

"Mrs. Walker?" His voice echoed off invisible walls, as if he were enclosed in a metal cylinder. "Mrs. Walker?" He tried again, but nothing, just the reverberation of his own voice. Tony could see through Mrs. Walker's eyes that

Clarence had taken a seat next to Maggie and they were waiting. He had carefully rehearsed the message that Clarence had asked him to deliver, but no one was home to receive it.

He panicked as a question came to mind: How was he going to get out of here? He hadn't thought about that. No one had. Maybe he would be stuck here, how long? The rest of her life? Or maybe when his body was through fighting at OHSU, his soul would join it? Neither possibility was particularly pleasant. And he warred with a rising sense of claustrophobia. Maybe if Clarence kissed her he would return. He wasn't sure, but the uncertainty made him uneasy.

But being here was right. He could feel it. When Clarence had asked, he had known it was the right thing to do, and it still felt like a good decision. He calmed as he thought about it. When was the last time he had done something for someone else with no strings attached, no agenda? He couldn't remember. Maybe he was trapped, but he accepted it with a sense of satisfaction, maybe even contentment.

Then the little line-dance hop thingy Grandmother had demonstrated occurred to him. He tried it. Tony now faced a dark wall behind him. His eyes adjusted, and he could make out what appeared to be doors along a dim barrier. Without being able to see himself, as if in a barely lit room, he made his way to the first door. It opened without resistance. A blast of light caused him to look away until his vision adapted. When it did he stood at the edge of a field of ripening wheat that stretched away as far as he could see, grain heads dancing in the breeze to a rhythm known only to them. A path through the field was before him, stretching into the distance and disappearing near a grove of stately oak trees. It was wondrous and inviting, but he closed the door and was again plunged into inky blackness.

Suddenly he heard a voice softly humming. He cocked his head from one side to another, trying to determine the source. It was farther ahead in the direction he was facing and he began to feel his way along. Glancing back in the soft and hazy light, he could still see Maggie and Clarence, holding hands and waiting.

The voice was distinctly behind the third of multiple doors, complete with a familiar latch type that he recognized from his own heart. It made him smile to find it here. It swung open easily, and he entered a cavernous grand and open room. The mahogany and cherry walls were lined with shelves bursting with books. Memorabilia of all sorts, including photographs and art, cluttered the unoccupied spaces. The humming sounded closer and he made his way past another wall of protruding shelving until he rounded a corner and stopped. There she was, the woman he had seen, but younger and very much alive and active.

"Anthony?" she asked, a smile brightening the room.

"Uh, Mrs. Walker?" He stood there, stunned.

"Amelia, please," she said and laughed. "Come, young man, and sit with me. I've been expecting you."

He did as she requested, startled to now be able to see his own hands and feet. She handed him a large cup of steaming coffee, black, which he gratefully accepted.

"How?"

"I am not alone here, Anthony. I have lots of company. It's all rather temporary and yet quite permanent. Hard to explain really, how one thing is woven into and yet an extension of another." Her voice was pure and tender, almost like a tune as she spoke. "The body wants to hold on to its connections as long as it is able. Mine, it seems, like my personality, is rather tenacious. *Tenacious*, I like that word. Has a better ring to it than *stubborn*, don't you think?"

They both laughed. Their exchange was uncluttered and straightforward.

"I'm not sure how to ask this, but are you able to leave here, this room?"

"For the moment, I am not. Even the door you came through shut behind you and I have no way to open it from the inside. But I am comfortable here. Everything I could possibly need while I wait is available to me. All this you see"—her arm orchestrated the air widely as she looked around—"these are my memories that I am cataloging and storing for the time of speaking. Nothing is lost, you know?"

"Nothing?"

"Well, there are some things not brought back to mind, but nothing is truly lost. Have you ever witnessed a sunset and you know there is a depth in that moment that no camera could ever capture, and you want to hold on to it, to etch it into your remembrance? Do you know what I'm talking about?"

Tony nodded. "I certainly do. It's almost painful, the momentary joy and then the sense of its absence and loss."

"Well, that's the wonder: it's not lost. Eternity will be the speaking and celebration of remembering, and remembering will be a living experience. Words," she said, smiling, "are a limitation when trying to speak of such things."

They sat for some minutes together, and Tony felt he could simply remain content here until it was time for something else, whatever that might be. Amelia reached over and touched his hand.

"Thank you, Anthony, for coming to see an old lady. Where am I, do you know?"

"In a care facility, a rather nice one, from what I saw.

Your family has spared no expense it appears. I don't know if you realize this, but I came with Clarence, your son."

"Really?" she exclaimed, standing up. "My Clarence is here? Do you think I might be able to see him?"

"Amelia, I'm not sure. I don't even know how to get out of here myself, not that I am in any hurry to leave. Clarence told me to tell you..."

"Then let's see, shall we?" she exclaimed, and grabbing his hand pulled him toward the door he had entered. As she had said, there was nothing that offered a way of exit, only a small keyhole head high. The door itself was old and oak, solid and sure, almost as if guarding the way. Tony could barely make out large figures etched on its surface.

"Cherubim." Amelia answered the question he had only wondered. "Marvelous creatures those. Powerfully comforting. They love to guard...doors and ways and portals and such."

It was then that it dawned on Tony. Of course! Reaching inside his shirt, he pulled out the key that he had chosen from the ring. Could it actually be? Hesitantly and holding his breath, he fit it into the keyhole and turned. A blue light pulsed through the thread holding it, and the door swung open, the inside light now spilling out into the room of her eyes. The key then vanished and Amelia and Tony stood, their mouths both agape.

"Thank you, Jesus!" whispered Amelia, quickly moving past him and into the room. Her Clarence and a woman she didn't recognize were clearly visible through the window.

"Momma?" Clarence looked directly at his mother's eyes. "Momma, did you say something?"

"Amelia, your eyes are the windows of your soul," Tony whispered. "Maybe if you talk they can hear you."

Amelia walked over and faced the transparent barrier, her feelings obvious. "Clarence?" she asked.

"Momma? Is that you? I can hear you. Do you know who I am?"

"Of course, I know you. You're my sweet boy all grown up. Look at you, you are surely a handsome man."

Suddenly Clarence was in her arms. Tony didn't understand how it worked, but it did. It was as if Clarence were inside with the two of them, and yet not. When she smiled on the inside, she was smiling on the outside. When she wrapped her arms on the inside, he was in her embrace on the outside. Somehow she was fully present, and Clarence was sobbing, months of loss all surfacing in a moment. Tony looked at Maggie, tears streaming down her face.

"Momma, I have so missed you, and I'm sorry we put you here, but none of us could take care of you, and I didn't get a chance to tell you good-bye or anything..."

"Hush, child, hush now, my baby." She sat down, a small, thin woman holding her man-son in a tender embrace, stroking his head.

Tony cried. Everything he missed about his own mother rose in his memory. But it was a good pain, a right longing, a true connection, and he allowed himself to be carried by its substance.

"My baby," she whispered, "I can't stay long. This is a gift from God, this moment, a treasure unexpected, a taste of what you can't imagine. Tell me quick how everyone is. Catch me up."

And he did, telling his mother about the babies that had been born, the jobs changed, what her children and grandchildren were up to, the everyday mundane news of life that seems trivial but has eternal weight. Only a breath came between laughter and tears. And then Clarence introduced Maggie to his mother and they became instant friends.

Tony was overwhelmed by the holiness of the everyday, the bits and pieces of light that surrounded and embraced the simple routines and tasks of the ordinary. Nothing anymore was ordinary.

An hour passed, and Amelia knew the time was approaching for good-byes. "Clarence?"

"Yes, Momma?"

"I have a favor to ask."

"Anything, Momma. What can I do for you?"

"When you come to visit me, would you bring your guitar and play for me?"

Clarence sat back, surprised. "Momma, I haven't played a guitar in years, but if that is something you would like, I'll do that."

Amelia smiled. "I would like that very much. To hear you play is something I miss terribly. Sometimes I am able to hear music when I can hear nothing else, and it is a comfort to me."

"Then Momma, I would love to play for you. It will probably be good for me anyway."

"I know it will," she predicted. "Just remember that regardless of where I am wandering in my inside world, I can hear you in the music."

She told Clarence that it was time and he nodded, their final embrace long and affectionate. Inside, Amelia reached her hand back and toward Tony, who took it. She squeezed tightly, then turned from the window toward him and in barely a whisper said, "Anthony, I will never be able to thank you enough. This is one of the single greatest gifts anyone has ever given me."

"You are welcome, Amelia, but it really was God's idea. It has been my honor to participate."

Amelia turned back and spoke. "Maggie, come here, sweet girl." Taking both of Maggie's hands, she said in the softest voice, "Maggie, you make a mother's heart sing. I am not prophesying anything, mind you." She said with a chuckle, "You are worthy in your own right."

Maggie put her head down. "Thank you, Mrs. Wal—"

"Momma will do, sweetheart; Momma will do."

"Thank you...Momma." Maggie had barely uttered the word and Amelia leaned down and kissed the top of her head. Again, Tony slid.

The car ride to their next destination was mostly quiet, each involved in his or her thoughts. Tony guided them back into southwest Portland, down by the river and into the parking garage that housed the abandoned janitorial closet, its unlocked entry barely visible, set as it was into the building's facade. He told them where to park and then directed them to remove the batteries from their cell phones as well as the SIM cards.

"Smart," grunted Clarence.

"Clarence, Tony thinks we need to put on gloves."

"We do," agreed Clarence, removing two pairs from his jacket pocket. "Tony, I only have two pair, so don't touch anything, okay?"

"Tony says keep your day job." Maggie chuckled. "He says his prints are all over this place anyway."

The two traversed the fifty feet to their destination, careful to walk exactly where Tony told them.

"Stinks in here." Maggie stated the obvious as she pulled

open the storeroom door. She felt along the wall and flicked on the switch, a single yellow bulb that barely cast light into the junk-filled space. "So this is your secret spy place? I expected more from you, Tony."

He ignored her and then noticed she was carrying a handbag. "Purse? Really? You brought your purse with you?"

"A woman don't go nowhere without her purse. What if we get trapped in here or something? I got a week's supply of everything."

"All right, sorry I said anything. Just go over to the corner over there. See that rusted box on the wall about three feet up from the ground? Yeah, that's it. Open the cover and you'll see a keypad." He waited until Maggie was ready.

"Now, push these buttons: 9, 8, 5, 3, 5, 5 ... good. Now, press the Enter button at the same time as the Power button, and hold them for six seconds."

Maggie did as she was instructed. Six seconds is longer when one has to wait, and she almost let go before a whirring and clicking started and the far wall slid back to reveal a shining steel fire door.

"Whoa!" uttered Maggie. "Now that's more like it. Dun, dun, dah, dah, dun, dun, dah, dah." She scatted the first bars to the theme from *Mission: Impossible.*

"Now," continued Tony, shaking his head, "Maggie, read off the numbers that you got from Loree and have Clarence enter them into the twenty-digit keypad."

"Okay: 8, 8, 1, 2, 12, 6 ... Now, Clarence, Tony says push the Enter button and hold it until you hear a beep. Good! Now press the numbers 1 and 3 at the same time and hold them until you hear another beep. Perfect!"

With the second beep also came the clanking of something in the wall mechanically shifting.

"It worked!" Tony breathed a sigh of relief. "You can go in now."

As the steel door easily opened, lights flashed on, revealing the hidden space: a modern but sparsely decorated apartment, complete with bedroom, bathroom, small kitchen and table, and large work area. The only things missing were windows, but art suitably decorated the walls. One wall was completely shelved, housing an array of books and documents, and an oversized oak desk sat in a corner complete with large-screen computer. The door closed automatically, and they could hear the wall outside slide back into place. Tony knew a timer would shut off the single bulb still shining in the closet space.

"Wow." Clarence whistled. "This is amazing."

"Yeah," grunted Tony. "It is crazy what a little paranoia can create."

"You like to read, huh?" Maggie had stopped to look over the books. "Stephen King fan?"

"Yup, that *Rita Hayworth and Shawshank Redemption* is a first-edition novella. Got more first editions downtown, but that's my favorite."

"And let's see...," continued Maggie, "you got some Orson Scott Card, that book by Emma Donoghue that I been wanting to read, and...Jodi Picoult? You read her stuff?"

"Not usually. Somebody left it on a plane in a seat pocket and I took it."

"Wow! Looks like you have a bunch of classics, too. Now that's more my style, along with Lewis, Williams, Parker, and MacDonald, and murder mysteries for fun."

"I haven't read most of those old books, not lately anyway," Tony admitted. "They are investments more than any personal literary interest. I pick up one now and then from

Powell's downtown. Did you know that they have an incredible rare book room?"

"All right, you two," interrupted Clarence. "This place is kinda creepy, no offense, Tony, and I would just as soon get what we came for and get outta here."

Tony agreed and directed them to the corner of the workspace opposite the desk. Built into the floor was the vault, with the traditional knob-turning tumbler. It took a couple tries of 9, 18, 10, 4, and 12, with the proper clockwise and counter spins before Maggie was successful and some internal hydraulics whished open the top. Inside were stacks of papers, documents, and cash, along with other items in small boxes of various sizes.

Maggie produced a black garbage bag from her coat pocket.

"What am I supposed to take?" she asked. "The cash?"

Tony laughed. "No, unfortunately. It's all counted and serial numbers recorded off-site. Secondary insurance that no one would be snooping in here unnoticed."

"Wow! You are paranoid, but I'm impressed."

"Thank you, I think," responded Tony. "But you might want to tell Clarence that he doesn't want to watch this part. Plausible deniability and all. And tell him not to use the water in the kitchen or bathroom. It will leave a record." Maggie did so and Clarence obediently went to explore more of the place.

"Okay, Maggie, see that big stack of documents on the right? Yeah, that one. Grab a big handful of them, but keep them in the same order as you pick them up. I have to find the right one."

She did so and placed a large pile of official-looking papers on the floor in front of her. Maggie read the top one. "Your Last Will and Testament? Is this the cat stupidity?"

"Yeah, like I said, not my best moment. Just take that one off the top and put it into the garbage bag." Internally, he slowly exhaled his relief, the sick feeling in the pit of his stomach subsiding as the tension eased.

"Okay, now take about ten of the stapled documents off the top and put them on the floor to your right."

"Are these all Last Wills and Testaments?" asked Maggie, confused.

"Yup! What can I tell you? I have been a rather fickle guy. Mood swings."

"Glad I didn't know you back then," huffed Maggie. "I don't think we would have been friends."

"Sadly that's true, and it would have been my huge loss, Maggie."

Maggie was speechless for a moment. Then she said softly, "So what am I looking for?"

"I actually don't need you to look for anything, Maggie. I just need you to turn the pages until I tell you to stop."

They slowly worked their way through another dozen of these wills, each one reviewed placed on the discard pile to the right.

"Stop!" exclaimed Tony. Something he was looking for had finally caught his eye. "This might be it. Maggie, just look somewhere, don't turn your head, but don't read, please, while I check this out."

"Okay?" She fought hard the temptation to see what it was that Tony was looking at. "Tony, I have curiosity DNA," she groaned. "Don't be doing this to me."

"Well, grab that photo that's in the safe over to the left of the docs you pulled out and look at that," he suggested. "Maybe that will distract you."

She reached for it, aged and inside a protective covering.

Turning it over, she was surprised. "Hey, Tony, I've seen this photo before."

"What?" He was shocked. "That's not possible."

"No," she continued, "Jake showed me the same photo a couple days ago. His was in lots worse shape than this one, all wrinkly and folded, but it's the same one. It's you and him and your mom and dad, right?"

"Yeah, it is." He was stunned. Jake had a copy of this picture?

"Jake said it's the only picture he has of your mom and dad. He used to keep it in a shoe so no one would steal it. He said it was one of the last happy days he can remember with your folks…I'm sorry, Tony, I didn't mean to…"

He found his voice again, and spoke softly. "It's okay, Maggie. Seems there are still lots of surprises in this world." Then a thought occurred to him. "Maggie, did Jake happen to tell you what we were laughing about in the picture? I've tried, but I can't remember."

"Ha!" She laughed. "He sure did. You were laughing because…" She stopped. "You know what, Tony, I think I'll let Jake tell you. I think that would be special."

"Maggie!" begged Tony. "Don't do that to me. Please, just tell me."

"You two almost done foolin' around in there?" came the voice of Clarence from the other room. "We've got to get outta here soon."

"Back to work, Tony!" whispered Maggie. "What am I supposed to do?"

"Well, thank God, I found what I was looking for and it is notarized and everything. Seems there was some value to my state of mind after all. Anyway, leave this one on the top, and return it along with the rest of the stack back to the same place you pulled it out from. Perfect! Now, the pile on the right, just throw those into the garbage bag. Have Clarence just give the whole bag to his friend to shred."

Maggie did as she was told and was about to push the Close button on the vault door, when Tony spoke.

"Wait! There are a couple other things I want to get out of there. Look over at the far left on the top shelf... See that envelope that says TWIMC on the top? Grab that, and... let me think. Oh yeah, on the shelf under where you found that letter there is another stack, on the left side. Yeah. Somewhere in there is a letter addressed to Angela. You found it? Great."

"Angela?" Maggie inquired.

"I had my moments. Sometimes I wrote to her things that I couldn't say, you know, asking for forgiveness and stuff like that. But I never sent them. This was my last one and if things don't work out, I want you to give it to her. Promise?"

She hesitated before answering. "Yeah, Tony, I promise," she said and added quickly, "but everything's going to work out just fine and you can tell her all these things yourself."

"I hope so." Tony faltered.

"Is that it? We done here?" asked Clarence sternly.

Tony made a quick decision. "Nope! There's one more thing. Do you see that small blue box over in the corner on the bottom left side? Would you take that, too? Please don't open it. It's rather personal. No one will know it was here, but I don't want to leave it here regardless."

"Sure, Tony." And without another question Maggie deposited the little felt-covered box, along with the two letters, in her purse.

"We're done," Maggie announced to Clarence and handed him the garbage bag.

He nodded that he knew what to do with it and helped her secure the safe, making sure it was properly locked.

"Don't worry about lights," Tony advised. "They are on motion detectors and will shut off automatically."

They exited the way they had come in, carefully retracing their steps to ensure that nothing appeared disturbed or out of place.

Back in the car Maggie broke the silence. "So, Tony, now what?"

"Now," he stated with complete certainty, "now, back to the hospital and do some healing."

18

CROSSED ROADS

I met you at the crossing
Where one road finds another
I did not even ask your name
I would not even bother

I looked at only what I saw
And did not see you fall
And even though I said I loved
I hardly loved at all

I didn't mean to leave you there
It wasn't my intent
I simply looked the other way
And said nothing I meant

I didn't choose to cross this road
Although it's what I wanted
Instead pretended you weren't there
Believed you never counted

Oh, see I have this golden chain
Tied round my throat and heart
A bond more real to me than you
Is keeping us apart

I need a Voice to answer me
I need Someone who's true
I need new eyes that let me see
That in my me is You

Oh, Someone please now guide me cross
This road betwixt between
And join my broken bits of soul
To real that is unseen

19

THE GIFT

Forgiveness is the fragrance that the violet
sheds on the heel that has crushed it.
—Mark Twain

Tony was more alive than he had ever been, but still he knew that he was tiring. He had slept, or rested, or something in between, without the memory of a dream but the lingering sense of being held when he awoke. Wherever he had been, it had been safe and would continue to be. Even if there was an explanation, he didn't want to know it. He was tiring. He was dying. He accepted that, with a consuming sense of peace. It was time to act.

"Maggie?"

"Hey you. I wondered when you were going to show. This place is not the same when you aren't around."

"Thanks for saying that."

"I don't say what I don't mean," she said affectionately, and then added with a snicker, "most of the time."

"So what's the plan?" he inquired. "When can we go up to the hospital?"

"Glad you asked. Well, I've been on the phone while you were gone, wherever it is you go, and we're all heading up there this afternoon."

"We?" asked Tony, curious.

"Yup, the whole gang. Even Clarence is coming." Maggie added quickly, "Now, don't you go worrying. I haven't told anyone what we're up to, just said it would be nice to be up there together."

"Who all are we talking about?" Tony still didn't quite understand.

"The whole caboodle of us, you know"—and she began itemizing on her fingers—"Clarence, me, Molly, Cabby, Jake, Loree, Angela"—she paused for effect—"and you. That's eight. Nine if you include Lindsay but she's already up there. Looks like we are starting our own church. Just better that no one knows that's what it is."

"You think that's a good idea? All of us up there?"

"One never knows if anything's a good idea. You just make a choice and go with the flow and see what happens. You only get one day's worth of grace, so why not spend it extravagantly."

"All right then," he acquiesced. That was a choice he could make, to stay inside the grace of one day. Everything else was just imagination anyway.

Maggie, who was busy baking as usual, suddenly stopped and asked, "Tony, you don't even know what day this is, do you?"

"No," he admitted. "I've sort of lost all track of time. I don't even know how long this whole coma thing has been going on. What's so special about today?"

"Today," she announced, "is Easter Sunday! Two days ago was Good Friday, you know, the day that we all poured out our wrath on Jesus hanging on the cross. The day he entered into our experience completely, got so deeply lost in all our crap that only his Father could find him...that's what day that was. God in the hands of angry sinners day."

"Seriously?" He was surprised. The irony did not escape him, or Maggie, who continued her preach.

"Tony, don't you get it? This is resurrection weekend!... And today we are going up to that hospital and we are going to raise you from the dead. By the power of God, we are going to raise you into a new life. Sunday's here! I can hardly stand how cool this is!" She let her Pentecostal roots show, waving a wooden spoon, sticky with a delicious-looking batter, and dancing a little jig. "Well, say something! What do you think?"

"How soon do we go?" he said, trying to match her excitement. It came out flat in comparison.

"Tony, how can you be so cold when something is this unbelievable! What's wrong with you?"

"I'm white—even out of body, what can I say." Tony laughed. "I'm grateful to be inside your head and not somewhere where someone might want me to dance or something."

Maggie laughed. Clean from the bottom of her toes and along with Tony. When she calmed she added, "Well, we should head up there pretty soon. I'm just waiting for some sweet dough to rise, and then you and I can go on up. Molly and Cabby are already there, probably the rest, too, but don't know for sure."

"Sounds good," he responded, but Maggie was already clearly focused on the tasks at hand, humming a tune that Tony barely remembered from somewhere. Everything was motion.

Maggie entered the waiting area outside Neurosciences ICU and was greeted warmly by Molly, Loree, and Angela. Jake and Cabby were off exploring the lobby Starbucks for a latte and hot chocolate. Clarence gave Maggie an appropriate but extended hug and she almost blushed. If only the others knew what they did.

A short time later Maggie dismissed herself to visit Tony in ICU alone, explaining that she wanted to pray for him and didn't want to embarrass anyone with her exuberance if she got a little carried away. Clarence gave her a knowing wink and whispered, "I'll be praying, too."

She checked in at the reception station, and as she approached Tony's room, an attending physician dressed in his whites emerged from inside.

"Maggie," Tony said, "do you still have that letter you took from the safe with you?"

"The one you wrote to Angela?" she muttered without moving her lips.

"No, not that one, the other one. Do you still have it?"

"Yeah?"

"Give it to that doctor who just came out of my room. Quick, before he's gone."

"Excuse me," she called out after the doctor. He stopped and turned. "I am sorry to bother you, but I was instructed to give"—she was rummaging through her purse and produced the envelope with TWIMC written on the outside—"this to you?"

"To me?" He looked surprised, taking the envelope from Maggie and opening it.

He scanned the pages and nodded. "Good! We've been waiting for this. Mr. Spencer's POLST document."

"What?" exclaimed Maggie, ripping it out of his hand. Sure enough, it was a signed and notarized Physician Orders for Life-Sustaining Treatment form. Tony had checked most of the boxes, recording specific preferences including feeding tubes, intravenous hydration, and oxygen ventilation. It not only permitted the hospital but directed them to remove him from the ventilator that kept him breathing.

"I'm sorry," the doctor said as he slowly reached over and pulled the sheet from Maggie's fingers, "but this will allow us to act according to the wishes of the patient and..."

"I know what it does," steamed Maggie, turning and walking away before she lost control. She entered Tony's room, which thankfully was empty of medical personnel or staff.

"Tony! What are you thinking?" she yelled in a hoarse whisper, not wanting to be ejected as she had been before. "This is insanity. Are you thinking that you can give them that form because it won't matter, that you aren't going to need the ventilator because you are going to be healed? Tell me that's what you're thinking."

When he didn't respond, Maggie walked to the bed and laid her hands on his body. "Pray, Tony!" And then she began to shake as the certainty of what was happening descended like the stage's final curtain. "Dammit, Tony, please... pray to be healed."

He was crying. "I can't!" he stated. "Maggie, my whole life I have lived for just one person, me, and finally I am ready to not do that anymore."

"But Tony," she begged, "this is suicide. You have a gift. You can heal yourself. You can help people who don't know what you know. You are taking your life into your own hands."

"No, Maggie, I'm not! Maggie, that's exactly what I'm not doing. I'm not taking my own life into my own hands. If

God has a purpose in me living, then God can heal me, but I just can't do this."

"But Tony," she was pleading, waves of sorrow pounding her. "But if you don't do this, you'll die. Don't you get it? I don't want you to die."

"Maggie, sweet Maggie, I get it. And you cannot begin to fathom what those words mean to me. But I get it. I have already been dead. Most of my life I've been dead, and didn't even know it. I walked around thinking I was alive and battering everyone in my world with my death. That's not true anymore. I'm alive. For the first time in my life, I'm alive and free and able to make a truly free choice and I've made up my mind. I'm choosing life...for me...and for Lindsay."

Maggie caved in, slumping to the floor in a sobbing heap. In this moment she wanted out, to not be here, to never have prayed that God would allow her to participate in his purposes. The weight of it was a crush, and she almost hated that a light of joy was simultaneously springing inside. The burden of what she had been carrying for Lindsay joined her grief for Tony and together lifted her to her feet. Her breathing came in ragged bursts as she fought to regain her composure. Finally she asked, "Tony, are you sure?"

It took him a moment to find his own voice, caught in both his and her emotions. "I am more sure about this than anything I have ever done. It's the right thing for me, Maggie, I know it is."

Maggie walked over to the sink and washed her face, hardly daring to look into the mirror and into Tony's eyes. She smiled finally and nodded.

"Okay, then, we don't have a lot of time. You're sure?"

"Yes, Maggie. I am sure."

"All right. You know you won't ever be able to have one of my caramel rolls, don't you?" She dabbed tissues at her eyes again. "Silly, huh! But I really wanted you to taste them."

"I will, Maggie, it just won't be for a while, but I will."

Maggie made her way back to the waiting area, where everyone immediately sensed that something had changed. She explained that the doctors now had the form directing their actions. Clarence raised his eyebrows but said nothing.

"They won't do anything until they have talked to the next of kin," she said and nodded toward Jake. Tears again welled up. "I want to go see Lindsay. I can't explain it, but I need to. Can you all wait until I get back? I'll only be a few minutes."

"I'm going with you." Clarence was not asking permission.

"Me, too," stated Molly, and she turned to Jake. "Would you watch Cabby for me until we get back? Please don't let him play hide-and-seek."

He nodded, a little bewildered, but ready to help in any way.

They were about to leave when Maggie suddenly turned back. "Cabby, come here for a minute, okay?"

It was obvious that he was aware of something, his demeanor subdued and gentle. He walked over to his Maggie-buddy, who put her arms around him, leaned forward until their heads were touching, and looked him in the eyes. In a quiet voice so no one else could hear she whispered, "Cabby, Tony says that someday is today, do you understand?"

Tears puddled in the corners of his beautiful almond eyes and he nodded. "Bye," he whispered, pulling Maggie's face down until their foreheads touched and he could look deep into her eyes. "Lub you!" and then turning he ran into Jake's waiting embrace, burying his face in the man's chest.

No words were spoken as the three made their way from the main building back to Doernbecher and to Lindsay's room. Clarence was stopped by the Pineapple Princess, but Molly granted the proper permissions, and after a short quiz about his health, he was also let into the area. Lindsay was awake and reading.

"Hi!" She smiled, raising her forehead toward Clarence and looking at Maggie with a sly grin.

"Yes, this is Clarence, the cop I was telling you about. Clarence, Lindsay...Lindsay, Clarence."

"*Very* nice to meet you, Clarence." She beamed as she shook his hand.

"The pleasure is all mine," he returned with a slight bow of his head, a gesture that Lindsay found entirely charming.

"Lindsay, we've come to pray for you, if that would be all right?" Molly reached out and touched Maggie's arm, a look of concern on her face. There was no lack of trust for her best friend, but she hadn't seen this coming. Maggie turned and hugged her, whispering in her ear, tears again flowing easily.

"Molly, this is Tony's gift to you, to all of us. Just trust me, okay?"

She nodded, eyes wide in question. "Lindsay?" Maggie asked.

"Of course." She smiled, a little disconcerted by the tears of the others. "I will take all the prayers I can get. I always feel better after somebody prays for me."

"Good girl," said Maggie, reaching into her purse. "Now, I am going to put a little of this oil on your forehead. It's not magic, just a symbol of the Holy Spirit, and then I am going to lay my hands on you and pray, okay?"

Lindsay nodded again and, leaning back into the pillows, closed her eyes. Maggie in two motions drew a cross in oil on her forehead. "This is the symbol of Jesus and very special today, since this is Resurrection Sunday." Her voice cracked and Lindsay opened her eyes.

"I'm okay, darlin'." Satisfied, Lindsay lay back and once more closed her eyes. Maggie then placed her hand on the teenager's forehead, where the oil still glistened, and leaned forward.

"Talitha cumi," she whispered, and Lindsay's eyes snapped open, looking into but as if through Maggie. Her eyes widened and tears began to seep from the corners. A moment later she focused and whispered back.

"Maggie, who was that?"

"Who was who, honey?"

"That man, who was that man?"

"What man? What did he look like?" Maggie was bewildered.

"That man, Maggie. He had the most beautiful brown eyes I have ever seen. He could see me, Maggie."

"Blue eyes," said Tony. "In case you are wondering, I have blue eyes. I think she saw Jesus. He told me once I couldn't actually heal anyone, not apart from him."

"That was Jesus, Lindsay," said Maggie. "You saw Jesus."

"He said something to me." She looked over at her mother. "Mom, Jesus said something to me."

Molly sat and enfolded her daughter in her arms, her own tears flowing. "What did he say?"

"He said something I didn't understand, and then he smiled and said, 'The best is yet to come.' What does that mean, Mom? The best is yet to come."

"I'm not sure, sweetheart, but I believe it."

"I'm sorry, Lindsay," interrupted Maggie, "but I need to go back over to Neuro ICU. Molly, it's time to say good-bye."

Clarence sat down next to Lindsay and began asking her about the book she was reading while Molly stepped to the corner of the room with Maggie. Molly tried unsuccessfully more than once to find words, but they stuck somewhere between her heart and her mouth.

"Maggie, just tell her that I am thrilled to be a part of this," said Tony, "any of this."

Molly nodded. "Tony?" she finally whispered. "Are you Jesus?"

"Ha!" He laughed out loud and Maggie grinned. "Tell Molly no, but we're tight."

This made Molly smile, but she leaned forward again. "Tony, I think there is more of him in you than you know. I can never thank you adequately."

"Tony says good-bye, Molly. He says you can thank him by keeping an eye on Jake for him, okay?"

"Yeah, okay." Molly grinned through the tears. "I love you, Tony!"

"I...I...love you, too, Molly." Simple words, but so unbearably hard to say, even though he realized that he meant it. "Maggie, get me outta here, please, before I totally fall apart."

A few minutes later Maggie and Clarence returned to OHSU and the waiting room. The two of them watched Cabby as the others, each when they were ready, slipped back to Tony's room to say their good-byes. It is a fragile and thin place, these moments between life and death, and Maggie didn't want to walk without compassion on this holy ground.

While Angela waited for her time, Maggie sat next to

her and handed her the letter from her father. For twenty minutes the young woman sat and bawled her way through what Tony had written to her, soon joined and comforted by her mother. Finally, she, too, entered ICU room 17, choosing to make the journey alone and later returned red-eyed and drained.

"You okay?" asked Maggie, taking her in her arms.

"I'm better. I told him how mad I was at him. I was so angry in there, Maggie, I thought I was going to destroy the place, but I told him."

"I'm sure he deserved it, Angela. He didn't know better; that was part of the hurt in him."

"Yeah, that's what he wrote in his letter, that it wasn't my fault."

"Well, I'm glad you got to tell him how angry you are. That is a healing thing."

"Me, too. And I'm glad I got to tell him that I love him and that I miss him, too." She pulled back to look into Maggie's eyes. "Thank you, Maggie."

"For what, darlin'?"

"I'm not sure, exactly." Angela smiled weakly. "I just wanted to thank you, that's all."

"Well, then, you are welcome. I'll be sure to pass it along."

Angela again smiled, not sure what Maggie meant, and then went to sit with her mother, leaning into her, exhausted.

Jake returned next, looking as if he had been through a grinder, but eyes still sparkling and alive.

"You sure you don't want to talk to him?" mumbled Maggie.

"I can't!" responded Tony, resigned.

"How come?"

"'Cause I'm a coward, that's how come. For all the changes, I'm still too afraid."

She nodded barely but enough that he would know and sat down next to Clarence, who simply leaned over and in the guise of a hug, whispered, "Thank you, Tony, for everything. Just so you know, whatever was in that bag was destroyed by an industrial shredder."

"Tell him thank you for me, Maggie. And please let him know what a good man I think he is. I'll say hi to his momma, however that works."

"I'll let him know," she returned.

The time had come and Maggie walked alone for the last time back to Tony's room. "So no cats!" she stated.

"Nope, no cats, thank God," replied Tony. "The will we left in the safe splits everything between Jake, Loree, and Angela. I got drunk one night and was listening to that Bob Dylan song, you know covered by that woman..."

" 'Make You Feel My Love'? Adele?"

"Yeah, that's the one. Well, I got all feeling bad and rewrote everything. Next morning, hungover and all, I still felt awful enough about myself to go and get it notarized. But then, like always, I changed my mind, you know..."

Maggie and Tony were by themselves as quiet descended, stillness breathing inside the ongoing and tireless repetition of machines.

Maggie finally broke the stillness. "I don't know how to do this. Tony, my life is changed because of you, for the better. You matter to me, and I don't know how to let you go, to say good-bye. I just know there is going to be this hole in my heart that only you fit."

"No one has ever said anything like that to me. Thank you." He continued, "Maggie, I have three final things that I need to talk to you about."

"Okay, but don't make me cry. I got nothing left."

He paused slightly before continuing, "Maggie, the first

thing is a confession. Someday you might want to tell Jake something for me. I couldn't do it. I really am a coward, but I…I just can't, I'm too afraid."

She waited while he was scrounging for words.

"My brother and I got separated and it was my fault. Jake always looked to me for everything and I was there for him, until there was this one family, this one particular foster family. From everything they were communicating to each other, and to me, too, I was certain that they were going to adopt. The problem was, they could only adopt one and I desperately wanted to be that one; I just wanted to belong again, somewhere." Tony had never told anyone about this and was fighting the shame that lay beneath the burden of the secret.

"So I lied to them about Jake. He was younger and sweeter and easier to manage than me, so I made up all sorts of terrible stuff about him so that they wouldn't adopt him. I sold out my own brother and did it in a way that he never knew about it. One day Children's Services pulls up and they take Jake away and he's screaming and kicking and hanging on to my legs and I'm hanging on to him like I really care, but Maggie, part of me was glad they were taking him away. He was all I had. I was destroying the love that I actually had for an imagination of belonging with someone else."

Tony took a moment to collect himself and Maggie waited, wishing there was some way she could wrap that little lost boy in her arms.

"A few weeks later the family all gathers and asks me to be there. They announce that they had made a big decision and that they were going to adopt. But it wasn't me they were adopting, it was a baby, and so the foster case-worker was coming by later that day to take me to another 'wonderful' family who was all excited about me coming. I thought I knew what it was like to be alone, but this was a whole new lost.

"Maggie, I was supposed to be there for Jake, especially because no one else was. I'm his older brother, and he completely trusted me and I totally failed him; worse, I betrayed him."

"Oh, Tony," entreated Maggie, "I am so sorry. Tony, you were just a little boy yourself. I am so sad that you even had to try and make those kinds of choices."

"And then Gabe comes into my life, and for the first time I am holding in my arms someone I actually belong to, and in that little boy I try to make it all right, but I couldn't even hold on to him. I lost him, too. Angela didn't have a chance. I was so terrified of losing her that I never even let her find a place inside my arms, and then Loree…"

He had spoken his heart, and now let his words hang in the air like a mourning fog, an unexpected sigh of an unburdened heart emerging and softly singing in the wake of his confession.

More silence as both waded through residual emotions. Tony finally took a deep breath and exhaled.

"Do you still have that little blue box?"

"Sure." She pulled it out of her purse.

"I want you to give it to Jake. It's the only thing I have from our mother; she gave it to me only a few days before she died, almost as if she knew she was leaving. She got it from her mom who got it from hers. She told me to give it someday to the woman I loved, but I was never healthy enough to love anyone. I can see that Jake has it in him, to love like that. Maybe he can give it someday to the woman that he loves."

Maggie carefully lifted the top. Inside lay a small gold chain and a simple gold cross. "It's beautiful, Tony. I'll do that. I'll be hoping to see it around Molly's neck one day. You know, just sayin'!"

"Yeah, me, too," Tony admitted. "That would be fine by me."

"And the last thing?"

"It's the most important of the three, I think, and probably hardest for me to tell someone. Maggie, I love you! I mean, I actually do."

"I know, Tony, I do know that. I love you, too. Crap, why did I even bother wearing makeup today?!"

"Okay, then, let's not make this any harder. Kiss me good-bye and go join our family."

"You want to know what you and Jake and your folks were enjoying in the picture?"

He laughed. "Of course!"

"I'm surprised you don't remember. Your mother accidently poured salt instead of sugar into her coffee, and when she took a sip, she sprayed it across the room in a most unladylike manner, and right onto a woman dressed to the nines. Jake can tell it better, but you get the idea."

"I remember." Tony laughed. "I remember how it made my day! How could I have forgotten, especially when..."

"Good-bye, my friend," whispered Maggie, tears spilling down her face as she leaned forward and kissed the man in the bed on his forehead. "I will see you again."

Tony slid one last time.

20

NOW

Everything we see is a shadow cast by that which
we do not see.
—Martin Luther King Jr.

The three of them stood on the side of the hill overlooking the valley that lay below. It was his property but barely recognizable. The river that had destroyed the temple had also demolished most of the walls. What once was burned over and devastated was now alive with growth.

Grandmother spoke. "Now that's better! Much better!"

Jesus responded, "It's good!"

What mattered in this moment to Tony was simply being here, inside the relationship with these two. There permeated in his soul an exhilaration and calm, a settled expectancy and wild anticipation clothed in peace.

"Hey," he wondered aloud. "Where are your places? I don't see either the ranch house or your..."

"Hovel," grunted Grandmother. "Never really needed them. All of this is now a habitation, not just bits and pieces. We would never have settled for less."

"It's time." Jesus smiled, stretching his hands into the air.

"Time?" asked Tony, curious. "You mean it's time to meet your dad, Papa God?"

"No, not time for that. You already met him anyway."

"I did? When did I meet him?"

Jesus laughed again and wrapped an arm around Tony's shoulder. Leaning close he whispered, "Talitha cumi!"

"What?" Tony exclaimed. "Are you kidding me? That little girl in the blue-and-green dress?"

"Imagery," added Grandmother, "has never been able to define God, but it is our intention to be known, and each whisper and breath of imagery is a little window into a facet of our nature. Pretty cool, eh?"

"The coolest." Tony nodded. "So, what is it time for then? Will Papa God be there?"

"It is time for the celebration, the life-after, the gathering and the speaking," answered Jesus, "and just to be clear, Papa has never not been here."

"So now what?"

"Now," said Grandmother triumphantly, "now, the best comes!"

A NOTE TO THE READERS AND ACKNOWLEDGMENTS

If you have not read *Cross Roads* yet, you might want to wait to read this note until after you have—there are a few spoilers here.

The name Anthony Spencer originated with our youngest son's game avatars. While characters tend to be composites of people I know, in the writing each begins to emerge uniquely. This is not true for Cabby, Molly's son. He is wholly built on Nathan, the son of friends, a young man who died only a couple of years ago when his hide-and-seek game took him outside of the arena where he was watching the Portland Trail Blazers, and out into the freeway where he was struck by two cars. Nathan had Down syndrome. There is nothing in the character of Cabby that was not true about Nathan, even his favorite epithet and his propensity to "lift" cameras and hide them in his room. While I was working on this story, I was in constant conversation with Nathan's mom, who provided me the details for the Cabby character. One afternoon she called me, explaining how one of our interactions stirred her curiosity and she went exploring through Nathan's personal items that are in storage. Sure enough, inside his toy guitar case she found an unfamiliar camera. She turned it on and to her surprise it was full of pictures of my family. Two years before Nathan died, he had been visiting our home and had "lifted" our niece's camera. All this time, we thought she had simply misplaced it.

There are so many to thank. Nathan's family, for allowing me the honor to write their son into a work of fiction. I hope I was able to capture both the simple wonder and some of the struggle that coexisted in Nathan's heart and in all families that face the daily challenges surrounding handicaps and limitations of one kind or other.

I had a lot of help and input on the medical side of the story. My thanks to Chris Green of Responder Life; Heather Doty, a Life Flight nurse and trauma nurse, who was an incredible resource to me with the collapse scenario; Bob Cozzie, Anthony Collins, and especially Traci Jacobsen, who let me invade their space at Clackamas County 911 in Oregon City, Oregon, and ask all the questions I needed to in order to make that part of the story accurate. The nurses and staff at both Oregon Health and Science University (especially in Neuro ICU) and Doernbecher Children's Hospital (especially in Hematology/Oncology), as well as friend and retired neurosurgeon Dr. Larry Franks.

Working on this part of the story introduced me to incredible people who are truly "in the trenches" of human hurt and crisis. Unless we are fortunate enough to know these folks in our personal lives, we don't usually intersect with them unless we are in a place of loss ourselves. From first responders, fire, ambulance, police, 911, to medical staff, techs, doctors and nurses, these are special hearts who work behind the scenes and help us cope with the tragedies that invade our everydays. On behalf of all of us who forget you are there or whose presence we so often simply take for granted, thank you, thank you, thank you!

Thank you, Chad and Robin, for letting me write at

your beautiful refuge at Otter Rock, and for the Mumford family, who gave me similar space to work up near Mount Hood. Without you, this story would not have made it to the presses in nearly as timely a fashion.

Thank you to my friend Richard Twiss and the Lakota— if you've read this book, you already know how you helped me. We all need a Grandmother and a tribe.

We are rich in friends and family, and it would take an even bigger book to list them all. I am grateful for how you are woven into our lives and for your participation in our becoming. Thank you especially to the Young clan and the Warren clan for your constant encouragement. To Kim, wife and companion, our six children, two daughters-in-law, one son-in-law, and six grandchildren (so far), I love you with all my heart... You make my heart sing.

Thank you to all of you who read and shared *The Shack* and then let me into precious and sometimes incredibly painful places in your stories. You have graced me beyond measure.

Thank you to Dan Polk, Bob Barnett, John Scanlon, Wes Yoder, David Parks, Tom Hentoff and Deneen Howell, Kim Spaulding, the incredible Hachette publishing family, especially David Young, Rolf Zettersten, and editor Joey Paul, and the many foreign publishers who have worked so diligently on my behalf and been powerfully consistent encouragers every step of the way. Special thanks to editor Adrienne Ingrum for her essential input and encouragement. The book is better because of her.

Special thanks to Baxter Kruger, PhD, my Mississippi friend and theologian, and photographer John MacMurray, who have been constant support and critics (in the best sense of the word). Baxter's book, *The Shack Revisited*, is the single best book written about *The Shack*.

Thanks also to our Northwest area family of friends, the Closners, Fosters, Westons, Graves, Huffs, Troy Brummell, Don Miller, Goffs, MaryKay Larson, Sands, Jordans, the NE folks as well as early reader/critics Larry Gillis, Dale Bruneski, and Wes and Linda Yoder.

I continue to be inspired by the Inklings, especially C. S. Lewis (better known to his friends as "Jack"). George MacDonald and Jacques Ellul are always good company. Love to Malcolm Smith, Ken Blue, and the Aussies and Kiwis who are forever part of our lives. Sound track to write by, supplied by a diverse group of musicians including Marc Broussard, Johnny Lang, Imagine Dragons, Thad Cockrell, David Wilcox, Danny Ellis, Mumford & Sons, Allison Krauss, Amos Lee, Johnnyswim, Robert Counts, Wynton Marsalis, Ben Rector, that trinity of old brilliant musicians Buddy Greene, Phil Keaggy and Charlie Peacock, James Taylor, Jackson Browne, Leonard Cohen, and of course Bruce Cockburn.

Any use of local area landmarks and haunts is entirely on purpose and for a reason. Oregon is gorgeous and a wonderful place to live and raise a family, and I am grateful to you.

Finally and at the center is the self-giving, other-centered love of Father, Son, and Holy Spirit, displayed extravagantly to us in the person of Jesus. Your grace is relentless affection independent of performance—a love that we are not powerful enough to change.

If you look for Truth
you may find comfort in the end.
If you look for comfort
you will not get neither comfort nor truth,
only soft soap and wishful thinking to begin
and in the end, despair.

—C. S. Lewis

Do you wish this wasn't the end?
Are you hungry for more great teaching, inspiring
testimonies, ideas to challenge your faith?

Join us at www.hodderfaith.com, follow us on Twitter
or find us on Facebook to make sure you get the latest from
your favourite authors.

Including interviews, videos, articles, competitions
and opportunities to tell us just what you thought about
our latest releases.

www.hodderfaith.com

 HodderFaith

 @HodderFaith

 HodderFaithVideo

HODDER
WHERE FAITH IS INSPIRED

If reading or listening to *The Shack*, or
Cross Roads, or *The Shack: Reflections*
has had an impact on you and you
would like to share your story with
the author, please e-mail it to:
wmpaulyoung@gmail.com or
mail it to:

PO Box 2107, Oregon City, OR 97045 USA

Please understand that you may or may
not receive a response due to the
volume of correspondence, but over
time we will read every e-mail and letter.
Thank you, in advance, for taking
the time to do this.

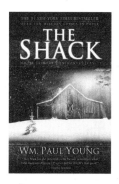

Mackenzie Allen Phillips's youngest daughter, Missy, has been abducted during a family vacation, and evidence that she may have been brutally murdered is found in an abandoned shack deep in the Oregon wilderness. Four years later, in the midst of his great sadness, Mack receives a suspicious note, apparently from God, inviting him back to that shack for a weekend.

Against his better judgment, he arrives at the shack one wintry afternoon and walks back into his darkest nightmare. What he finds there will change his life forever.

In an age where religion seems to grow increasingly irrelevant, THE SHACK wrestles with the timeless question: Where is God in a world so filled with unspeakable pain? The answers that astounded and transformed Mack will do the same for readers.

We invite you to continue your experience of *The Shack* with *The Shack Revisited* by C. Baxter Kruger (foreword by Wm Paul Young), the book that guides readers into a deeper understanding of God the Father, God the Son, and God the Holy Spirit, to help readers have a more profound connection with the core message of *The Shack*—God is love.

The powerful story found in *The Shack*, written by Wm Paul Young, stole the hearts of millions and rocketed to fame by word-of-mouth,

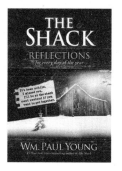

making it a phenomenon in publishing history. Now, *The Shack: Reflections for Every Day of the Year* provides an opportunity for you to go back to the shack with Papa, Sarayu, and Jesus.

This 365 day devotional selects meaningful quotes from THE SHACK and adds prayers by writer Wm Paul Young to inspire, encourage, and uplift you every day of the year.